The
Lost Letters
of Ireland

BOOKS BY SUSANNE O'LEARY

The Road Trip

A Holiday to Remember

SANDY COVE SERIES

Secrets of Willow House

Sisters of Willow House

Dreams of Willow House

Daughters of Wild Rose Bay

Memories of Wild Rose Bay

Miracles in Wild Rose Bay

STARLIGHT COTTAGES SERIES

The Lost Girls of Ireland

The Lost Secret of Ireland

The Lost Promise of Ireland

The Lost House of Ireland

Susanne O'Leary

The
Lost Letters
of Ireland

bookouture

Published by Bookouture in 2022

An imprint of Storyfire Ltd.
Carmelite House
50 Victoria Embankment
London EC4Y 0DZ

www.bookouture.com

ISBN: 978-1-80314-734-5
eBook ISBN: 978-1-80314-733-8

For Mary Collins Griffin

1

Edwina was dragged out of a deep sleep by a loud jingle. She opened her eyes, looking wildly around the bedroom, her head pounding. This was one hell of a hangover. And where was her phone? She had to find it to make it stop ringing. She groped around on the thick carpet and finally found it under her bed.

'Yes?' she mumbled. 'Who is this so early in the morning?'

'It's me, Jonathan,' a voice said cheerily. 'And it's nearly lunchtime, by the way.'

'Oh.' Edwina blinked and stared at the ceiling, trying to wake up properly, relieved it was only Jonathan on the phone and not someone she would have to impress.

Most women had best girlfriends but Edwina had Jonathan, whom she had known for over three years now, ever since that mess with the country house in Kerry that had caused her such misery. Since then he had been her friend and advisor, and sometimes even her safety net when she needed an escort to a party she didn't want to be seen alone at.

'It feels like the middle of the night to me,' she mumbled after a long silence.

'You sound a little ropey,' Jonathan said.

'Hungover,' she muttered. 'Party last night at... someone's penthouse. Were you there? I can't seem to remember...'

'No, I wasn't.' Jonathan paused. 'But I'm nearby now, and there's something I want to discuss with you. Would it be all right to come up to your apartment in about half an hour or so?'

'But I have to go to work.'

'It's Sunday, Edwina. And you quit your job last week.'

'Oh God, you're right. What a relief!' Edwina laughed but stopped when it made her head hurt. 'Okay. I think I can pull myself together in half an hour.'

The thought of even getting out of bed made her wince, but Jonathan's warm voice was so comforting. He had been an estate agent with Sotheby International when they first met, before he had started his own estate agency, selling apartments and houses. He and Edwina had clicked instantly and a very special friendship had begun – a friendship that had become stronger and closer as time passed.

'Take two Alka-Seltzers and jump in the shower,' Jonathan's voice said in her ear. 'See you in a tick. And I'll bring breakfast.'

'I'm not sure I can eat anything,' Edwina protested, feeling sick at the thought of food. But Jonathan had already hung up.

Clutching her head, Edwina got out of bed and dragged herself into the kitchen, searching in the cupboards for the Alka-Seltzer. She found them behind a packet of muesli and plopped two into a glass of water. Then she stood there while the tablets dissolved, squinting against the bright sunlight that was streaming in through the tall windows. The apartment, on the top floor of a Georgian building in Donnybrook, a swish Dublin suburb, was newly decorated and had everything Edwina had wished for: a large bedroom with an adjoining dressing room and spa-like bathroom, a state-of-the-art kitchen and a spacious living room with a balcony overlooking a beautiful garden below.

Bought five years ago with some of the money from her trust

fund, the apartment was the first home Edwina had ever owned. She had decorated it sparsely with just a few pieces of furniture: a huge sofa in the living room, a queen-size double bed, various side tables and a big glass-topped table in the kitchen-diner, where she often entertained friends and colleagues, serving food delivered from top restaurants in the area. The fridge was crammed with white wine and bottles of champagne but very little food, as she never really cooked anything and didn't spend much time at home when she wasn't entertaining.

As a fashion icon and buyer at Brown Thomas, the Irish equivalent to Harvey Nichols, Edwina had been very much in demand at fashionable parties and premieres. She was also well known for her podcast called 'How to be Fabulous', which had thousands of followers, before she closed it down. It had been the glitzy lifestyle she had always dreamed of. But now, standing here, she was beginning to see the cracks in the glossy image she had spent so much time and effort building up. She was nearly forty, after all. She couldn't keep on partying like this forever. She needed something fresh and new. Her sell-by date was running out – a frightening thought.

Edwina squinted at her image reflected in the wall-mounted oven door. Even in this blurry reflection, she knew she looked awful. She wasn't conventionally beautiful, but what she lacked in beauty she made up for in style. Now, however, there wasn't even that to fall back on. Her dark blonde hair with caramel highlights, cut in a shoulder-length bob, was flat and lank, and her usually sparkly green eyes had bags no amount of eye cream could shift. And Jonathan would be here in twenty minutes. Not that she needed to dress up for him, but she'd like to look at least human before he arrived.

Having gulped down the Alka-Seltzer, Edwina walked into the bathroom, peeled off her silk pyjamas and, after a quick shower, dried herself with a thick fluffy towel. Then, twenty minutes later, dressed in a soft pink cashmere jumpsuit, her freshly washed hair tucked behind her ears, her face bare of make-up, she opened the door to Jonathan, who, impeccably dressed in a bomber jacket, light blue shirt and chinos, looked businesslike and dapper. His hair was cut short and, with his clean-shaven face and horn-rimmed glasses, he looked the picture of a successful estate agent. He was carrying two paper mugs of coffee and a bag of croissants, and a folder under his arm.

Edwina smiled wanly as she let him in. 'Hi. I know I look like death warmed over, but I feel a lot better now than when I woke up.'

'Then you must have felt *truly* awful,' he said with the hint of a teasing smile. His grey eyes behind his glasses were warm as he studied her.

'I did, that's for sure.' Edwina took one of the paper mugs. 'Latte?'

'Yes. And an Americano for me.'

'Let's go and sit on the sofa,' Edwina said, leading the way into the living room. She sat down and pushed a few of the multicoloured silk cushions behind her, leaning back, sipping the coffee. She held out her hand. 'Actually, I think I can force down a croissant while you talk. And maybe you want to show me what's in that folder?' she suggested as Jonathan handed her a pastry. 'I take it it's not the Sunday papers.'

'No.' Jonathan sat down beside her and sipped his coffee, putting the bag with the croissants on the coffee table. 'It's something I think would be a great investment.'

'Really?' Edwina bit into her pastry. 'Please, not some apartment block you want me to buy into? You know I don't want to be a landlady.'

They had discussed the idea that Edwina would invest in some kind of property and Jonathan had promised to find something interesting and lucrative for her, as she had told him she desperately wanted a fresh start. Fashion and style were beginning to feel a little tired and her job had come to a dead end when the last collection she had picked out at the London Fashion Week didn't sell as well as she had hoped. In fact, it had bombed and her company had been left with a lot of expensive clothes that had to be included in the summer sale, at a loss for the store. Feeling quite hopeless, Edwina had handed in her resignation before they could fire her. This, on top of her recent break-up with a man she had thought was her perfect match, added to her sense of failure. That was when she had asked Jonathan for help. And now he looked as if he had come up with something.

'Is it in Dublin?' she asked.

Jonathan shook his head. 'No, it's something completely different. A row of houses for sale. Not in Dublin, but in Kerry.'

Startled, Edwina opened her mouth to speak. The mention of Kerry conjured up painful memories of when she had plotted to get the big family house in Strawberry Hill sold after her great-aunt's death. She had backed off at the last minute, however, when she realised what she was about to do to her cousin Gwen and her brother, Max, who both loved the house. It had been a hugely painful moment filled with shame, yet another disappointment to add to the list. Jonathan had been a great help then, even though he had been disappointed not to have got the sale. He had understood her dilemma and that had made them bond as friends.

'No,' she said. 'Please don't tell me it's some row of houses near Strawberry Hill.'

'It's in Sandy Cove,' Jonathan said.

'Not there!' Edwina exclaimed. 'You know how I feel about that whole area. It's...'

Jonathan held up a hand. 'Just listen to me for a moment. I know what you're thinking. It's the back of beyond and just down the road from Strawberry Hill and Max and Allegra. I know all about that trouble you had with your family and the inheritance. But—'

'They will always *hate* me for that,' Edwina cut in glumly. She was still sad about what had happened, cringing with guilt every time she thought about it. They had made some kind of peace but there was still a coldness between them. The bad vibes between her and her brother upset her so much that she avoided visiting them, despite longing to see her little nephews.

'That was nearly four years ago,' Jonathan said calmly. 'Surely they have moved on since then?'

'So they say,' Edwina replied. 'But we're not really close at all any more. Max is still very sour with me. And Allegra is always sweet, but that might be all pretence just to keep the peace.'

'Maybe you're just very prickly?' Jonathan suggested with a smile. 'You've been asking me since then what to do with the money from the sale of the land and what Max and Gwen gave you when they bought you out. I haven't found anything worth investing in until now. And this is it,' he said as he took a large brochure from the folder and laid it on the table.

Edwina stared at the photo on the front cover and instantly recognised the row of houses on the edge of a cliff, below which huge waves crashed against rocks. There was a little beach beside those rocks with white sand and slopes leading down to it, covered with wild roses. *Wild Rose Bay*, it said in the description. It was a stunningly beautiful place, but one with a lot of memories attached to it that she couldn't erase.

'Do you know where it is?'

'Yes. It's... it's the old coastguard station called Starlight Cottages,' Edwina murmured. 'The place where Allegra was staying when...'

Jonathan nodded. 'That's right.'

'And there's a house for sale there you want me to buy?'

Edwina looked at him, bewildered. 'Why is that such an investment? It's just a small cottage.'

The beautiful spot was suddenly vivid in her mind. More than beautiful, she remembered now, nearly feeling the sea breeze against her face. Unique and wild, with that end-of-the-world feel that had momentarily blown her mind when she had last seen it.

'No, not just one cottage.' Jonathan opened the brochure. 'The whole row of *four* cottages is for sale.'

Edwina stared at him. 'And...?'

'And you could buy them and do them up, and either sell them or rent them out.'

Edwina shook her head and pushed the brochure away. 'No, that's crazy. I don't see the investment there. It's a remote, backwards place. Nice, I agree, but not with what I'd call huge potential.'

Jonathan sighed. 'I have a feeling you're not very well informed when it comes to places that are becoming popular in Ireland.' He paused and pushed the brochure towards her. 'Forget about your own family history and try to think more like an investor. Sandy Cove is a hidden gem on the Wild Atlantic Way. It has two amazing beaches, great for surfing and swimming. Wonderful walking trails, and then there's this amazing wellness centre. All small-scale and discreet, and that's what people with money who love the great outdoors want.' He drew breath and looked at her expectantly.

Edwina blinked and then laughed. 'Oh yes, I get it now. For those people who don't play golf and want to wander in the wilderness in designer gear.'

Jonathan nodded. 'Exactly! I see it as getting in on the ground floor before property prices there shoot up. And these four cottages, once they've been done up, will be a true gold mine for you, whether you sell them or let them for huge rents in the summertime. I've heard people pay around a thousand euros a week for a nice holiday cottage during the high season.'

'You're pitching it to me,' Edwina said. 'So you want a quick sale to get the commission, and you thought I'd be easy to convince?'

'No.' Jonathan suddenly laughed. 'I always knew you'd be a hard nut to crack. I've had several offers already, but I thought I'd tell you about it before I decided. It's a great chance to get in on this particular market.' He leaned forward and looked deep into her eyes. 'Edwina, I know this will be good for you. It'll be fun and exciting and it will also help mend a lot of fences. Right now, you're at some kind of crossroads. You've quit your job, you had this painful experience with Matthew, and...'

'Please,' Edwina pleaded as the memory of her recent break-up made her shudder. 'Let's not go there, okay? That was horrible and I just want to forget it.' She stopped and met Jonathan's gaze. 'Let me think about it.'

He leaned back and sipped his coffee. 'Okay.'

Edwina put her mug on the table and took the brochure, flicking through it while Jonathan waited. 'Most of the cottages look fine to me. Why do they need to be done up?'

'They're not in the style that people want these days. They need to be turned into something very special, with all the comforts and class these people would expect. I'm thinking seaside chic with a Cape Cod touch. But let's leave that for the moment.'

'All right. I'll just have a look through these...'

Edwina gazed at the photos of the houses, their back gardens with stunning views, and suddenly remembered that day when she had stood on the terrace of the house Allegra was renting just before she had moved in with Max. It had been a cold, windy day in late October and Edwina had been feeling miserable after all that had happened between them. Allegra had been so kind that day, as if she understood how lost and lonely Edwina was feeling. She had felt so broken then but standing there, looking out to sea, she had felt oddly comforted.

Edwina closed her eyes as the memory of that place slowly came back to her. The clean, cool air with a tang of seaweed, the views across the bay, the deep blue water, the plaintive cries of the seagulls and the shimmering outline of the Skellig Islands against the setting sun. She had had a glimpse of a place that was heavenly, magical and romantic. A place that had briefly mesmerised her during a very painful time in her life. She had forgotten how it had made her feel until now, as the photos in the brochure jolted her memory.

Edwina put the folder back on the table and met Jonathan's eyes and saw the challenge there. He was daring her to get into something new and risky, something that could fail – or might succeed with flying colours. And there was something else about going back to that place. Maybe it was a chance to heal the rift between her and her brother, an opportunity to get closer to him, Allegra and the children again and have a family at last.

It was suddenly like standing on a diving board looking into deep water, deciding whether to jump or not. She felt a dart of fear. Then she took a deep breath.

'Okay. Let's do it. Let's go to Sandy Cove and take a look at the coastguard station.'

2
_____

Jonathan's jaw dropped. 'What? You mean you've decided just like that?'

Edwina nodded. 'Yes. To take a *look*. Not to buy it yet. I want to go there and see...'

She didn't quite know what she meant, except that she wanted to stand on that spot and look out over the ocean again and feel the peace that had been so soothing when she had been so desperately sad and lonely.

'This is not like doing something fun on an impulse,' she added. 'It seems like a huge undertaking to me. So don't get your hopes up.'

'Yeah, of course. But I thought you'd refuse to even *see* the place. What did I say to make you change your mind?'

'It was nothing you said,' Edwina replied. 'It was something that hit me just now. A memory, a feeling... I was suddenly standing there, at the back of that little house Allegra was renting when she first came to Kerry. And I felt the wind on my face and heard the seagulls and saw the sun setting behind those islands.' She shook her head and smiled. 'I felt that place calling me.' She laughed. 'Now you're going to think I'm bonkers.'

'No,' Jonathan said, looking pleased. 'It's the magic of Sandy Cove. Once you've been there, you'll never forget it.'

'Well, I did forget,' Edwina argued. 'But those photos took me back there.' She drained her mug and put it on the table, picking up the brochure again. 'So, four houses, you said. Who's selling them?'

'The first two belong to a couple who need something bigger for their grandchildren who come to visit often. They've bought a house with a garden nearby – the cottages aren't really suitable for small children because of the steep cliffs.'

'I can imagine.' Edwina turned the page to the third cottage. 'And this one?'

'That one is owned by a Dutch woman who is moving back home to live near her family.'

'And the fourth?'

'It belonged to an artist who has bought a bigger house in the area so there's room for her mother-in-law. The owner of that last cottage was very reluctant to leave, apparently.'

'I can understand that.' Edwina turned her attention to the photos of the interiors of the cottages. 'They're all different. The first one is very cosy but a little old-fashioned, and the second one is too bare and the kitchen décor doesn't fit the seaside setting. It's too modern, I think. As for the third one...' Edwina studied the photos of the living room and kitchen that had been combined by taking down a wall. 'This open-plan layout is a little dated. It doesn't really work here. And the fourth one is quite run-down.'

'I know,' Jonathan agreed. 'My idea would be for you to do up all the cottages in a similar style. Bleached wood floorboards, exposed beams and furniture that matches the seaside. Beach-comber feel, in a very elegant way, if you see what I mean.'

Edwina nodded. 'I do. Cape Cod, the Hamptons and all

those classy houses with simple but expensive furniture. And the little gardens at the back... Something with a nearly Japanese look. Gravel, the odd potted plant...' Her creative side started to kick in and she began to feel excited at the prospect of doing up the houses and turning them into bijou residences. It would be an amazing project, something she could be proud of, finally proving that she could do something serious.

'So, what if you want to make an offer on the houses?' Jonathan asked.

'I'm not sure I want to buy them at all,' Edwina protested. 'I'd have to talk to my accountant in any case. He might not think it's a good investment.'

'I think he will,' Jonathan argued. 'Anyway, the price is at the back of the brochure. Show it to him and then we'll discuss it.'

'Okay.' She turned to the back of the brochure and hiccupped when she saw the amount. 'Oh, heck, it's nearly a million euros. That's a lot of money. And then all the work that has to be done...'

Edwina felt a dart of disappointment. The thought of buying the cottages and doing them up had seriously piqued her interest. She had always loved anything to do with interior design, and watched house makeover programmes with huge interest, trying to imagine what she would do with an old house. The idea of turning these cottages into charming little gems was beginning to capture her. It would be the most exciting thing she had ever done. But when she saw the price, she realised what a risk it would be.

'It's open to negotiation,' Jonathan said. 'But there isn't a lot of wiggle room. So let me know what you want to do.'

'I will.' Edwina sat back and took another croissant from the bag. 'I haven't even seen the place yet, but I'm feeling suddenly brighter.'

'I can see that.' Jonathan smiled. 'Your colour is a lot better already.'

'Oh, Jonathan,' Edwina said wistfully. 'You know how I always wanted to do something like this. And now, remembering the ocean and the seagulls, and the islands in the distance... I just have a feeling Sandy Cove is a very healing place.'

'I think it is,' Jonathan replied. 'I often take a trip there when I'm in Killarney.'

'You're really hooked on Kerry,' Edwina remarked.

'It's kind of growing on me, I suppose,' he said. 'And I'm sure it will grow on you too.'

'My mother wasn't from Kerry, like yours.'

'No, your mother is from Belgravia.'

Edwina laughed and leaned back against the cushions. 'She isn't *really* from Belgravia, she just seems to spend a lot of time shopping there. And other posh parts of London. When I was a little girl, I thought she was born in Harrods.'

'A very glamorous woman, I have to say.'

'I suppose.' Edwina's thoughts drifted to her mother, who, born in England, had been married twice since the divorce from her Irish husband, who had died in a car crash a few years after the divorce. Her father's death had been traumatic for Edwina as she had been in boarding school and about to spend the Christmas holidays at Strawberry Hill.

She still remembered what a sad place it had been, and Max's devastated face at the funeral and those weeks afterwards in the cold, dark house. Not to mention their mother not being there for them, which Edwina had still not managed to forgive. Their relationship was fairly friendly these days, but far from the mother-daughter bond that Edwina felt she needed. Her mother divided her time between Dublin and her native London, flitting back and forth like a colourful butterfly. She was in town right now and had called Edwina and asked her to lunch the following day.

'Glamorous and cold like the diamonds she likes to wear,' Edwina murmured.

'Maybe she's sad and lonely deep down?' Jonathan suggested.

'Could be,' Edwina said with a shrug. 'But she'd never admit it.'

'It's a pity you don't get on. For both of you,' Jonathan said.

'I know, but there's nothing I can do about it. Anyway, let's not dwell on that.'

'Not today anyway.' Jonathan gathered up his folder. 'I'd better get going. I'm driving down to Killarney later today. I'm going to spend a week looking at offices. I'm thinking of moving my firm down there.'

'Oh?' Edwina looked at him in surprise. 'Is this a new thing?'

'I've been thinking about it for a while. I want to handle properties down there. It's a growing market, especially the holiday homes.'

'But I thought you loved Dublin? You're doing so well here.'

'Yeah,' Jonathan said. 'Dublin is great, but it's not where I want to spend the rest of my life.'

'I never thought of it that way,' Edwina said, startled by this revelation. 'I haven't a clue where I want to spend the rest of my life.'

She had no answer to that question and wondered why she hadn't spent much time thinking about it. But now that Jonathan had raised the issue, she was beginning to worry. Where *did* she want to spend the rest of her life? She hadn't found that place yet, and maybe she never would.

Jonathan got up. 'Maybe you should think about that?'

'Yes, maybe,' Edwina said. 'As I'm about to hit the big four-oh soon. Like you said, it feels as if I'm at some kind of crossroads in my life. But I'm suddenly excited about this new project... I'll call you as soon as I've spoken to my accountant. And then I'll go to Sandy Cove to take a look.'

'Great.' Jonathan started to walk out of the room. 'I'll let you know when I'm back in town and we'll have dinner. See you soon.'

'Bye, Jonathan. Have a good trip to Kerry,' Edwina said and waved.

As the front door slammed behind him, Edwina lay back against the sofa cushions, her thoughts drifting. The investment he had put before her was unusual – not something she had planned to do – but it had grabbed her interest after her initial hesitation. It would be amazing to turn those cottages into something truly unique that would have her stamp on it.

What she had said to Jonathan about being at a crossroads was true. She needed a change and a challenge, and maybe something more. When he had given her the brochure with those photos it was as if it was *meant* to happen, as if he was showing her the way to a whole new life where she would not only start a new career, but also get closer to the only family she had. She didn't realise how much she missed them until Jonathan had reminded her of the rift between her and Max.

And now, as she thought about the project and what it would bring, she felt a spark of excitement. The memory of that unique little village on the edge of the Atlantic drifted back into Edwina's mind. *Yes*, she thought, *it feels right and exciting and exactly what I need. It might also bring me closer to Max, the brother I lost many years ago...*

The conversation with Jim, her accountant, on Tuesday morning did not go the way Edwina had hoped. He wasn't as enthusiastic about investing in the four cottages as she had anticipated, telling her it would involve spending most of her capital, which he strongly advised against. He had been her accountant and handled her financial affairs ever since her grandmother set up her trust fund when she was twenty-one, and he had been a rock of good sense all through the years.

Edwina was astonished to hear that she didn't actually have the cash flow she needed to safely invest in the cottages. And when he pointed out to her that it would be foolish to sink all her capital into a project that carried many risks, she felt disappointment settle on her like a damp cloth. As she listened to what he had to say, her beautiful dream of a whole new career slowly faded. But when he had finished, she sat up and fixed him with a steely look.

'Okay. You've doomed and gloomed enough,' she told him. 'And you might be right. But you know what? Life's too short to be careful.'

'Maybe.' Jim shrugged. 'But you know what I've said about putting all your eggs in one basket.'

Edwina laughed. 'Yeah, but I rather like the idea of cracking them to make a delicious omelette.'

He peered at her. 'You're in a strange mood. You're not usually this reckless. What's happened?'

'I don't know, but I feel I need something different. I want to live a little, take a walk on the wild side. You know what I mean?'

He shook his head. 'Not really. But I have a strange feeling you're going to do it, despite all I've said. Maybe you could find someone to help you out? Someone who might want to join you in this project?'

'But then it wouldn't be *mine*,' Edwina protested. 'I can't think of anyone who'd be willing to help me out, in any case. I'll have to do this on my own, or not at all.' She paused and took a deep breath before she continued. 'Look, Jim, I know you think I should be sitting on that pile of money for the rest of my life, but it's beginning to feel like a burden instead of a blessing. So what if I lose it all? That could be another kind of blessing. So now I'm even more determined to do this. It could be the making of me! Or the worst disaster. But I'm going to do it, no matter what.'

'In that case, be careful, is all I can say.'

'Careful seems so *boring*.' She leaned forward and kissed his cheek. 'Bye, Jim. Thanks for all you've done through the years.'

'That sounded like you're not coming back.'

'Oh, I'll be back.' Edwina laughed. 'But only for you to handle my taxes. The rest I'll take care of myself from now on.' Then she smiled, waved and walked out, feeling as free as a bird and oddly grown up for the first time in her life. She was in charge of her own affairs at last.

She suddenly realised, as she left the building and walked down the street on her way to meet her mother, that something was shifting in her life. She didn't quite know what it was, but it felt good. She would buy those cottages and spend the summer doing them up. And then, who knew? Something else might come up. But this was now, and she would raise the money to buy the coastguard station, even if it meant blowing all she had.

During her stay in Sandy Cove she would not only work on this exciting project, but also try to mend her relationship with her brother and his family. She had two baby nephews she hardly knew. Now she had a chance to get to know them properly and try to be a fun aunt they would love to spend time with. A fresh new beginning seemed to wait for her around the corner. A new life with an exciting challenge. And it was waiting for her in Kerry.

The only spoke in the wheel was that cash flow problem Jim had mentioned. She needed a lot of money and it would mean using up her entire capital, which seemed quite risky. If she was to succeed in buying the cottages and getting started on the project, she needed help. She knew it was a little crazy to make such a decision without viewing the property first. But she had been there and remembered how magical that place was. The more she thought about it, the more she wanted to go there and do this project. But how was she going to realise it without going completely broke? There was only one solution, not one Edwina was happy about but, if she wanted to go ahead, she had to take the proverbial bull by the horns and...

Edwina gritted her teeth, wondering if it was worth it. But yes, she wanted it so badly she was prepared to do anything to get it.

Anything at all.

3

Lunch at the small, exclusive and wildly expensive restaurant was a tense affair. Pamela Smythe-Delahunt, Edwina's mother, looked her usual polished self. Her gleaming light-blonde hair was cut in a short sleek style, her Chanel suit fitted her slim body to perfection and, despite having recently turned sixty-five, she didn't look a day over fifty.

'Hello, Mummy,' Edwina said as they air-kissed on both cheeks. 'You look fabulous as always.'

'Thank you, darling,' Pamela said, her bright blue eyes sweeping over Edwina as she sat down. 'You've put on a little weight. But you look well,' she added, making it sound like a criticism.

'I haven't gained weight actually,' Edwina said, feeling the usual annoyance with her mother. 'I weigh exactly the same as last time.'

Pamela's perfectly arched eyebrows shot up. 'Really? But you look a little puffy. Are you not sleeping?'

'I sleep like a baby,' Edwina said, trying her best not to snap. 'Can we stop the comments on my appearance now? I'm fine, everything is great and I'm very happy,' she added with a stiff smile.

Pamela sighed. 'I'm sorry. I didn't mean to criticise. I'm just worried about you, that's all. I'm not at all happy that you quit your job without a thought of what you're going to do next.'

'But I have,' Edwina announced. 'I'm thinking of getting into a whole new project that I'm very excited about. A bit of a financial risk, but I think it will all work out in the end.'

Edwina paused and took a breath, wondering if putting it like that was the right way to go. Asking her mother for help to realise her dream felt both right and, at the same time, very wrong. Pamela wasn't one to part with her cash easily, and their mother-daughter relationship was already fraught with conflict. Edwina knew that asking for help would make her look vulnerable instead of strong and independent. But it was out there now, so she had to make the best of it.

'What project?' Pamela asked.

Suddenly getting cold feet, Edwina smiled and shrugged, trying to look as if she had been joking. 'Oh never mind. It's just an idea. I might not do it at all. Forget I said anything.'

Pamela's blue eyes were suddenly serious. 'You're getting into something risky? What is it?'

'Not *risky*, exactly. But you probably wouldn't approve, so...' Edwina sighed and gave up. It was no use. Her mother would not understand how much it would mean to her. She would have to look for another partner.

'Tell me!' Pamela insisted.

'It's something I've always dreamed of doing.'

'Like what? Edwina, you have to tell me what it is.'

'I don't think you'll like it.'

'Why not?' Pamela's eyes softened. 'If it's something that will cheer you up, I'd be willing to help you out.'

'Okay, I'll tell you. I want to invest in some property in Kerry.' Edwina groped in her tote bag, pulled out the brochure and laid it on the table. 'It's a row of coastguard cottages in Sandy Cove.'

'Oh?' Pamela picked up the brochure and started to flick through it. 'This looks interesting...' she muttered to herself. 'Sweet little cottages in... where did you say?'

'Sandy Cove, not far away from Strawberry Hill. It's a very unique place on the coast, as you might know.' Edwina babbled on while Pamela slowly turned the pages and studied the photos. 'That area is becoming quite fashionable with people who like to surf and walk in the mountains, and really beginning to take off with the wealthy crowd. The cottages could be made into bijou houses and let for a lot of money, you see? Or sold on for twice the price when they've been refurbished.' Edwina drew breath, on tenterhooks as she waited for her mother's reaction.

'Hmm,' Pamela said, looking at the photos. 'Nice area. Gorgeous views. Great potential, I have to admit.' She flicked to the back, her eyes widening as she saw the purchase price before handing the brochure back to Edwina with a curious expression in her eyes. 'And you're doing this with whom?'

'Eh, just me,' Edwina said. 'I thought I'd buy them and organise the renovations on my own.'

Pamela looked startled. 'All alone? You can't be serious. That would mean spending what's left of your trust fund, and more. You might have to take a loan.'

Edwina stuck out her chin. 'Yes. And I will if I have to.'

'Not if...' Pamela murmured.

'If what?' Edwina asked, the rest of sentence hanging in the air.

'Not if you get someone else on board.'

'Like who?' Edwina held her breath, realising her mother was actually in favour of the idea. Was Pamela really going to help her out financially? It was the ideal solution on the one hand, but on the other it might mean a lot of interference that could make things even worse between them in the end. 'Are you saying...?' Edwina started.

'Yes. Someone like me,' Pamela replied, as if reading Edwina's thoughts.

Edwina swallowed, not quite believing it was happening. 'Are you serious?'

Pamela nodded. 'Yes. I suddenly had this mad idea that you might like to do this with me. That we could have fun and maybe get a bit closer while we work on it.'

'Oh.' Edwina was stunned to hear her mother utter those words. 'Yes, it would be a nice thing to do with you. I mean, you're so good at interior design. Like a professional.' Edwina sighed and put the brochure back in her bag. 'But maybe it's too much of a financial risk for you? Silly of me to even mention it...'

'Yes,' Pamela said, looking thoughtful. 'And no.'

Edwina looked at her mother. 'No? What?'

'Not so silly.'

'Really?' Edwina said, feeling a mixture of hope and dread.

She wasn't really sure she wanted her mother to get involved, but at the same time she needed the financial backing, and perhaps also the support of someone who might have more experience than her. Pamela had bought and sold a number of apartments over the past few years, always coming out better off than when she started. This project was not about apartments in the best part of town, however. It was a completely different idea, the outcome of which was not predictable.

'Could be risky,' Edwina repeated.

'But fun,' Pamela said. 'Not my thing at all – that outdoorsy stuff and seaside sports. Too frisky for me, but I know it's all the rage now. And Kerry is becoming quite the in place these days. It might be an idea to get in on the ground floor, so to speak. I'm not keen to get involved with builders and decorators in a place like that, though. But I have a feeling you'll be hands-on and want to run the whole thing?'

'Yes, that's my plan. You wouldn't have to be near the place at all.' Edwina looked pleadingly at her mother, feeling like a six-year-old. 'I so want to do this,' she said. 'If you could help me, I'd be so happy.'

'It could all go belly-up, of course,' Pamela said, looking thoughtful. 'And I'd end up with a lot of money down the drain.'

'Or it could be a huge success and we'd be better off than when we started,' Edwina filled in.

'It's a gamble,' Pamela said, sounding doubtful. 'And I never gamble.' She picked up the menu. 'Let's get something to eat and think about it. What would you like?'

'Something plain.' Edwina's stomach was suddenly in a knot as she knew that Pamela could change her mind and back out very quickly. She looked through the menu. 'Lemon and herb chicken salad looks nice.'

'Sounds good.' Pamela ordered the same for herself when the waiter arrived and waved away the bread basket. 'Just water, please, and then camomile tea for two.'

When the food arrived they ate in silence for a while, Edwina chewing the chicken without tasting it, while Pamela prattled on about her visit to Dublin and the friends she had met up with.

'I had dinner with Max last night,' Pamela said. 'He was in town for a business meeting early this morning, but he's driving back to Kerry straight away.'

'Oh? He didn't call to say he was here,' Edwina said, feeling hurt that her brother hadn't been in touch.

'Didn't have the time, I'd say,' Pamela replied. 'He was in a hurry to get back to Allegra and the boys.' Pamela shook her head disapprovingly. 'Utter madness to move to Kerry, I think. And living in that old wreck with two small children, what are they thinking? Such a pity it wasn't sold.'

'They love the house,' Edwina said, defending her brother.

'So why shouldn't they live there? I'm glad the house wasn't sold. I still feel guilty about trying to force them...'

Pamela put her hand on Edwina's. 'I know you do, but there's no need to feel guilty. I think you were quite right about that.'

'Oh, but you don't understand how they feel about Strawberry Hill,' Edwina argued. 'I didn't either, until Max explained it to me.'

And I didn't understand how they felt about Sandy Cove, until I stood on that terrace and looked out over the ocean, she thought.

Having finished her salad, Pamela put down her knife and fork and looked at Edwina. 'You're looking a little sad. Is it because of that awful man?'

'What awful man?' Edwina asked before she realised what her mother was talking about.

'Matthew O'Donnell,' Pamela replied.

'Oh him,' Edwina said, feeling a dart of pain at the mention of his name. 'No, that was just a huge mistake. I shouldn't have become involved with someone like that.'

'I don't blame you, though,' Pamela said. 'He was quite the looker – not to mention the money, the car, the villa in the south of France... What a couple you were.' She sighed. 'So sad you let him go.'

'I didn't let him go,' Edwina said hotly, the memory of the break-up suddenly hitting her like a stab in the chest. 'He broke up with *me*.'

Edwina had been swept off her feet by a handsome, charming man she had met on holiday in Saint-Tropez. She had been completely bowled over by his film star looks, dark wavy hair, bright blue eyes and deeply tanned perfect body. His name was Matthew O'Donnell, a stockbroker and entrepreneur from Dublin who was supposed to be one of the most eligible men in Ireland. Their eyes had met across the dance floor in a nightclub and he had walked over to where she was sitting with her friends and asked her to dance. They had danced until the small hours of the morning, ending up in bed in his villa nearby. After that, they had spent every moment of the following week together until Edwina had to get back to Ireland.

Matthew had followed her home and they'd had a whirlwind romance that lasted until the end of the summer, when he suddenly broke it off. He couldn't give her the commitment she wanted, he said, and he didn't want to be tied down. Edwina had cried herself to sleep every night for a month, and then had slowly come to her senses and told herself he wasn't worth her tears. It had been so hard to face everyone afterwards and notice the pitying looks sent in her direction. She was only now, at the start of the following summer, beginning to enjoy herself again.

'I was *dumped*, Mum,' she said, to emphasise what had happened.

'That's not what I heard,' Pamela protested.

'That's not what you're telling your friends, you mean,' Edwina said bitterly.

'I didn't really know what happened,' Pamela said. 'I thought *you* left *him*.'

'So you made up a story that sounded better?' Edwina leaned forward and looked at her mother. 'You know what? He wasn't even nice to me. We never really knew each other properly. We just partied like there was no tomorrow and then, well, I saw what was behind the glossy façade and it wasn't pretty. Maybe he saw the real me too and didn't like it? Who knows? But I'm glad it ended, even if it hurt me at the time.'

'I wish you'd settle down,' Pamela said, shaking her head. 'With someone suitable and dependable.'

'That kind of man is thin on the ground.' Edwina pushed her half-eaten chicken salad away. 'I'm suddenly not hungry any more. Maybe I should go.'

Pamela put her hand on Edwina's arm. 'Please don't leave just yet. I haven't told you what I think of your project.'

'I know what you're going to say. It's not the kind of thing you'd like to invest in. To small, too rural, too—'

'No. You're wrong. I want us to do it,' Pamela interrupted. 'I want to help you buy it and then you can do what you like with it. And I'll only help if you need me.'

Startled, Edwina stared at her mother. 'What? Are you serious?'

'Never more serious in my life,' Pamela declared. 'You want to do this, and you think it'll make you happy. It might be the start of something new for you, developing properties. You're intelligent and creative. This could make you or break you.'

'Yeah.' Edwina sighed. 'Probably break me. I don't know much about renovating work or building. So it'll probably fail spectacularly.'

Pamela shook her head. 'Possibly. But you won't know until you try. So go for it, darling. I think it's a great chance for you to move on from everything you've been through.' Pamela sat back and looked at Edwina, her mouth breaking into a smile. 'I bet you never thought you'd hear me say that.'

'Never in a million years,' Edwina admitted, still flabbergasted as she wondered what had made her mother turn around like that in just a few minutes. 'Why are you doing this?' she finally asked.

Pamela sighed and squeezed Edwina's hand. 'Because I don't want you to end up like me,' she said in a near whisper. 'I never achieved much in my life, except marrying men with lots of money. And I'm too old to change that, but I want to watch you do what I never did.'

'Oh,' Edwina said, stuck for words. It made her happy to hear what Pamela had just said, and she had a feeling it had come from the heart. But as she looked into her mother's eyes, she saw a sadness there she hadn't noticed before. 'Are you okay?' she asked.

'I'm fine.' Pamela shook her head and straightened up. 'Let's have that tea and iron out the details. Then we could go to my solicitor and get an agreement drawn up to do the conveyancing, once we've made an offer. And then we'll sort out the money and how much we should agree to spend. How's that?'

'Perfect,' Edwina said, suddenly feeling a wave of love for her mother, a love she had never really felt before.

Why had it taken so many years for that to happen? She knew the road ahead would have many turns and bumps, and that there would be anger and arguments and irritations. But she was ready for that, and for the challenge of taking on a project in that wild, wonderful place. It had been like a curtain parting to show her something beautiful before it closed because of her own blindness to what was truly there. She needed to go and see it again and feel that soft wind on her face and hear the seagulls and the waves crashing against the rocks.

'This is going to be quite exciting,' Pamela said. 'Don't you think?'

'Oh yes.' Edwina looked at her mother as tears welled up. 'Thank you,' she whispered, feeling as if she had been given a wonderful gift.

Sandy Cove here I come, she thought, the anticipation making her heart beat faster. A new adventure was beginning and she couldn't wait for it to start.

4

A month later, in early June, Edwina was driving down the country road towards Sandy Cove after picking up the keys to the cottages at Jonathan's new office in Killarney. She had intended to drive straight to the village, but on a whim, decided to call in to Strawberry Hill on the way. She hadn't told Max or Allegra she was coming or why, as she didn't want to jinx the project. And her mother had advised against her telling Max anything. He might be against it and, even if he wasn't, he'd interfere with everything they wanted to do. Architects were like that, Pamela had said, which was probably true.

It had looked as if it wouldn't happen at all, but now it was all done and Edwina was taking possession of the four cottages the following day. There had been a lot of wrangling and nego-tiating during the past month between Edwina and her mother, which had threatened to turn into a serious argument, but Edwina had stood her ground and told Pamela, when she started to dither, that she had to be either in or out. That had threatened to lead to a serious falling-out until Pamela finally agreed to put up half the purchase price, plus thirty per cent of the renovation costs. After that they had hugged and cried a little, and all was well again between them.

Jonathan had been a surprisingly tough negotiator, but then he had to think of his clients and the commission for his firm. But if Jonathan was tough, Pamela was even tougher and she had finally managed to get the purchase price down by nearly ten per cent. It was all sewn up to everyone's satisfaction and they had a celebratory drink at the Shelbourne when all the papers had been signed. Pamela cosied up to Jonathan and declared him to be a true gem of a man, which made him blush furiously.

Edwina smiled at the memory and felt a dart of happiness that she was getting closer to her mother. She knew that they would have tiffs and arguments, and that she would need a lot of patience, but it was a very positive step forward all the same. And now she would have to tackle Max and explain what she was doing, which wouldn't be easy.

She wasn't staying at Strawberry Hill with her brother, but in a small flat over a shop she had seen for rent in Sandy Cove. It was simple but looked clean and comfortable and it would do while she oversaw the renovation of the cottages. The rent was very reasonable and it would be fine as a base for the summer. It would also be fun to live in the centre of the village and get a feel for the people and their daily lives. Edwina hoped they wouldn't see her as an outsider, but part of Max's family as she had heard they were very much liked there, which was probably all Allegra's doing. Getting on with everyone would make her work on the project easier as well. She was looking forward to spending the summer there, and hoped to have time off to enjoy the beautiful beaches and walks in the mountains.

She had also traded in her rather big car for an Audi A3 Sportback, which, being smaller and more compact, she figured would be easier to drive on narrow country roads. Now, as she made her way through the twists and turns on the back roads, she congratulated herself on her choice. She had picked a red model with beige leather upholstery, which was pretty rather than practical, and not exactly ideal for country living, but she had fallen in love with it at the showroom and thrown caution to the wind. Life was too short to *always* be practical.

As she neared her destination, Edwina turned the car around a tight bend and gasped as a battered Toyota Yaris suddenly came hurtling towards her at breakneck speed. Oh, no! It was going to hit her brand new car. Gasping, she pressed on the brake as hard as she could. The tyres squealed as she swerved and nearly went into the ditch before she managed to come to a stop. Shocked and furious, panting hard, she stared out the window at the driver in the other car, a man with dark hair and eyes that blazed with anger as he stared back at her.

Shaking, Edwina got out as the man emerged from the other car. 'What the hell do you think you were doing, driving like an idiot?' she exclaimed.

The man walked towards her and stopped, still glaring at her. 'Oh yeah? What about the way you came around the bend like a bat out of hell?' He glanced at her number plate. 'A Dubliner. Typical.' He looked her up and down. 'Where do you think you are? Grafton Street?'

'That's a pedestrian street,' Edwina retorted, while noticing how handsome he was. 'So it would be impossible to drive down. But of course a Kerry yobbo wouldn't know that.'

He suddenly laughed, his brown eyes softening. 'Yeah right.' He eyed her white jeans and pink linen shirt. 'And what is a Dublin princess doing in the back of beyond?'

'None of your business. You could have killed me!'

'Ditto,' he said.

'My car nearly went into the ditch!' Edwina touched the back of her neck. 'I think I have a touch of whiplash, as well. I could sue you, you know.'

'You could try,' he said, looking suddenly amused. 'But then I could sue you right back. Or I could call the Guards right now and get you arrested.'

'For what?' she asked. She would have enjoyed their repartee if she hadn't been so annoyed. But despite her annoyance, his good looks were making her feel flustered.

'For reckless driving. You must have been doing at least eighty coming around that bend.' He paused and shrugged. 'But hey, I'll let you off this time if you could reverse back a few hundred metres so I can get past you. The road is a bit wider back there.'

'Why should I?' she snapped, still seething at the fright he had given her, even though she was beginning to feel seriously attracted to him. 'Why don't *you* reverse and let me pass you a bit further on? There's plenty of room.' She pointed at a place in the road behind him where there was a gap beside a gate.

'I'm in a hurry.'

'To do what?' she asked, looking at his dark blue bomber jacket and beige chinos. 'Play golf?'

'To see a patient,' he said. 'I'm a doctor.' He held out his hand. 'My name is Shane Flaherty and I'm the GP in Sandy Cove.'

'What?' Edwina said, feeling confused. 'I thought the GP in Sandy Cove was a woman. At least, that was what my brother told me.'

'She was – is. But she's on leave and I'm filling in for her this summer.'

'Oh, okay.' Edwina reluctantly shook his hand. 'I'm Edwina Courtney-Smythe.'

'Courtney-Smythe? Are you related to Max?' Shane asked when they had shaken hands. 'He told me he had a sister in Dublin, I think. So that would be you?'

'Yes.'

'Nice to meet you. Now if you could just move your car...'

'Okay,' Edwina sighed. 'But only because you're on your way to see a sick person. Otherwise I'd refuse.'

'How very charitable of you,' he said sarcastically and started to walk back to his car.

Edwina didn't reply, but got into her car and backed it slowly around the bend, annoyed that he had forced her to make this difficult manoeuvre on a narrow country road with poor visibility. When she was finally at the point in the road with enough room for two cars, Shane drove around her and tooted as he passed. She could see his wide smile before he drove off and was about to make a rude gesture but changed her mind. She would probably bump into him in the village from time to time. No need to make a bad impression, even if she thought he was arrogant.

She started the car and drove slowly up the road until she came to the entrance to Strawberry Hill. The tall iron gates had been repaired and painted and the two eagles on the pillars restored. The gate lodge was still a wreck, and the avenue up to the house had as many potholes as before. But flanked by green fields where horses grazed, and huge oaks that provided shade from the hot summer sun, it was a lovely drive all the way to the big house that sat on a hill overlooking beautiful countryside.

Edwina pulled up in front of the house and looked up at the façade. It was an imposing early Georgian house with wide steps leading up to the massive front door. A lovely house with beautiful grounds that impressed most people. But Edwina had very mixed feelings about it. Her childhood holidays here had often been traumatic, as they had come here after her parents' divorce, and then when her father died only a few years later. She had never been happy here – unlike Max, who had loved spending holidays here, riding with their great-aunt Davina and their cousin Gwen, who now ran a horse training and breeding business from the house and stables. And Max had moved his architect firm here when he married Allegra, whose website design business was also based from the house. It was a hive of activity and a home for Max and Allegra and their two little boys, Patrick and Christopher.

Edwina felt a dart of dread. It was strange to be back after all that had happened and she wondered how Max would react when he saw her. There was still tension between them, from the harsh words that had been said years ago and, even though they had somehow made peace, there wasn't much affection between them. That was why she had stayed away and not seen her little nephews that often. But now she was here and she wanted desperately to be part of this family. But she didn't know quite how to handle them – especially her brother.

After a moment's reflection, Edwina drove around the corner to the back of the house, as the front door was rarely used. She parked the car in the courtyard and got out, walking to the open back door and stepping into the utility room where two large black dogs rose from their beds and started to bark. Edwina snapped a curt 'sit' and the dogs stopped barking and sat down, looking sheepishly at her.

'Good dogs,' Edwina said and gave each of them a pat on the head before she entered the large kitchen, where two little boys with blond hair were circling the huge table on their tricycles, shouting at each other at the tops of their voices while a small white Jack Russell barked loudly, running after them.

'Hello!' Edwina shouted. 'Patrick and Christopher, please stop making that noise.'

The boys stopped cycling and stared at her. 'Who is that?' Christopher, the smallest of the two boys asked, pointing at her.

'It's... it's our auntie,' Patrick, the older boy, said. 'Auntie Edwina.'

'Auntie 'wina?' Christopher said.

'*Ed*wina,' Patrick corrected. 'I know her, but you don't 'cos you were just a baby when she was here before.' He looked at Edwina. 'I'm three,' he said proudly.

'Congratulations,' she said and bent down to smile at the smallest boy. 'Hello, Christopher. I'm your auntie. I saw you when you were a baby but now you're a big boy, aren't you?'

Christopher nodded, staring at her with his big brown eyes.

Patrick got off his tricycle and ran towards her. 'Did you bring sweeties?'

Edwina jumped back, worried about sticky fingers on her pristine white jeans. 'No.'

'Why?' he asked.

'I forgot.'

They were interrupted by Allegra arriving into the kitchen with an armful of laundry.

'Edwina?' she said, looking startled. 'Hi. I had no idea you were coming. Max didn't tell me.'

Edwina looked at her pretty sister-in-law, her long strawberry-blonde hair ruffled by the wind and her rosy cheeks. 'Hi, Allegra. I haven't told anyone. I thought I'd surprise you all.'

'Well, you did.' Allegra put the pile of laundry on the table and picked up Christopher. 'Say hi to Auntie Edwina, Chris.'

'Hi,' Chris said and stuck his thumb into his mouth. He looked adorable with his blond locks and big brown eyes.

'Are you here for the weekend?' Allegra asked. 'Or a bit longer? I'll make up the bed in your old room if you like, or you might want to stay in the blue room further down the corridor. Not as close to the nursery, so a bit quieter.'

'I'm not staying here at all,' Edwina said. 'I'm on my way to Sandy Cove.'

'You are? Why?' Allegra asked, looking confused. 'What are you doing there?'

'Long story,' Edwina said. She paused, remembering what her mother had said: to keep quiet about why she was there as long as she could. Max would probably not approve and then he'd try to get involved and argue about everything Edwina planned to do with the cottages. 'I'm here for a good rest and to do a health and fitness month at that Wellness Centre in Sandy Cove,' she lied. 'And, of course, to spend time with my gorgeous nephews. I felt I had to get to know them properly.'

'You... what?' Allegra let a wriggling Chris onto the floor. 'Where is Noirin?' she asked.

'Upstairs,' Patrick replied. 'In the nursery, tidying up 'cos we made a mess.'

Allegra nodded. 'Okay. Paddy, please take Chris with you and go and help Noirin tidy up. And then come down here for your supper. I want you in your pyjamas when Daddy comes home so he can read you a story before you go to bed.'

'Okay-dokey,' Paddy said and took his brother by the hand. 'Come on, Chris. We have to find Noirin.'

Allegra smiled fondly as the two little boys trotted out of the kitchen with the little dog at their heels. 'See you later, boys. I'm going to have tea with Auntie Edwina and then I'll make you supper.' She turned to Edwina. 'Please sit down while I put the kettle on. And then you can tell me all about what you're doing.'

'I will.' Edwina sat down, having checked the chair for stains or blobs of jam.

'It's perfectly clean,' Allegra remarked.

Edwina sat down. 'I know. It's just that with the kids...'

'You don't know what to expect?' Allegra laughed while she filled the kettle. 'You're right. You never know what you might find. White jeans might not be the best thing to wear in this house.'

'That little dog is nice,' Edwina said. 'Is it new?'

'We got her about a year ago. Her name is Maureen O'Hara and she's a right little diva, but the boys adore her.'

Edwina laughed. 'Maureen O'Hara? That's a hoot.'

'It was a joke really, but the name stuck. I think it suits her.'

Allegra turned on the kettle and started to fold the laundry on the table. 'I'll just tidy these up while the kettle boils.'

'You have so much to do,' Edwina said. 'And then you have your web designer business as well. How on earth do you manage it all?'

'It can be stressful,' Allegra replied. 'But I have a strict schedule and get a lot done in the mornings while Noirin takes the boys out for walks. She's a life-saver. I don't know what I'd do without her. And Max is very hands-on too.'

'And Gwen? How does she cope with the boys?'

'Beautifully,' Allegra said. 'She's quite gruff with them but they know she loves them to bits. She has promised them a pony when they are a little older. They can't wait, especially Paddy.' Allegra turned to the kettle that had just boiled and busied herself with making tea. That done, she placed a teapot, two mugs and a plate with slices of lemon sponge on the table. 'Try this cake. My friend Maura made it. She's amazing at baking. And she has four children as well. You think I'm managing? Compared to her I feel quite a slacker.' She turned around as the door opened and a tall man with dark-blond hair walked in. 'Max! Look who's here.'

Max's eyes widened in surprise as he discovered his sister at the table. 'Edwina! What a surprise. Is that your fancy car outside?'

'Yes. I bought a new one,' Edwina said as she rose and kissed her brother on the cheek. 'Hi, Max. How are things with you?'

'Eh, fine,' Max said. 'Didn't expect to see you here. How long are you staying?'

'At least a month, it appears,' Allegra cut in. 'She's here for a rest and some kind of health and fitness thing. Isn't that what you said?'

'Something like that,' Edwina replied glancing nervously at Max, who stared back at her.

'Rest and fitness?' he finally said. 'In this house?'

'No, in Sandy Cove,' Edwina replied, feeling increasingly apprehensive. Max looked so stern standing there frowning at her. She knew he thought her a bit of a ninny, only interested in fashion and make-up, but she was much more than that. And she was going to prove it. But she wouldn't tell him the real reason she was here until she had to. 'At the Wellness Centre. They do a whole month of health and yoga and diets and stuff. I heard it's a great place to come to de-stress and rest.'

'Rest from what?' Max asked with a touch of irony. 'Having nothing to do?'

'I have plenty to do, thank you,' Edwina snapped. 'I'm not working at the moment, but I'm planning to get into something very challenging soon.'

'Great,' Max said and sat down at the table. 'What kind of thing would that be?'

'Something to do with design?' Allegra asked as she went to get another mug from the cupboard over the sink.

'You could say that,' Edwina said. 'But it's in the early stages, so I can't tell you much more.'

Max poured himself tea from the pot on the table. 'So you're here for a while?'

'At least a month.' Edwina nibbled on her slice of cake. 'I saw an ad for the Wellness Centre and looked at their website, and then I was hooked.'

'I designed that website,' Allegra said.

'It's amazing. The photos, the layout and the video clips are so enticing,' Edwina said. 'But then of course I've been to Sandy Cove before.'

'That wasn't exactly yesterday,' Max cut in.

'No,' Edwina admitted. 'But it's still so fresh in my mind. Sandy Cove is a unique spot.'

'It's gorgeous,' Allegra said dreamily. 'I'll never forget the few weeks I spent there...'

'There are some changes afoot in Sandy Cove, I've heard,'

Max said, frowning. 'I've just heard that someone has bought Starlight Cottages. The whole row. Someone said they'll be turned into some kind of boutique place or something. Maybe they'll be knocked all into one and made into an exclusive living space and sold on for millions.'

'Can they do that?' Allegra asked. 'I thought those buildings were listed, like historical monuments or something. Those cottages are unique the way they are. I would hate to see them too modernised.'

'Oh yes, me too. That would be horrible,' Max agreed. 'I think you're right, though. They are listed buildings. So whoever is doing it will have a problem getting planning permission for any kind of extension.'

Edwina was about to protest, but changed her mind. No need to reveal all yet. She'd have to keep her cards close to her chest for a while. Just until the work she had planned to have done in the cottages was underway.

'I'm sure it won't be that bad,' she said. 'The new owner will probably do something nice with those houses. They're in such a pretty spot and quite unique just the way they are.'

'I agree,' Max said. 'But they are also in a prime location and I'm sure they can be rented out for huge sums once they've been tarted up. I bet they'll have Jacuzzis on the back terrace and the sunrooms will be turned into champagne bars with fancy furniture. And then they'll build high walls so famous people can hide from the paparazzi.'

Allegra let out a giggle. 'Paparazzi? In Sandy Cove? Where did you get that idea?'

Max shrugged and got up from the table. 'Well, you never know. Sandy Cove is one of those sleepy villages that will be discovered by jet-setters one day. It's bound to happen.'

'Sounds scary,' Allegra said. 'I'd hate that.' She looked at Edwina. 'Would you like to stay for supper?'

Edwina pushed her mug away. 'Thanks, but I'd like to go and settle in.'

'Where are you staying?' Max asked.

'I'm renting a small flat in the village,' Edwina replied. 'I think it's over the grocery shop.'

'Oh yes,' Allegra said. 'That's Sorcha's old flat. She lets it in the summertime. It's very nice. She did it up herself and the bedroom has great views of the bay and the islands. Not as good as Starlight Cottages, but nice all the same.'

Max shot Edwina a suspicious glance. 'So you're renting a small flat in Sandy Cove? And you're going to do some kind of health thing at the Wellness Centre?'

'Yes,' Edwina said, meeting his gaze levelly. 'Why are you looking at me like that?'

'I don't know,' Max said. 'But I have a feeling you're up to something... I mean, you'd usually be on the French Riviera right now. Or some other hotspot with those fancy people you hang out with. I can't help wondering what you're doing renting a small flat in the village and doing some kind of health and fitness course at the Wellness Centre, which is about as far from being a luxury spa as you can come.'

'I want to get back to nature,' Edwina said. 'I need to find myself and recharge my batteries in a place that's fresh and clean and beautiful. Is that so hard to believe?'

'After all the trouble you've caused around here, yes,' Max said with a grunt.

'But that was years ago,' Allegra argued. 'What could she possibly get up to in Sandy Cove anyway?'

'I'm sure she'll think of something,' Max replied. 'Anyway, nice to see you. Come for dinner another day. Or Sunday lunch or something,' he said in a tone that told Edwina he didn't mean it.

'Oh yes,' Allegra agreed with an excited glint in her eyes. 'We could invite a few friends for you to meet. And maybe an attractive man or two? The new GP in the village is single and he's great fun.'

'I've already met him,' Edwina said. 'He nearly hit me with his car just now. We had a bit of an argument. I don't think he's my type at all.'

'I would agree,' Max said. 'I can't see you hitting it off. You're too high maintenance.'

Edwina laughed, not the least bit offended. 'Yeah, you're right. I can't see myself with a country doctor either.'

'Don't be a stranger, in any case,' Max said, sounding a little more friendly. 'It would be nice for the boys to get to know you better.'

'And for me,' Edwina said, nodding. 'I'm not that into kids, but they are my nephews so I'm willing to learn. I really want to get to know them and be part of their lives, you know?'

'That will be a steep learning curve,' Max said with the hint of a smile as he walked to the door that led into the corridor. 'I have a few things to check through on my laptop in the study, so I'll say bye for now.'

'Bye, Max,' Edwina replied. 'I'll be off, too,' she said when he had left. 'Thanks for tea.'

'Lovely to see you,' Allegra said and went to kiss Edwina on the cheek. 'Please keep in touch. But I'm sure we'll see you in Sandy Cove often. We could have a picnic on the beach with the boys, if you like?'

'Sounds like fun,' Edwina said, trying to sound enthusiastic. She suddenly realised that keeping the real reason for her stay a secret would be nearly impossible. She'd better book onto that detox course or whatever it was just to stick to her story a bit longer. 'See you soon, then,' she said.

'Have a great first evening in Sandy Cove,' Allegra said. 'I think you should go and have a meal at the pub in the harbour tonight. You'll meet a lot of people and the food is great.'

'Good idea.' Edwina picked up her bag and started to walk out of the kitchen.

'I'll see you out,' Allegra offered.

'No, that's okay. You have to cook supper. I'll be grand,' Edwina said. 'Bye for now.'

Edwina walked out of the house feeling a lot happier than when she had walked in. Max had been a little cool, but he seemed pleased to see her all the same. Allegra had been sweet as usual and Edwina had a feeling she was trying to make peace between brother and sister. Edwina felt suddenly sad about all the arguments and misunderstandings in the past. Was there too much water under the bridge for them ever to become friends? Or would her project with Starlight Cottages make Max hate her forever?

So many problems, Edwina thought as she drove away from Strawberry Hill. *Why is life always so complicated?*

As she continued down the road towards Sandy Cove, Edwina thought of the weeks ahead. The project would be challenging and difficult, but she was still looking forward to working with the decorators she had lined up to do the new interiors. They were part of a firm called Seabreeze Constructions and would take care of all aspects of the renovations, from architectural designs to interiors, plumbing and electricity. It would be amazing to see the houses restored with a beautiful, modern finish. She would also try to have a little fun and enjoy all the things Sandy Cove had to offer.

She remembered the pretty village with the charming mix of cottages, Victorian houses, quaint shops with beautifully painted signs and the main street that sloped all the way to the ocean, as well as the view of the islands. She hadn't been there for a few years but she hoped nothing had changed. The backdrop of the village would enhance the cottages once they were done up and they blended with all the beauty around them.

Edwina drove on, imagining the summer ahead with a

happy smile. Then, suddenly, as she was nearly at the village, the memory of her encounter with the young doctor popped into her mind. She had to admit he was attractive, even if he had been incredibly rude. But if ever they met again, which was highly likely, she would be cool and distant and not let those brown eyes distract her. She didn't want any romantic notions clouding her judgement or distracting her from her project.

5

Edwina pulled up outside the grocery shop in Sandy Cove just before closing time. There were a lot of people around and they all stared at the car, and then at her, as she got out. She tried to look as if she didn't notice the probing glances and walked into the shop, looking for Sorcha, the owner, as instructed in the email correspondence. A smiley girl with dark hair standing behind the counter greeted her.

'I'm Pauline,' she said. 'Sorcha's assistant. She had to go out on an errand and told me to give you the keys to the flat, and then she'll call in to check if you need anything later. And welcome to Sandy Cove, of course.'

'Thanks,' Edwina said as Pauline handed her the keys. She looked around the shop. 'Do you mind if I pick up a few things to put in the fridge? I'll be eating out most of the time. But I need things for breakfast and snacks and so on.'

'That's absolutely fine,' Pauline said. 'I'm closing now but I'll stay around until you've got what you need.'

'Thanks,' Edwina said. 'You're very kind.'

'Sure, it's what we do here,' Pauline said. 'Why wouldn't we?'

'They don't do that in Dublin.' Edwina laughed. 'I mean, let people buy things after closing time.'

'Ah, Dublin,' Pauline said with a wistful glint in her eyes. 'That's the big city. You would expect that sort of thing there. But hey, isn't it a grand town all the same? The shops, the restaurants, the pubs... I was there for Paddy's Day this year. The craic was fantastic. But I was wrecked afterwards and couldn't wait to get home to have a rest.'

'I can imagine,' Edwina said as she picked up a basket from a stack by the door. 'That's why I'm here. To rest. I'm doing this fitness and health course at the Wellness Centre.'

Pauline nodded. 'Oh yeah, I've heard of that. It's tough going, though. Not so much the working out and the strict diet, but all that exercise. Yoga, Pilates... I was exhausted just reading the brochure.' She leaned on the counter and peered at Edwina. 'You don't look as if you need it. You're as thin as a rail.'

'It's not about weight,' Edwina argued. 'It's about health, energy, fitness and healthy eating.'

'No boozing, though,' Pauline said, looking glum. 'That would be my Friday nights at the pub out the window. Can't imagine not drinking a drop for a whole month. Not that I'm a big drinker,' she added. 'But I like my Prosecco and a few tequila shots. Then we dance all night and wobble home at the crack of dawn.'

'Dance?' Edwina asked. 'Where?'

'At a disco in Killarney,' Pauline replied. 'I go there on Friday nights and meet up with friends. I stay with my sister who lives there. Great fun.'

'Oh, I see.' Edwina nodded. 'I didn't think there'd be night-clubs in Sandy Cove.'

'Nah, this place is too small,' Pauline said as she went to the cash machine. 'But the pub in the main street has fun evenings on Saturday. Trad music and Irish dancing and singing. Anyone can join in. You should go.'

'I might.' Edwina went down the aisles to pick up the food she would need. When her basket was full, she went to the counter and handed it to Pauline, who checked the items through and put everything in a paper carrier bag.

'How do I get upstairs to the flat?' Edwina asked when Pauline had handed her the change.

'Oh.' Pauline laughed. 'I should have explained. You go outside and then there's another door a little to the left and then you go up the stairs to the landing. There's only one door. The big key is for the entrance downstairs and the smaller one for the front door.'

'Great, thanks,' Edwina said and took the bag with the groceries.

'Do you need help with your luggage?' Pauline asked. 'I could give you a hand if you like?'

'Thanks, but I think I can manage.' Edwina smiled at Pauline. 'You've been very helpful.'

'Ah, sure, it was nothing,' Pauline said with a shrug. 'Have a nice evening. I hope you'll have a great stay here. And give me a shout if I can help you with anything.'

'I will,' Edwina promised and went to settle in to her new home.

She smiled as she unlocked the entrance door, thinking how kind and cheerful Pauline had been. If this was how people were around here, she would have a lovely summer. If they didn't disapprove of her renovation plans, that was... She climbed the stairs to the floor above the shop, finding the door wide open, and a large bouquet of white lilies, pink roses and red peonies on the table in the tiny hall with a note that said:

Welcome to Sandy Cove, Edwina.

Sorry I wasn't here to help you settle in, but I'll call in later to say hello. I hope you'll have a wonderful stay.

Best wishes,

Sorcha

Edwina smiled, sniffed at the bouquet and sneezed violently. She had momentarily forgotten about her allergy to certain flowers, lilies being one of them. They would have to go immediately. Not in the bin, but out the window so the smell would disappear completely. She tried to hold her breath while she picked the lilies out of the bouquet and, in a panic, ran to the window and threw them out. Sneezing again, her eyes streaming, she closed the window without looking at what was below and then, blowing her nose on a tissue, turned to look around.

She found she was standing in a small living room with a busy red carpet, on which stood a chintz sofa in front of the fireplace, an armchair upholstered in green velvet, a coffee table and a smaller side table holding a lamp with a pink tasselled shade. By the window was a small desk, a standing lamp and a padded stool. There was a low bookcase crammed with books beside the fireplace and the walls were covered with posters and paintings of various kinds. The room, despite the mishmash of styles, was cosy even though the décor was terrible. Edwina felt a pang of longing for her living room in Dublin with the huge white sofa full of cushions and the view across the city rooftops. She even missed the traffic noise and occasional sound of sirens – the silence of the quiet village street unnerved her.

Edwina turned and opened the window again to see if there was a view, but all she could see was the main street. The bedrooms at the back must have the nice views Pauline had mentioned. Then she looked down at her car and gave a start as she saw someone standing beside it. A man was lifting the lilies she had thrown out the window.

'Oops,' Edwina exclaimed, laughing at the sight. 'Sorry about that!' she shouted.

He looked up and their eyes met for a split second. Edwina froze as she recognised him. It was that rude doctor she had nearly crashed into earlier. 'Oh God. It's *you*,' she blurted out.

'I'm flattered,' he said. 'But I haven't reached God status yet. Thanks for the flowers, though. I assume someone sent them to you and you didn't like them – or him?'

'No, it's not like that,' Edwina protested. 'Sorcha put them in the flat to welcome me, but I'm allergic to lilies so I had to get them out quickly or I'd have sneezed the pictures off the walls. Should have put them in the bin, but I panicked. I didn't mean to hit you.' Feeling beyond embarrassed, she quickly closed the window and stood there breathing hard, trying to regain her composure.

Why did that man have this effect on her? She was usually cool and collected with men, assessing them while she smirked and batted her eyelashes. She had even done that with Matthew before she had fallen for his looks and, yes, money and lifestyle. But that had ended in disaster and she had vowed never to be fooled by a man again. But here she was, feeling hot all over after only a few seconds of a weird conversation. *Get a grip, Edwina*, she told herself and glanced out the window to see if Shane was still there. But the street was empty.

Pulling herself together, she explored the rest of the flat and found the main bedroom, which, with its double bed, fluffy rug, oak floorboards, flowery wallpaper and yellow curtains that clashed with the pink candlewick bedspread, made her wince. Not the work of an interior designer, that was for sure. But the bed looked very comfortable and there was a clean smell of freshly washed bedlinen.

Edwina looked out another window and discovered it had a padded seat and a lovely view of rolling green hills that sloped down to the glittering ocean. This was a lot better than the view from the living room and she knew she would sit here with a cup of tea in the morning. Next door was a smaller bedroom with a single bed and the same wallpaper, curtains and bedspread. Then there was the kitchen, which was compact but had everything she would need. The bathroom was very small with a shower, basin and toilet. Well, it would have to do, even if this was a huge change from her own enormous spa-like bathroom at home.

Edwina put the groceries away and went to get her luggage from the car. She was just dragging her second suitcase into the flat, when she heard someone coming up the stairs.

'Hello?' a pleasant voice called. 'Anyone home?'

'Yes!' Edwina called as a woman with short red hair and a cute face full of freckles came into view.

'Hi,' she said and held out a hand. 'I'm Sorcha. Sorry I wasn't here when you arrived. Had to run an errand for my husband. He's the chemist and couldn't get away so I volunteered. He delivers prescriptions to old people outside the village who can't get to the chemist easily. Anyway, here I am,' she ended as they shook hands.

'Hi, Sorcha,' Edwina said. 'Thanks for the flowers,' she added, hoping Sorcha wouldn't notice that some of them were missing.

'You're welcome. Did you manage to get everything you need from the shop?'

'Yes. Pauline was very helpful.'

'And full of chat, I bet.' Sorcha laughed. 'That girl could talk the hind legs off a donkey if you give her a chance.'

'She was lovely,' Edwina said.

'She is,' Sorcha agreed. 'So, do you have everything you need? The sheets and towels are in the hot press, which is in the kitchen. No room for it anywhere else, I'm afraid. I will give you fresh sheets and towels every Monday. And if you have anything else to wash, I'd be happy to do that for you. But there's a clothesline in the garden behind the shop where you can hang things you've washed by hand. No washing machine, I'm afraid. It's a tiny flat, but I hope you'll be comfortable here.'

'I'll be grand,' Edwina assured her, even though she knew it would take her a while to feel at home in such a small place with that kind of décor. 'I won't spend much time here, though. I plan to do a lot of outdoorsy stuff and I'm also doing the health and fitness course at the Wellness Centre.'

'Gosh,' Sorcha said, looking impressed. 'That's like boot-camp, I've heard. And I know for a fact that Billy, the new fitness teacher, is very strict. No cheating or you'll be doing extra push-ups and sit-ups.'

Edwina laughed. 'I know the type. My PT in Dublin is like that. Takes no prisoners.'

'Oh, you should be fine then,' Sorcha remarked. 'If you're used to working out.'

'Eh, well, I would be if I'd attended the gym regularly. But I haven't been there for over a month. I've been too busy with... stuff,' she ended, not wanting to reveal the real reason for her stay. She knew it would come out eventually but she wanted to keep it quiet as long as she could.

Sorcha nodded. 'I know what you mean. I'm madly busy myself. I thought that once my son moved out I'd have a lot of time to myself, but I find I'm doing even more than before.' She paused, looking at Edwina thoughtfully. 'You and Max are very alike, I realise now. The same eyes, nose and chin. But your eyes are green and his are blue and he doesn't have that little dimple. Apart from that, you could be twins. Is he older than you?'

'Yes. He's nearly three years older,' Edwina replied.

'Nice man,' Sorcha remarked. 'And Allegra is a darling. We're all so fond of them both. So lovely that the Courtneys have finally started to come to the village. They'll be opening the house to the public next year, I heard. Won't that be fabulous? And now you're here too for the summer. I think that's so wonderful. I'm sure you'll be up at Strawberry Hill a lot to see your little nephews.'

'Well, yes, I'll try to find the time.'

'You should. They grow up so fast.' Sorcha looked around. 'Is there anything else you want to know before I head off?'

'Yes. What about cleaning?' Edwina asked, wondering what day of the week the cleaners would come.

'Oh,' Sorcha said apologetically. 'I forgot to tell you where everything is. There is a cleaning cupboard in the kitchen where you'll find a small Hoover and some Ajax and other cleaning materials like a brush and a mop for the floor.'

'Great.' Edwina, who had never cleaned anything in her entire life, tried to look happy. In Dublin, her cleaning lady came in twice a week and did everything, including the washing and ironing. But here she would have to do all that herself. 'That's fine,' she said, wondering if that Hoover thing came with instructions. She'd have to look up hoovering on YouTube.

'Okay. If that's all...' Sorcha moved to the door. 'I must go. Tom, my husband, will be heading home for supper. Let me know if you need anything else. I'm down at the shop most days. Have lovely evening!'

'Thanks,' Edwina said. 'I'm planning to go to the Harbour pub for a meal tonight. Allegra said it's a great place to meet people.'

'It is, that's a great idea. Bye for now, Edwina. So nice to meet you.'

'And you,' Edwina said, and smiled at Sorcha as she left.

She turned to her suitcases and wondered where on earth she would put all the clothes she had brought. And why had she brought so much? But being of the 'just in case' school of packing, she always ended up with bucketloads of clothes she never wore. Well, she would just have to stuff most of them into one suitcase that she'd put under the bed in the spare room and then try to fit the rest into the miniscule wardrobe in the bedroom.

How on earth had Sorcha managed to live here without ample storage space? Maybe she was one of those minimalists?

Edwina forgot about Sorcha and her lack of outfits as she did her best to sort out her clothes, shoes, handbags, jackets, scarves and exercise outfits – one for each day of the week – and stuff them into every available cubby hole she could find. That done, she changed into a pair of dark jeans, a white cotton shirt and a navy sweater, which she threw across her shoulders. Her white Adidas trainers finished off the casual, sporty look she thought would fit in with whatever the locals wore when they went to the pub. She brushed back her hair, put on a pair of gold hoop earrings, applied fresh red lipstick and a coat of mascara and was ready for dinner at the Harbour pub. She smiled at herself in the mirror and nodded, her green eyes glittering. *Yes, baby, you look truly fabulous*, she thought. She picked up her handbag and ran down the stairs, looking forward to meeting a whole new group of people. She stopped for a moment in the dark hall downstairs, wondering how they would take the news of her makeover of Starlight Cottages. Would they love it or hate it? She would have to be careful and not reveal too much...

6

It didn't take Edwina long to find her way to the pub as there was a green sign that said 'Harbour pub' pointing to the end of a narrow lane. Once she was there, the lane opened onto the pier and the harbour, and she saw little fishing boats riding at anchor in the bay, their hulls painted in bright colours. The late evening sun bathed the scene in a golden hue and the only sound was the clucking of water against the boats and the cry of a seagull. Edwina stopped for a moment taking in the sight, wishing she could paint. But, short of a paintbrush, she picked up her phone and took a photo, even though she knew it wouldn't quite capture the mellow light, the stillness, the soft air laden with the tang of seaweed, and the feeling of complete peace. It was as if time stood still here, and nothing bad could ever happen.

She stood there for a moment, drinking in the scene, until she continued further down towards the pier, where she spotted the pub in a large, low building just off the harbour. As she walked closer, she could hear the din of voices and smell herbs and garlic wafting from the kitchen. Her stomach rumbling, she picked up her pace and entered the pub, which was cosy and welcoming, with wooden panelling, wide oak planks on the floor and a large array of bottles on shelves behind the bar. The place was packed and, looking around, Edwina had a sinking feeling she would have to wait a long time to get a table. The smell of food was making her nearly faint with hunger and she looked pleadingly at a waiter approaching with a tray loaded with plates of steak and chips.

'Any chance of a table?' she shouted above the din.

'Afraid not, love,' the waiter said. 'Unless you booked?'

'No, I didn't,' Edwina said.

The waiter looked over his shoulder. 'I can see a place at the bar. Would you mind eating there?'

'Not at all,' Edwina said, even though she would never have accepted this in a restaurant in Dublin.

'You better grab it while it's free,' the waiter said and continued through the throng with his tray.

Edwina pushed through the crowd, who were drinking pints and talking loudly at each other, and managed to claim the empty spot at the bar. She eased herself up on the barstool, hitched her handbag higher on her shoulder and put her elbows on the counter, smiling at the waitress at the other side.

'Hi,' she said. 'I was told to sit here. Can I order something to eat?'

'Of course.' The waitress pushed a menu towards Edwina. 'Take a look and I'll get back to you. What do you want to drink?'

'A glass of red, please,' Edwina replied. 'Chateau Margot if you have that.'

'Eh, we don't...' the waitress said. 'Would a pinot noir do?'

'Okay,' Edwina said, feeling she would have to lower her standards a little around here. She loved a good Bordeaux, but a decent Burgundy was okay if there was nothing else.

Someone sat down beside her, jolting her with his shoulder. She glanced at the person, giving a start as their eyes met. It was *him*, that obnoxious doctor. He shot her a lazy smile that was enhanced by his white, even teeth and the mischievous glint in his brown eyes.

'Of all the gin joints in all the towns in all the world, she walks into mine,' he drawled, quoting that famous line from *Casablanca*.

Edwina sat up straighter. 'Well, this is not a gin joint,' she said primly. 'And it's not yours either.'

'Oh, we're a nit-picker, are we?' he said, still smiling.

'I'm not, but you might be. I just like facts to be correct.'

He laughed. 'Oh, of course. I just thought my Humphrey Bogart act might break the ice. You did throw flowers at me earlier and called me God, so I hoped you might be softening towards me.'

'I have no feelings whatsoever about you,' Edwina said in a haughty tone. She grabbed the glass of wine the waitress put before her and saw that Shane already had a pint of Guinness.

He held up his glass. 'Here's looking at you, kid.'

'Oh, please,' Edwina groaned and rolled her eyes.

She sipped her drink and glanced at the menu only to show she was not interested, which was very far from the truth. Sitting so close to him, she could see his face in detail: the unruly dark curls, the slightly crooked nose that seemed to have been broken at some stage, the smattering of freckles, the thick eyebrows and long dark eyelashes fringing deep brown eyes, the beautiful mouth and the strong chin. Those looks, his strong body and the clean smell of soap was a heady combination and she found herself drawn to him so strongly it shocked her. She took a swig of wine as the waitress came back and asked her what she wanted to eat.

'I'd like the fillet steak,' she managed to reply. 'Medium rare.'

'And chips?' she asked.

'No, just a salad,' Edwina said.

'Great.' The waitress looked at Shane. 'And for the doctor?'

'I'll have the fillet of pork,' Shane replied without consulting the menu and downed what was left of his pint. 'And another one of these and one more of that red for the lady beside me.'

'You don't have to buy my drinks,' Edwina protested. 'I can get my own, thank you.'

'I'm sure you can, but I was just trying to be friendly. You can buy the next round.'

'What round?' she asked, beginning to feel annoyed. 'We're not on a date or anything. And in any case, I'd say two pints are quite enough for anyone. What would you do if you were called out on some kind of emergency?'

'I'm not on call tonight,' he replied. 'I have a deal with the GP in Ballinskelligs. We alternate nights to give us both a break.' He stopped as his phone rang and he glanced at it. 'Excuse me, but I have to take this.'

'Okay.' Edwina tried not to listen to the conversation that followed but couldn't help hearing what Shane was saying to whoever was calling him.

'What do you mean?' he muttered under his breath. 'You need more money? What for?' He listened for a while, then said: 'No, absolutely not. I've told you already. And don't give me the thing about your mother telling you to ask me. The subject is closed. In any case, it's the middle of the week so you're not going and that's final.' Shane ended the conversation and pocketed his phone, glancing at Edwina. 'I suppose you couldn't help hearing that.'

'Er, no,' she said. 'Not that I usually listen to private conversations, but it was quite loud.'

'I know.' Shane sighed and took a swig of his pint. 'That was my son, Daniel. He likes to play me and his mother off each other.'

'Must be difficult,' Edwina remarked, her heart sinking, a reaction which surprised her.

Why did the thought that he was married with a son upset her? They had just met, so why should this man's marital status matter? But it did, because she found him madly attractive despite his slight arrogance. Allegra had said he was single, but she might be mistaken. Typical. All the dishy men of her age were usually taken, and he was a prime example. She had initially been offended by his hostile attitude towards her and his teasing had been annoying; she felt that he saw right through her. But she couldn't deny that he was very attractive in a wild Irish way, quite the opposite to the smooth continental charm of the men she usually dated. There was a hint of a challenge in those dark eyes that made her feel she wanted to prove herself to him. But now she had found out he was a husband and father...

'It's not easy.' Shane interrupted her thoughts as he looked glumly into his pint. 'Teenagers are hard to handle. Especially this one. But I suppose he's had a tough time while we were arguing about custody during the divorce.'

'Oh,' Edwina said, feeling a dart of guilt at how much the mention of his divorce cheered her up. 'I'm sorry. Divorce is always horrible.'

'You've been there too?' he asked, looking sideways at her. 'Marriage on the rocks and then divorce?'

'No, but I've been through it with my own parents. So I've seen it from that side.'

'That's not easy either,' Shane said with a hint of sympathy in his eyes.

'No,' Edwina replied, wishing they could get back to their sparring earlier, which she had begun to enjoy, even though she had pretended to be hostile. 'But hey, there are worse things in life,' she said, trying to lighten the mood.

'Oh yeah,' he agreed. Then he looked at her with more interest. 'So back to you. What is a girl from the posh part of Dublin doing in a place like this? Just visiting family?'

'No, not really,' Edwina replied. 'I mean, of course I'll be going to see Max and Allegra and the children while I'm here, but I've come for a holiday and to do a health course at the Wellness Centre. I saw it on their website and it looked great. Very different from a spa or any other fitness programme. And as I've recently quit my job, this will give me a chance to recharge and get my energy back.'

'You lost your energy?' he said, looking at her with an amused glint in his eyes.

'Yeah, well,' Edwina said, squirming as she tried to think of an explanation that would sound feasible while hiding what she was really up to. 'I had a bit of a burn-out recently.'

'I can imagine,' he said. 'You seem to have a really hectic lifestyle.'

Edwina stared at him, her heart beating. 'What do you know about my lifestyle?'

'I flicked through the magazines in the waiting room and spotted an article about you in that VIP mag,' he said. 'Totally by accident as I was tidying up.'

'But that article was in the Christmas issue,' she said, taken aback.

'Well, we get those magazines from the library and they're often years old. So last Christmas would be very recent in this case. At least I didn't google you like some people might have done. Come on, Edwina. Don't tell me you haven't googled me.'

'Well, no. Sorry to disappoint you.' She was telling the truth, but only because she hadn't had the time. She had planned to do that later, though.

'I'm crushed,' he said, pretending to look hurt.

They were interrupted by the waitress bringing their food and drinks. Edwina saw that Shane's order was medallions of pork in mushroom sauce served with chips and haricot beans, all of which looked delicious. Her fillet steak topped with parsley and garlic butter smelled heavenly, too. She couldn't help starting to eat at once and found that the meat melted in her mouth and the flavour of parsley and garlic was so delicious it nearly brought tears to her eyes. The salad was crisp, the dressing wonderfully tangy.

'This is fab,' she said, as she took another bite of steak.

'Best restaurant in town,' he agreed. 'Although the fish at the Wild Atlantic Gourmet is also worth a try.'

They ate in silence for a while, Shane looking as if he was enjoying his meal just as much as she was.

'How's your steak?' he asked.

'Great,' she said, as she took the last bite.

'I bet you'd love it even more with chips.' He pushed his plate towards her. 'Feel free to have some of mine. They always give me more than I can handle.'

Edwina hesitated. Then she smiled, took a chip and put it in her mouth. 'Thanks. They're really good,' she said and took another one. 'I don't usually eat chips.'

'I suppose a healthy diet is important. And you look as if you follow that to the letter. But it's good to break out occasionally, isn't it? Like slumming it with a lowly GP.'

'Oh yes,' she retorted in a haughty tone. 'It's good to mix with the peasants from time to time. Very refreshing.'

The waitress came back and asked them if everything was all right and if they were enjoying their meal.

'Yes, everything's amazing,' Shane replied. 'Especially the company.'

The waitress laughed. 'You're a gas man, Doctor Shane. Hey, have you heard the latest news? Some big property developer has bought Starlight Cottages. They're going to demolish them and build some kind of motel there. Or was it a shopping centre?' She thought for a moment. 'No, that couldn't be true. I think I heard something about a nightclub, though. Wouldn't that be a hoot?'

'A *nightclub?*' Shane said, looking shocked. 'In Sandy Cove? That should wake this village up.'

The waitress shook her head. 'That's just one of those rumours. But in any case, something's going to happen over there. Could be that they'll build some kind of high-rise.' She shivered. 'Horrible thought. I mean that's such a lovely spot and those cottages are so wonderful.'

'I'm sure it won't be too bad,' Edwina cut in, feeling a knot of fear in her stomach. She was beginning to realise that people around here were very fond of Starlight Cottages, and might not approve of her big plan. 'Whoever bought them must have seen the potential to leave them as they are and just rejig them a bit to make them more...' She stopped, trying to think of something that would calm the girl down and stop the rumours.

'Commercial?' Shane suggested, looking curiously at Edwina.

'Something like that,' she said.

'It's all about money, isn't it?' the waitress said as she took their plates. 'Would you like anything else, lads?'

'No thanks,' Edwina said. Her phone rang and she fished it out of her bag, sighing as she saw it was her mother. 'Hello, Mum,' she said over the din in the pub. 'What's up?'

'How are you getting on?' her mother said. 'Have you been to the cottages yet? Or met the designer?'

'I only just arrived,' Edwina said. 'I'm in a very noisy pub right now having dinner. I'll call you later.'

'No need,' Pamela said. 'I just wanted to see how you're doing and to tell you that I ran into your ex-boyfriend.'

'Who?' Edwina asked. 'Sorry, can't hear what you said.'

'Your ex!' Pamela shouted. 'Matthew O'Donnell. He was asking about you. Said he was still trying to recover from the break-up.'

'What?' Edwina glanced at Shane and then slid down from the bar stool with an apologetic smile. She pushed through the crowd to the door and went outside, where the cool breeze soothed her hot face. 'Did I hear correctly?' she asked. 'Matthew O'Donnell said that he's trying to recover from dumping me?'

'Well, he didn't put it quite like that,' Pamela admitted. 'I think he said he realised what a mistake it had been to break up with you and that he missed you. He asked where you were and I—'

'You *told* him?' Edwina hissed into the phone. 'Oh God, Mum, why did you do that? I have been trying to move on and begun to feel really good about myself again. I had put it all behind me and was looking forward to doing this project and to...' She stopped, knowing it was no use. Her mother would never understand. 'I thought you didn't even like him,' she added. 'You called him a dreadful man just recently.'

'That was to cheer you up. He seemed so sad yesterday. He said he'd tried to contact you, but that you must have blocked him everywhere. Maybe he's changed and seen the error of his ways?'

'That would be the day,' Edwina said with a snort. 'I hope he's not coming here. I don't need that kind of complication right now. Please tell him I don't want to see him. Ever.'

'How can I?' Pamela said with a little self-pitying sniff. 'I don't have his phone number. I just bumped into him at this restaurant. He said hello and wasn't I your mother and then we talked about you, and how he felt, and how sorry he was for what he'd done to you and...'

'Oh please,' Edwina said with resigned sigh. 'That's such a load of rubbish. If you see him again, just tell him you were mistaken and that I've gone to France or something.'

'But that wouldn't be true,' Pamela protested.

'No, but neither is that spiel he gave you. I've no idea why he said it or what he's up to. But I do hope he's not planning to come here for some kind of reunion.'

'But maybe he's really sorry,' Pamela argued.

'No, trust me, he's not,' Edwina snapped. 'I don't believe that for a second. Listen, Mum, I have to go back in and pay for my meal and then I'm going to bed.'

'How is that flat you're renting?' Pamela asked.

'It's fine. Bye, Mum. I'll call you when things are up and running.' Edwina hung up without waiting for a reply.

She stood there in the dark for a while, breathing hard. What was going on with Matthew, and why was he trying to contact her? And why was her mother suddenly so interested in him? While they were dating, her mother had been wildly enthusiastic about their relationship, hoping for a society wedding. She had been very disappointed when they had broken up, turning on Matthew and calling him a 'cad'. And then she had urged Edwina to start afresh and do something worthwhile, and had even delved into her coffers to help finance the new project. But now she seemed to be encouraging Matthew to get in touch again, the mere thought of which made Edwina shudder.

The memory of the break-up was still fresh in her mind, but the pain had begun to lessen recently and she had felt ready to move on. Now, this new project and the summer in Sandy Cove ahead felt like the beginning of a new life. The friendliness of the people around here had lifted her spirits. She knew she had come to the right place to start again, and she didn't want anyone from her old life to come here and drag her back, least of all Matthew.

She closed her eyes, remembering the moment when they had first met and Matthew's flirty eyes had looked at her across a crowded room. Then he had walked over and introduced himself, which was unnecessary as she already knew who he was. His deep voice, his handsome face and his athletic body, always dressed to perfection, had all seemed so seductive. She had been swept away by all the glamour, his money that paid for everything and that easy charm. They'd had that summer she would never forget.

But then, when it was over, so was their romance. Matthew had used the cliché 'it's not you, it's me' and looked at Edwina with sad eyes across the table in the wine bar he had picked as the spot for their break-up. 'It's not working for me,' he had said. 'You're a lovely woman and you deserve someone better.' Then he had kissed her cheek and left, while she sat there, devastated, trying to understand what she had done wrong.

It had taken her a long time to recover, but now she was finally moving on, feeling free, strong and happy. She didn't want to see Matthew ever again but, if she did, would it reopen the wounds that had begun to heal?

7

Edwina shivered in the cool night air, pulled herself together and went back into the pub and her place at the bar, where Shane was chatting to a group of people.

He turned to her when she joined them. 'Hi, again. I've met up with some friends. Let me introduce you.' He gestured at a tall woman with light brown hair and a man with dark hair. 'This is Maggie and Brian, who's our local vet. Maggie is a PE teacher, among other things.' He turned to the other couple, a beautiful woman with dark curly hair and a blond man who looked slightly familiar. 'And then we have Tara and Mick, who's our local politician and former minister and Tara's a photographer. Tara's twin sister Kate is the doctor I'm filling in for this summer, actually. And this, folks, is Edwina Courtney-Smythe, Max's sister, who's here for some kind of sabbatical.' He drew breath as Edwina shook hands with them all.

Edwina turned to Shane. 'Thanks for introducing me, but I'm afraid I'm very tired after the long drive from Dublin. I haven't even unpacked all my bags yet. So I'll just pay the bill and get going.'

'I'd pay, but I have a feeling it would annoy you,' Shane said.

'You're right. It would,' Edwina said, turning to the waitress who had just appeared. When she had paid, she smiled at the group. 'Nice to meet you all.'

'Lovely to meet you, Edwina,' the tall, dark-haired woman called Tara said. 'Where are you staying?'

'I'm renting a flat over the grocery shop,' Edwina replied. 'There are no hotels or B&Bs in this village, so that was the best option.'

'We have guest cottages for walkers at our farm,' Tara said. 'But they're all booked up for the summer.'

'There's a hotel in Ballinskelligs and one in Waterville, though,' Maggie said. 'But in this village there are only houses for rent. Willow House used to be a guesthouse, but the family took it over and it's a private house again. So you're right. There are no B&Bs or even a guesthouse here.'

'But that might soon be remedied,' Shane cut in. 'If rumours are to be believed. Someone has bought Starlight Cottages and it's supposed to be turned into a hotel – or was it a nightclub?'

'A hotel?' Tara asked. 'There's hardly room for that. Unless they're planning to add more floors, or maybe even pull the cottages down altogether.'

'I heard it was going to be a nursing home,' Maggie's husband Brian said.

Shane suddenly burst out laughing. 'The guessing gets more and more incredible. Why not wait and see? In any case, if they're planning to build any kind of extensions, they'll have to apply for planning permission. And then we can find out what's going on and the name of the applicant when the notice goes up.' He glanced at Edwina. 'I'm sure this isn't really that exciting for you, as you've only come for a holiday.'

'Well...' Edwina hesitated, that familiar knot of anxiety tightening in her stomach. 'I know the cottages,' she said, trying to sound casual. 'My sister-in-law stayed there when she first arrived in Ireland. Very nice place.'

She hadn't expected this amount of interest in her project, nor had she envisaged the kind of gossip she would encounter. Allegra had once said she was happy to live a good distance from the village, away from probing eyes, and Edwina now realised what she meant. Even though there was a cosy feel to the village and everyone was so friendly, it was a quite a culture shock to have so many eyes on you. Edwina slid away into the crowd, heading for the door and hoping nobody would notice her leaving.

Shane caught up with her outside. 'I'm heading home too.'

'Where do you live?' Edwina asked.

'In the same building as the practice. It's a nice family house. Kate and Cormac, her husband, thought it was the best option for me to live there while she's away. She's doing an obstetrics course in Australia for a year, and the whole family went with her.'

'And when the year is up, what will you do?' Edwina asked as they walked down the lane to the main street.

'Not sure. I might go somewhere else they need a GP. Or I might stay here and share the practice with Kate. It's a large area and should be served by two doctors, really. I like looking after the elderly, and she's brilliant with young mothers and kids. My summer will be a bit stressful, though,' he continued. 'I have to take Daniel for the whole break. Maybe you could give me a tip on how to cope, as you were in his situation when you were young?'

Edwina glanced at him in the dim light. 'Not saying you *have* to take him might be a good place to start,' she remarked dryly. 'That kind of comment doesn't exactly make anyone feel wanted.'

'Good point,' Shane said softly. 'Must remember that.'

They had arrived at the door that led to the flat. Edwina

took her key from her bag. 'Well, thanks for seeing me home. Good night,' she said, holding out her hand.

He took her hand and held it for longer than was necessary. 'Good night, Edwina. Thanks for the company. And good luck with whatever you've come here to do.'

He walked away before she could ask him what he meant. She looked at his figure disappearing into the darkness and thought about their conversation in the pub. Their banter had been fun, even if it was laced with a certain amount of negativity. Edwina shrugged. They had only just met and in any case, she didn't want to get involved with someone who seemed to have as much baggage as she did. Her project was number one on her agenda and she was looking forward to meeting the interior designer the following morning. Then they would start the work of turning the cottages into exquisite hideaways for people with good taste.

And a lot of money.

Edwina woke up at six o'clock the following morning. Not by choice, but because a delivery truck in the street below the flat arrived with a load for the grocery shop. Even though the bedroom was at the back of the house, the noise through the open window was loud enough to wake her up. She sat up in bed, looking wildly around at the flowery wallpaper and the pictures of dogs and sheep in sunlit meadows and wondered if she had died and gone to décor hell from 1982, or if she had mistakenly checked into some crazy B&B.

Then she remembered and lay down again, snuggling under the duvet as a chilly early morning breeze wafted into the room. She was in Sandy Cove, and this was the flat she had rented for the summer. Of course there would be early morning deliveries from time to time; that was to be expected. She should have realised this. But despite the early morning wake-up call and the décor, the flat was cosy and convenient for everything. She would just have to get used to waking up at this hour. And to the wallpaper.

Unable to go back to sleep, Edwina got up, made herself a large mug of tea and several slices of toasted soda bread with a generous layer of local honey, and brought it all on a little tray back into the bedroom where she settled on the window seat and looked out at the view of the ocean, its water turquoise in the morning sunlight. Seagulls glided over the waves and tiny clouds drifted across the baby-blue sky. *What a beautiful morning*, she thought to herself.

The sight made her want to go down to the sea, and maybe even swim. It was the perfect opportunity to inspect the cottages, she decided, and quickly finished her tea and toast. There would be nobody around this early, so she could slip inside and then go down to the little private beach and swim before the design team arrived. Nobody would see her go in and she could easily sneak out afterwards, as she knew the cottages were quite isolated and not overlooked. Plus, Jonathan had told her that the owners of the fourth and last cottage in the row had moved out. It was early June and the renovations would all be finished by late August and then she'd be on her way back to Dublin. That was nearly three months away, which gave them plenty of time to do all the work that would be required.

Everything would work out fine, she told herself as she got dressed. Denim shorts and a T-shirt seemed the best option today as the forecast was promising a hot day. Edwina put on a pair of trainers and pushed a towel and her swimsuit into a bag that already held her phone, wallet and keys and left the flat, opening the entrance door slowly, peering out at the empty street. The truck had left and there was nobody around, not even a dog or a cat. Perfect.

Edwina closed the door behind her and walked down the street, feeling a dart of excitement. This was the first day of her new life as a property developer. All the frustrations and pains of the past seemed to disappear as she walked on, glancing at the pretty front gardens of the little houses that lined the street, round the corner and then down the track that led to Starlight Cottages. As she arrived at the first cottage, she stopped for a moment and looked down the row. She could see the finished houses in her mind's eye: the newly painted façades, each door painted a different colour, and new windows. She opened the door and walked inside, her footsteps echoing in the empty rooms as she made her way through the sunroom and onto the terrace, where she stood looking in awe at the stunning scenery. This was heavenly. The light, the ocean, the islands shimmering in the distance, the clean, fresh air... She felt as if she could float away on the breeze and fly over the sea to the islands.

She remembered standing here on a cold day in late October four years ago. She had been upset and angry and then she had come out here and seen this wonderful view and felt a sense of magic and healing. It wasn't Allegra's soothing words or Max's forgiveness that had helped her come to her senses then. It was this place, this view. It had stuck in her mind and now, here she was, owning it. The view, the air and the light were even more beautiful in the summer. Edwina turned and looked up at the house. She knew she couldn't live here; it was too small and too remote. But oh, what a wonderful place to develop and restore. She felt instinctively what she could do and how it would look when it was finished. It was going to be incredible.

8

As the sun rose higher in the sky, Edwina remembered her plan to swim at the little beach below the cottages. She glanced down the slopes covered in wild roses and saw the private beach, with its golden sand and crystal-clear water. She grabbed her bag and left the terrace, opened the gate in the fence and carefully made her way down the steps.

The beach below was deserted and Edwina quickly changed into her swimsuit behind a boulder. Then she waded in and threw herself into the waves and swam a few strokes before she turned on her back and floated, staring up at the blue sky, enjoying the feel of the cool, clean water. She closed her eyes and felt a strange calm come over her, finding an unexpected buoyancy that didn't demand any effort at all.

Flotsam and jetsam, she thought. *I could float away on the waves until I reach the other side of the ocean.*

Edwina laughed at herself and turned, swimming back with long, easy strokes, feeling refreshed and rejuvenated. As she reached the shore, something bobbed against her in the water. An object made of green glass. She caught it in her hand and looked at it more closely. It looked like a beer bottle sealed with a cork. When she could stand on the sand, she examined it and discovered there was something inside. Something that looked like a folded piece of paper... A message in a bottle? She suddenly laughed. This was like something out of a movie. She'd heard of messages in bottles and people meeting each other as a result, but she had never believed it was really true. This must be some child having a bit of fun. But she just had to read the message.

Excited, she held the bottle in her hand and waded onto the beach, but stumbled on a rock and fell, the bottle slipping out of her hand and breaking on her knee as she fell, the glass splitting open a deep wound that immediately started to bleed.

The intense pain and the sight of the blood gushing from the gash made Edwina nearly faint, but she managed to stumble to where she had left her clothes. Without hesitating, she picked up the towel she had brought and wound it tightly around her leg. Then she sat on a rock and examined the bottle, the neck of which was broken, but the rest intact. Despite the pain and shock, the piece of paper in the bottle intrigued her. She sat on the sand, the blood seeping through the towel, and fished the message out of the bottle, unfolding the piece of paper and reading the faint letters.

To someone beautiful and far away.

The darling girl who left me broken-hearted. It's the end of this century, New Year's Eve 1999. I drank the beer in this bottle standing on a pier in Dingle, where we met. I wrote her letters after the terrible accident to say sorry and that I love her, but she didn't reply.

Tonight, as we partied, I tried to blot out the pain with beer and booze, but it wouldn't go away. Then I decided to pen a little note and put it inside the bottle and throw it into the water, hoping it might reach that sweet girl who lives some-where across the ocean.

I hope you will have a happy life in the next century, my darling. If you should happen to read this, please call the number below and say hi to a lonely guy who will never forget his first love.

Best wishes from Ireland and Pearse.

35366744258

Edwina sighed and folded the note, pushing it into her bag. How sad. Poor guy who lost his girl and then probably, a little drunk on New Year's Eve, decided to send a message in the beer bottle that he had sealed with a cork. That bottle had been floating around here on the currents back and forth for over twenty years, not getting any further than just down the coast to Sandy Cove. This man called Pearse had probably hoped to get a phone call from some girl in America who'd contact him.

She wondered briefly if he was still around in Dingle, but then the throbbing in her knee made her forget anything except the need to get to a pharmacy to get something to clean and bandage it properly. She carefully peeled off her wet swimsuit and managed to get dressed without dislodging the towel wrapped around her knee. Then she limped up the steps and reached the cottage just as a car pulled up outside. Oh no. It was them. The design team had arrived. She limped through the house to the front door and opened it, trying to look cheerful despite the pain that was now becoming nearly excruciating.

'Hi!' she called to the two people alighting from the car. 'Thanks for being on time. I had a little accident, so I'll just have to pop over to the chemist and get some plasters. But please come in and look around and then we can talk when I come back.'

The team, consisting of a dark-haired woman wearing a Versace T-shirt and a man with greying hair, walked towards her, looking concerned.

'You're bleeding,' the woman said, pointing to Edwina's leg.

'It's nothing,' Edwina said quickly. 'Just a little cut.' She pressed on the blood-soaked towel with one hand and held out the other. 'Hello. I'm Edwina by the way.'

'I'm Karen,' the woman said. 'I'm the interior designer, and this is Andrew, who's the architect.'

'Hi, Karen.' Edwina shook her hand.

'But I see your wound is quite serious,' Karen remarked, looking concerned. 'Maybe you need a stitch?'

'I'll be fine.' Edwina tried to look as if it was nothing.

'I could take you to the doctor, if there is one in this village?' Andrew offered.

'Doctor?' Edwina said, beginning to panic. She didn't want anyone to know what she was doing, least of all Shane. 'I'm sure that's not necessary.'

'I'm sure it is,' Andrew interrupted. 'You're bleeding quite badly.' He picked up his phone and tapped in something. 'Okay... GP surgery... Sandy Cove... Here it is. Seems to be nearby. And it opens at nine thirty. It's just past nine, so I suggest we head over there right now. Karen can take a look at the cottages and then we'll all talk when you've had your injury seen to,' he continued in a tone that didn't allow argument.

Edwina knew that what he suggested was the only sensible option, despite her reluctance to see Shane right now. She nodded and started to hobble out the door.

'Okay, let's go then,' she said.

'I'll drive you there,' Andrew said and opened the door to the car for her when they were outside.

'Thank you.' Edwina eased herself into the passenger seat, wincing as the movement made the pain worse. 'I might bleed on the seat, though,' she said, looking at the cream leather upholstery.

'No problem,' Andrew said and got in, starting the engine.

'Nice car,' Edwina remarked, impressed with the smooth ride of the BMW.

'It belongs to the company.'

'You must be doing well, then?'

'Can't complain,' Andrew grunted.

It only took them a minute or two to reach the tall Victorian building that housed the surgery. Andrew helped Edwina to the door and rang the bell. The door opened a minute or so later and Shane looked out.

'We're not open—' he started, then stopped when he saw Edwina. 'What are you doing here at this hour?' His gaze travelled down her leg. 'Holy mother, what have you been up to?' he asked, looking annoyed.

'I haven't been up to anything,' Edwina retorted. 'I fell on some glass. I didn't actually do it on purpose.'

'I suppose you didn't,' Shane said, his voice suddenly softer. 'Come inside and I'll take a look. The nurse isn't here yet, but we'll manage.' He took Edwina's other arm and with Andrew's help got her into the surgery and onto the examining table. Then he looked into Edwina's eyes. 'I'm going to take the towel off now, okay? Don't look if it makes you feel sick.'

Edwina nodded and closed her eyes. 'I won't. I can't stand the sight of blood.'

'Lucky for you, I can,' Shane said and slowly eased off the towel, letting out a whistle as he saw the wound. 'This is quite nasty. That glass went in very deep. I'll clean it first and then I'll see what I can do.'

'I'll wait outside,' Andrew said, looking suddenly pale.

'What on earth happened?' Shane asked when the door closed behind Andrew.

'I was at the beach swimming and then stumbled on a rock

and cut myself on a bottle,' Edwina mumbled between her teeth.

'Bloody kids,' Shane said. 'They should be punished for leaving bottles and glass around like this.'

'It was an old bottle,' Edwina explained. 'Floating on the waves. I picked it up and stumbled on a rock as I got out of the water and then I fell onto it and it shattered.' She was going to tell him about the message, but found it hard to get the words out.

'What kind of bottle?'

'An old beer bottle. Actually, it had a...' she started but then the pain got the better of her and she let out a groan.

'A what? Oh never mind. I can see you're in pain,' Shane said. 'I'll give you a local anaesthetic once I've cleaned it, and then I'll put in a couple of stitches once the anaesthetic has kicked in. You won't feel a thing.'

Edwina looked into his brown eyes that were now full of concern and nodded. 'Thank you,' she whispered.

Shane quickly washed his hands at the sink and then prepared the injection. He approached Edwina, holding up a syringe. 'This will only take a second. It'll sting a little bit. Are you ready?'

'Yes,' Edwina whispered and immediately passed out.

When she came to, the round friendly face of a woman with blue eyes and curly grey hair swam before her. Edwina blinked and sat up.

'Hello,' she said. 'Where am I?'

'On the sofa in the living room,' the woman said. 'I'm Bridget, the surgery nurse. You fainted when you had that wound stitched up. Shane and the other young man carried you out here.'

'Oh.' Edwina looked at her knee that now had a big white dressing on it. 'It feels better.'

'Of course,' Bridget said. 'The anaesthetic is still working. But it shouldn't be too bad when it wears off. Shane put in five stitches. He also wrote a prescription for antibiotics and gave you a tetanus shot in the... you know,' she said and pointed at her ample behind.

'In my...?' Edwina said, alarmed. 'Bum?'

'Yes, that's where tetanus shots are usually given,' Bridget replied matter-of-factly. 'You were out cold so he thought it better to do it when you wouldn't feel it. Had to be done or you could get very sick indeed.'

'I suppose,' Edwina said, blushing at the thought of Shane giving her an injection in that part of her body.

'He's a doctor,' Bridget said. 'And all he thinks of when he's with a patient is what ails them. Nothing else. Even if the patient happens to be a good-looking young woman.' She handed Edwina a steaming mug. 'Here. Drink this and then I think you'll be fine.'

'What is it?' Edwina asked.

'Tea, of course,' Bridget replied. 'Hot tea with lots of sugar. The best thing in the world for shock and fright and sadness, and all kinds of thrills and spills life hits you with. Now, drink up and then you can go home with your young man.'

'What young man?' Edwina asked.

'He said his name is Andrew. He's waiting for you in the car.'

'Oh, *him*. He's not mine – or even very young,' Edwina said, letting out a laugh. 'He's a... business associate. Why do people always assume every man I'm with is my boyfriend?'

'Probably because you're so attractive,' Bridget said, getting up. 'And to me, any man under fifty is young. Dr Shane, here, is just a boy at forty-two. But you're right. I shouldn't have assumed the man who brought you was your boyfriend.'

'If I were a man you wouldn't have,' Edwina remarked.

'I think you're right. Very sexist of me, I suppose. Women still get a raw deal in the world, don't they? As if you're nobody without a boyfriend.'

'So true,' Edwina said, smiling at Bridget. She looked like the kind of woman that would be lovely to sit and chat with for hours and tell her all your worries and secrets. She had such a cosy, sweet face. Edwina drank the tea and even if it was sickly sweet, it instantly made her feel better. She put the mug on the table and got up. 'Thanks for the tea. I'll be off now. Would it be all right if I came back later to pay the bill? I left my bag in the... car,' she said, not wanting to reveal that she had anything to do with Starlight Cottages.

'Of course,' Bridget said.

'Great,' Edwina replied.

'Shane wants a word before you go, though,' Bridget said. 'He had a patient just now, but I'll go and see if they're finished. Wait here.'

'Okay.'

'You're renting Sorcha's flat for the summer, I heard. And you're Max's sister. So we know where you are,' she added with a wink.

Edwina took a tentative step forward to test her leg and found it didn't hurt much at all. She felt foolish about having fainted like that, but the sight of a needle always did that to her. The shock and pain had also made her feel weak, but Bridget's tea had already helped a lot. She gave a start as Shane, dressed in scrubs, a stethoscope strung around his neck, entered the room.

'Feeling better?' he asked.

'Yes, much better, thanks,' Edwina replied. 'Sorry about passing out like that.'

'The sight of a needle does that to some people,' he replied. 'You should have told me.'

'I forgot.'

'Yes, well...' He hovered by the door. 'Must get back to my patients. I just wanted to tell you to come back to get the stitches out in a week and to be careful until then. No jogging or swimming or anything strenuous. Keep the leg up as much as you can for the next few days. I phoned through a prescription for antibiotics to the pharmacy.'

Edwina nodded, trying not to look too deep into his warm brown eyes. 'Thanks for looking after me so well.'

'That's what I do,' he said with a smile.

'I know.' She wanted to say more, to tell him what a good doctor he was, how his gentle hands and voice had soothed and calmed her until the incident with the syringe. But she was too overwhelmed by everything that had happened.

They looked at each other for a few awkward moments until Shane moved to the door. 'I've got to go. See you soon. Hope you'll feel better, Edwina.'

'I'm sure I will. Bye, Shane,' Edwina said. 'And thanks again.'

'You're welcome,' he said and walked out.

Edwina stood there for a moment gathering her thoughts, her gaze drifting to the mirror over the fireplace. She brought her hands to her face. What a fright she looked, her hair still wet and tangled from the swim, her face pale and her T-shirt wrinkled. She had better go and tidy herself up before the meeting that was now running horribly late. She walked out of the surgery and found Andrew sitting in his car, looking at his phone.

'Hi,' she said, easing herself into the passenger seat. 'Sorry about all this and thank you for all your help. I know the meeting is now an hour late, so maybe you want to reschedule?'

'No, that's fine,' he replied, starting the car. 'Karen is still looking at the cottages and wants to talk to you about some ideas she has. But maybe you'd like me to drive you somewhere where you can freshen up first?'

'Freshen up?' Edwina said with a hollow laugh. 'I need a total makeover. But yes, please, that would be great. I'll at least try to look human.'

'I think you look terrific,' Andrew said. 'Just a little shaken up.'

'You're a sweetheart,' Edwina said.

It didn't take long to drive to the flat, where Edwina, with Andrew's help, climbed the stairs. He waited in the living room while she quickly changed into blue linen trousers and a white shirt. Then she did a quick blow-dry and dabbed on blusher and applied mascara, all of which made her look a lot better, even if not as polished as usual. But it would have to do.

She was anxious to get back to the cottages and the rest of the design team so they could get the project started. She couldn't wait for the work to begin. If she could just keep it a secret a little longer...

9

_____

A little later, after Andrew had driven her back to the cottages, she stood on the terrace of the first house again and listened to Karen, who had been investigating the houses and the sites and come up with a few ideas.

'This is a *superb* setting,' Karen said, looking out at the view. 'It will be a fabulous place for someone to relax and hide from the probing eyes of the press and other media. Far from the madding crowd and all that.'

'That's what I thought,' Edwina agreed.

'The houses are small.' Karen opened a folder with notes and sketches. 'But I have a few ideas about how to use the indoor space more efficiently. I think that the living room can be split into two rooms, and this way, make one smaller cosy space with that fireplace. The other room would then be a bedroom. Knock through to the utility room beside the kitchen and make an en suite shower and toilet. Then put the washing machine into the kitchen and make that room more compact. That would create a three-bedroom house with two bathrooms.'

'Oh,' Edwina said, impressed. She glanced at Andrew. 'Would that be hard to do?'

'I'd have to take a look at the walls, but I think it's perfectly doable,' he replied.

'Sounds great,' Edwina said. 'Any other ideas?'

'Yes,' Karen said. 'There is also the option to knock through the walls of all the cottages and combine them into one big house. But then you'd be limited to just one property after that. And we're not sure we'd get planning permission, anyway.'

'I think that could be tricky,' Edwina remarked.

'I think the four cottages will be better as individual houses anyway,' Karen announced. 'Planning applications can be slow and difficult and you might get protests from the locals.'

'I agree,' Edwina said. 'Jonathan, the estate agent, said the houses are listed, so we wouldn't be able to do many alterations to the exteriors. I don't want to enter into any kind of argument about it. Nobody in the village knows I'm the owner of the cottages and I'd like to keep it that way for as long as I can. But I'm sure it's only a matter of time before the cat is out of the bag, so to speak.'

'You want to keep it a secret?' Karen asked, looking surprised. 'In a small village like this? I'd say that would be nearly impossible.'

Edwina laughed. 'Yeah, I'm afraid you're right.'

'You could always say you've been hired as project leader or something?' Karen suggested. 'And if I were you, I'd create a limited company and come up with some name and then say that they're employing you.'

'I'm not sure I want to do that,' Edwina argued. 'It would be lying.'

'Are the people around here really that against these houses being done up? Or is it because they'll be turned into holiday lets instead of residential homes?' Andrew asked. 'I mean, what Karen just proposed won't really alter them much from the outside.'

'Except for these little gardens,' Karen cut in.

Edwina turned to Andrew. 'What do you suggest we do with them?'

'Ah, yes, we nearly forgot about those,' Andrew replied. 'We thought we'd build decking right to the end and put in a hot tub on each one. And we need to have a fence between each house for privacy. Or maybe a bamboo screen. I don't think that'll require planning permission.'

'I hope not,' Edwina exclaimed. 'I don't want to have to put up any kind of notice with my name on it.'

'I'll look it up,' Andrew promised.

'Did you say hot tub?' Edwina tried to imagine what it would be like to sit in one under the stars. 'What a brilliant idea.'

'Yes, we thought so.' Karen closed her folder. 'So now that you've heard the different ideas, we'll head off. Let us know what you want to do and we'll get started on plans and drawings and then round up builders and decorators. We have a whole team lined up, so you don't have to do anything really, other than sign the cheques.'

'Well, I want to see the quotes before I give you the green light,' Edwina said quickly. 'We might have to compromise on some things. But right now I can tell you that what you said about adding a bedroom and new bathroom seems to be a great idea. So if you could draw that up and then give me a list of what needs to be done and then we can decide on the details later. Bathrooms and kitchen interiors and stuff like that.'

'Absolutely,' Karen replied. She and Andrew moved away to leave.

'We'll be in touch very soon,' Andrew promised. 'And maybe you'd like to come to our office in Tralee next week where we'll have a mock-up of the design, as soon as I've finished the drawings?'

Edwina nodded. 'I'd love to. I can't wait to see it.'

'Take care of your leg,' Andrew said as he turned to leave. 'I hope it feels better soon.'

'Thanks for driving me to see the doctor,' Edwina said, smiling at him. He had been such a great help and she couldn't thank him enough for being there for her, even though they hardly knew each other.

'You're welcome,' he replied. 'Glad to help. That was a bad gash.'

'Yes, it was. But it'll get better very quickly. Hope to see you soon, Andrew,' she said, feeling to her surprise that she meant it. There was something nice and solid about him that she liked. And he had been such a brick when she needed someone to lean on. Men like that were thin on the ground in her circle.

'Good luck,' he said before he followed Karen out to the car.

Edwina stayed on the terrace for a while, digesting what Karen had said. Her suggestions were fabulous and Edwina knew it would work out really well. The cottages would be little gems that people would queue up to lease and she could charge huge rents and make a lot of money once all the work was done. She couldn't wait to see them finished.

As she stood there, looking down at the little beach in Wild Rose Bay, she remembered how beautiful and peaceful it was. There was a kind of serenity there she had never felt before. Not on the fashionable beaches on the Riviera or in the Bahamas, or anywhere in the world she had ever been to. Was it really right to commercialise this spot in this way? But there wouldn't be that many people here, she reasoned. It was the exclusivity she would be selling, the away-from-it-all aspect that was so rare these days.

Edwina suddenly winced, feeling a slight stinging in the wound on her knee as the anaesthetic began to wear off. Her thoughts strayed to Shane. Now that she had seen him in action as a doctor, she was even more intrigued by him. He had been the opposite of the slightly arrogant man she had been sparring with at the pub. Was the caring, compassionate doctor the real man behind the façade? she wondered. Not that she hadn't enjoyed the teasing between them – that had been fun, too.

She pulled herself together and turned to leave. *Forget about men*, she thought, *this project has to be at the top of my agenda right now.* As she stood there, looking down at the beach, the message she had found in the bottle popped into her mind. She could nearly see the young man standing on the pier in Dingle, sad, forlorn, possibly a little drunk, wanting something to happen, something romantic and sweet, like that young girl across the ocean finding his note and then trying to contact him. There had been a name and a number... Edwina wondered if she should call it and see if the young man—now twenty years older—was still around and had recovered from whatever sadness had happened to him. But that might be a foolish thing to do. Better to just send him a kind thought and not stir up what might be a bad memory.

After a quiet weekend resting and reading and looking at the drawings the design team sent her via email, Edwina went to the Wellness Centre on the Monday after her arrival. She couldn't exercise just yet, but she wanted to let them know she wouldn't be able to attend for at least another week. She was greeted by a tall willowy woman with light brown hair that tumbled to her waist. She was dressed in a black T-shirt and leggings and spoke in a soft, gentle voice Edwina found soothing.

'Hello, Edwina,' the woman said when Edwina had introduced herself. 'I'm Billy.'

'Oh,' Edwina said and laughed. 'I didn't know what to expect. But as I heard you were tough, I was imagining a muscular man with tattoos and a shaved head who took no prisoners.'

Billy smiled. 'I can be if my clients don't work hard enough. But that's when I'm working as a PT. In my classes, you will work at your own pace. Although I will know if you fake it, and then I take out the whip.'

'That sounds scarier than the guy with the muscles I thought you were,' Edwina replied. 'I booked online for the health and fitness course. But I'm not going to be able to work out this week or even the next. I had a bit of an accident the other day and had to have stitches. The doctor said not to do any exercise until it's all healed up.'

'Where is your injury?' Billy asked.

Edwina lifted her leg. 'Just below my knee. I fell on some glass at the beach and cut myself quite badly.'

'Oh, that must have been painful,' Billy said.

'Yeah, awful.' Edwina paused. 'But Shane was brilliant, I have to say. Got it all stitched up in no time.'

'Shane is an angel,' Billy said with a fond smile.

'Well, I wouldn't go that far,' Edwina remarked. 'He wasn't exactly angelic the first time we met.'

'Oh, he can be moody,' Billy agreed. 'I know because we go way back. We both come from Cahersiveen, you see. I've known Shane since he was a teenager. He went through some tough times recently.'

'Oh,' Edwina said, taken aback. 'I had no idea.'

'He hides it well,' Billy said. 'But aren't we all hiding some kind of sorrow?'

'Yes. I suppose that's true.' Edwina paused. 'But enough about him,' she breezed on. 'I just came here to explain. I thought it would be more polite to do it in person. And I wanted to see this place,' she said, looking around the reception area. What had looked like a large shed from the outside was an inviting, calm space on the inside. With wide, bleached-wood planks on the floor, whitewashed walls covered in posters with photos of the ocean and pots with flowers and exotic plants dotted around, the room oozed calm and tranquillity. The faint scent of lavender and soothing music from a loudspeaker added to the peaceful atmosphere. 'It's actually lovely,' she said in awe.

'You sound surprised,' Billy said.

'Well, I didn't expect something so... sophisticated around here,' Edwina confessed. 'And it just looks like a shed from the outside.'

'Simplicity is what we aim for here,' Billy replied, smiling. 'In any case, I didn't do this. It's all Cormac's doing. He's a healer and herbalist and this is his creation. But he's gone to Australia for a year with his wife, who is the doctor here. So I'm holding the fort until he comes back.'

'So I've heard,' Edwina said. 'Funny how just one evening at the pub will fill you in on so many things in the village.'

Billy smiled and nodded. 'That's true. I already knew who you were when you came in. Quite normal for a small place like this. I heard you're here for a break after being stressed out in Dublin. And you're Max's sister and the two of you don't get on, so you're staying in Sorcha's flat and then you have some kind of business around here but nobody knows what it is. Yet.' Billy winked. 'But we'll get that out of you sooner or later, right?'

'Probably,' Edwina said, wondering how long it would take before everyone knew her secret. 'And it's not true that Max and I don't get on. We do, to a fashion. It's just that there's some... stuff between us that needs to be sorted.'

Billy nodded. 'Yeah, I know about stuff. Every family has a bit of that. But back to your fitness programme. There is a lot you can do around your injury. We do chair yoga here, and then you can work out with weights which will not put any pressure on your bad leg. Could be an option until you're up and running again? And of course, we have the meditation room, where you can just chill and let your thoughts float around. Very relaxing if you're feeling stressed.'

Edwina met Billy's large hazel eyes and considered the

suggestions. Then she nodded. 'That all sounds great. So yes, I'd love that.'

'Wonderful,' Billy said. 'I'll draw up a plan for you and email it to you. I think I have your email address on file as you booked the course. You could start with the chair yoga tomorrow morning, if you like?'

'That would be great,' Edwina said.

Billy nodded and looked at the timetable on the counter. 'Okay. It starts at nine. We do it on the deck at the back of the building if the weather is fine. I'll get back to you by email later today with the plan for the next two weeks. And after that, you'll probably be all healed up and ready to take part in all the classes.' She looked up as a group of people of various ages entered through the open door. 'But now I have to go and whip a few people around the gym.'

Edwina smiled. 'I'll leave you to it, then.'

'See you tomorrow.' Billy turned her attention to the newcomers. 'Hi, lads. Ready for a little pain and torture?'

They all laughed and said they were looking forward to it.

Edwina watched them disappear through the door that led to the gym and felt a dart of disappointment that she couldn't join them. She had a feeling Billy was just the kind of inspirational fitness teacher she needed. She looked forward to the chair yoga the following morning, even if it seemed like something for the elderly and infirm. But she had to be careful not to open the wound again. At least until Shane had taken the stitches out next Friday. She was no longer in any pain, even if the wound was a little tender to the touch. Not being able to swim had been the most difficult part as the weather was still lovely.

But today, there would be no time to swim, even if she could, as she was driving to Tralee for a meeting with the design team, to see their computer drawings and the mock-up model they had made. She couldn't wait to see the cardboard model of the finished cottages. Then, when she had agreed on everything, the contractors would move in and the work would start in earnest. And then... What would happen next, when it was all finished? Would she sell it all and move on to another project? She stood outside the Wellness Centre looking out over the sea, trying to figure out what she was actually doing here and what would happen after this project was over. Where would she go? Would she ever find a place where she could settle and be finally happy?

As she stood there, Edwina suddenly felt strangely lost, like a plant pulled out of the earth with all the roots dangling in the air. She knew Dublin wasn't really her true home, the place she wanted to live for the rest of her life. But where did she *really* belong? She had been in Sandy Cove less than a week but already felt a peace here that was truly soothing. It was a lovely spot, but not where she felt she could make a life. The quiet country lifestyle didn't suit her restless mind.

She suddenly remembered the note she had found in the bottle, the message from a deeply sad young man. More than twenty years had passed since he threw it into the sea, hoping it would float away across the ocean. But instead, it had been bobbing up and down the coast on the currents only to be found across the bay twenty years later by a lost and lonely woman trying to find herself a spot to call home.

She wondered what had happened to that young man. Had he found solace and happiness since that night when he had been so sad? Maybe she should go to Dingle and try to find him? She only knew his first name. Pearse. Not that common. But not so unusual, either. But the phone number might still work. It was a number to a landline, though, so maybe it didn't exist any more. She decided to go to Dingle town for a visit when she had the time, just to stand on the pier and send a thought to the man called Pearse, and make a wish that all had been resolved and he was finally happy.

She remembered what Billy had said about Shane: that he had been through something in his life he found hard to deal with. Was it the divorce? Maybe he was still in love with his ex-wife. And then had to deal with a difficult teenager who was, like she had been, probably angry with his parents about the divorce. She had been very attracted to Shane from the start, but now she realised it might be better not to get involved. An ex-wife, a prickly teenager and some possible other heavy baggage was too much to cope with. Edwina knew it would be a huge mistake to try to take that on. Better to nip it in the bud before it started. Even if flirting with a dishy man had been great fun.

10

After her consultation with the design team in their elegant office in Tralee and her approval of their plans, the project started rolling the second week in June. The builders turned up as planned, and the work was in full swing very soon after that. The hammering and banging and drilling could be heard throughout the village and the rumours about what was going on were even more outlandish than before.

'Exciting times around here,' Shane said when Edwina called in to the surgery to have her stiches out. 'Starlight Cottages are being gutted, I hear. God only knows what they'll be turned into.'

'I'm sure they're going to be fabulous,' Edwina said.

'Really?' Shane put on latex gloves and took the dressing off her knee. 'I believe you're involved with the project,' he said offhandedly as he examined her wound.

'What?' Edwina stared at him. 'How... I mean, who told me that?'

Shane shrugged. 'Can't remember exactly. Someone who saw you at the cottages with two strangers. A man and a woman who were looking around.'

'Oh yes, that's the construction company who are doing the renovations.' Edwina realised there was no use denying she had something to do with it, but at least she could hide the fact that she was the owner.

'So you're part of that team?'

'Yeah, well, in a way,' Edwina said, feeling awkward about lying to him. 'I was offered the job as project leader a while back.'

Shane lifted an eyebrow and looked at her for a moment before he turned back to her injury. 'So that's the real reason you're here?'

'Amongst other things. What about the wound?' she asked, in order to change the subject. 'Does it look okay to you?'

'Yes. It looks good. Healing very well. So you took the antibiotics like a good girl.'

'Of course,' Edwina said, bristling at the way he addressed her. 'And I'm not five years old.'

'Sorry. Force of habit, dealing with kids a lot of the time.' Shane took a long, thin pair of scissors from a dish and started to snip off the sutures, then pulling them out with a tweezer. 'Good,' he muttered. 'No sign of infection. There'll be a hairline scar but that won't mar your beauty. Barely visible, actually.' He put a plaster on the wound. 'There. Take this off in a couple of days and then you can go back to whatever you did before. Running, swimming, whatever.'

'I'm doing a fitness course at the Wellness Centre,' Edwina said. 'Right now, only chair yoga and meditation. But as soon as I can, I'll join Billy's classes and workouts.'

He looked up from her knee. 'So you met Billy?'

Edwina nodded and put her leg down, getting off the examining table. 'Yes. She's lovely. She told me you know each other from way back.'

'Yes, we do. She's been a great help to me,' Shane said, looking suddenly serious. He got up from the stool he had been sitting on, pulling off his gloves. 'So that's it. You can go back to running that building project. I'm sure it's quite exciting. Even if it causes a lot of talk around here.'

'Talk?' Edwina asked. 'What kind of talk?'

'People are worried about what's being done to the cottages.' Shane threw the used gloves in the bin. 'The coastguard station is very important to them, and they wouldn't want it to change in any way. And I agree with that, to tell you the truth.'

'Well,' Edwina started. 'I do know that they won't be that different from the outside. They're just going to be freshened up.'

'I hope that's all that's being done. But I'm sure it's an interesting job.'

'Well, yes,' Edwina said, hesitating at the door. 'I'm enjoying it. And it's not going to be something hugely awful like people seem to think.'

'Ah, well, they're a bit suspicious about anything like that after the furore of the proposed hotel project a few years ago. I wasn't here then, but I believe there was quite a row about it and the guy who was planning it was run out of town. By a lynch mob with torches.'

'Yeah right,' Edwina said with a snort.

Shane smirked. 'I made the last bit up. But there was a lot of bad feeling around here, I believe. So whoever is really behind this thing should be careful.'

'I'm sure they know that,' Edwina replied. 'Bye, Shane.'

'Bye, Edwina. I'm glad I was here when you needed help.'

'You seemed almost annoyed when I arrived at your door,' she said, not wanting to show how much she had appreciated his care.

'I had just woken up,' he countered. 'And I thought you had been careless. But I was wrong. Sorry about being so brusque when you came in that day.'

'That's okay,' Edwina replied. An awkward silence ensued

while they looked at each other across the room. 'Well, I'll be off then,' she said finally. 'See you around.'

'Okay. Bye.' Shane nodded and Edwina slipped out of the room while he went to the sink to wash his hands.

As she left the surgery, Edwina wondered why she always felt so stiff and self-conscious around him. She couldn't be sure having only recently met him, but she guessed there was a turmoil going on behind his calm, confident exterior. She found herself more and more attracted to him but tried her best not to make it obvious. In any case, he didn't seem that interested, just slightly amused by her as if she were someone he enjoyed to tease.

Edwina had a feeling he thought she was stuck-up and spoiled, both of which could be true, if she was honest with herself. She had arrived here full of ideas about what she was entitled to and ready to look down her nose at country people. But even after just one week in this little village, she felt herself softening and found that she was beginning to see people through different eyes. She was quite awestruck by the kindness of strangers who were nice to her without expecting anything in return. Because of this, she felt she had to keep her real role in the refurbishing of the cottages under wraps.

These nice people might treat her differently if they didn't approve.

Edwina managed to keep up the pretence of working as an employee of some building firm until one evening in the beginning of July at the Harbour pub when she happened to mention the refurbishment work that was being done to Tara and Mick, the couple she had met during her first evening in Sandy Cove. They had quickly become friends and Edwina had especially bonded with Tara, who, with her high-profile career in photography, was interesting to talk to. And Mick was charming and funny and wonderful company. She remembered seeing him in a play at the Abbey Theatre in Dublin many years ago, and had been impressed with his political career after he gave up acting. With his fair hair and bright blue eyes, he was good-looking in a careless way and his expression of true love as he looked at Tara was endearing. The three of them had fallen into the habit of meeting for a drink from time to time, grabbing a coffee or getting together for a bite to eat and a glass of wine.

'What is actually going on down there at Starlight Cottages?' Tara asked as they sat together in the Harbour pub eating pizza and sharing a bottle of wine.

'The four cottages are being completely refurbished,' Edwina replied. 'I'm kind of leading the project for the developers and I've seen all the plans.'

'Oh,' Tara said, her dark eyes glittering with excitement. 'So *that's* what you're doing here.'

'Yes, among other things,' Edwina replied, looking at Tara to see if she was upset about the project. 'I hope you're not worried?' she asked.

'Me?' Tara laughed. 'No. I'm not from around here. I'm a blow-in from Dublin like you. I got a lot of negativity when I first arrived here to do a photo shoot for a travel magazine back in the US. So it isn't a huge shock-horror thing for me that those cottages are going to be modernised, or whatever.'

'They're just being restored and done up a little,' Edwina said, attempting to downplay what was going on.

'We were all wondering,' Tara remarked. 'So it's going to be some kind of exclusive holiday place, then?'

'Something like that,' Edwina said. 'It's not quite decided whether they'll be sold or let. In any case, the plan is to do them up to five-star standard inside and build a deck with a hot tub at the back of each cottage.'

'Sounds heavenly,' Tara said, nudging her husband. 'Hey, why can't we have a hot tub at our place?'

'We have the river,' Mick replied. 'You love bathing there on hot days.'

'Yes, but on cold days, wouldn't it be fabulous to sit in a hot tub and look at the stars?' Tara said dreamily.

'Until one of the kids decide to jump in with you,' Mick said dryly. 'Or the dogs want to play or the new kitten drowns in it...'

'Spoilsport,' Tara said, giving him a shove.

Mick laughed and put his arm around Tara. 'Okay, darling. You can have that hot tub when the kids have grown up and we have no dogs or cats.'

'Which will be never.' Tara sighed and drank some more wine. 'Maybe we should rent one of those cottages when they're finished and use it as our very own hideaway.'

'If we can afford it,' Mick replied. 'I've heard it's going to be very luxurious. Gold-plated taps and silk wallpaper.'

Edwina laughed. 'No, that's wrong. There are no gold taps or silk wallpaper. The interiors will be very traditional. A "Cape Cod meets the Hamptons" kind of look. The furniture is simple and tasteful, which suits the seaside setting. It's all being shipped from the States.'

'Sounds expensive,' Mick remarked.

'Yes, it is,' Edwina admitted. 'But if you're doing exclusive you can't skimp on anything.'

'It'll be a far cry from what those cottages looked like when they were inhabited by real coastguards,' Tara remarked. 'Those families were poor. They had to work hard to make ends meet. Every family member had some kind of job, even the children. The houses were very basic.'

'They were solidly built, though,' Mick said. 'And they really stand out along this coastline. It's such a beautiful spot. But if you want my honest opinion, I think this is not going to be hugely popular with people around here. I mean, they should have consulted with the village, don't you think?'

'But why? I mean, we knew we didn't need to apply for

planning permission when we bought them,' Edwina blurted out without thinking.

'*We?*' Mick asked, looking intrigued. 'You mean *you're* one of the developers?'

'Yes, I...' Edwina stopped, horrified, putting her hand to her mouth.

She hadn't meant to admit anything. It had just slipped out because she had felt so relaxed in the company of this nice couple. She looked around the pub and noticed people had stopped talking and were all now staring at her.

Oh God, it was out now. What was she going to do?

11

Edwina looked at Mick and Tara and let out a fake laugh.

'Just messing with you,' she said, trying to hide her dismay.

'No you weren't. You're the person who bought the cottages. Aren't you?' Tara said, looking highly amused as she stared at Edwina.

Edwina squirmed. 'Well, okay, since you ask, yes. I own the cottages and I have hired this building and design firm to do them up.'

'I've suspected something like this all along,' Tara said. 'I *knew* there was more to your story than you let on. I mean, you don't look like someone who's just an employee at some construction company.'

'How do you mean?' Edwina asked, staring back at Tara.

'You look like a boss.' She leaned forward across the table, smiling at Edwina. 'This is so fabulous. I do understand why you're keeping it a secret, though.'

'Secret no more,' Mick said, looking around the pub at the people who were now staring at Edwina. 'That was quite a showstopper, my dear.'

'Feck,' Edwina exclaimed.

'Is it true?' a man standing by the bar asked. 'You're the owner of Starlight Cottages?'

'Yes,' Edwina croaked.

'So that's what you're doing here?' a woman standing at the bar said in a loud voice. 'You're here to wreck the coastguard station?'

'No,' Edwina protested. 'Don't worry, they're not going to be wrecked. Just spruced up a little.'

'Spruced up?' the woman asked. 'Is that what you call brand new windows and doors, that fancy deck and a hot tub, no less? I took a walk along the back yesterday and it's all going to be like Beverly Hills. Fancy, schmancy,' she added, taking a sip from her bottle of beer.

'Beverly Hills?' Edwina asked, feeling near tears. 'No, it's being restored in the best possible taste. It's going to be simple but very beautiful.'

'As long as there is no hotel or high-rise apartment block going up,' the man said.

'I wouldn't put that past a smart-looking career woman from Dublin,' the woman remarked in a nasty voice. 'I'm sure they're going to be tarted up beyond recognition. There might even be some horrible extensions.'

'Of course not,' Tara retorted, coming to Edwina's help. 'That would be ridiculous.'

'We have just heard it's going to be very exclusive and classy,' Mick cut in. 'And you won't notice much of a difference, except for the swish people who'll be spending lots of money in all the shops around here.' He raised his wine glass. 'Here's to the new, and even better, Starlight Cottages. Isn't it great that someone is improving them and attracting the right sort of person here? A win-win for us all, I say.'

'A win-win for the rich, you mean?' someone shouted after a brief silence.

'Sure won't they be great customers,' someone else shouted.

'I'd say cheers to that.' And then some of the people raised their glasses and drank to the new, refurbished cottages, while others looked sourly at Edwina.

'Don't mind them,' Mick whispered in her ear. 'It'll be fine once everyone gets used to the idea.'

Edwina was relieved to see that, apart from a few, the general feeling was positive, all thanks to Mick. But then he was a very popular politician and a former actor with tons of charm. She looked at him, feeling a surge of gratitude.

'Thank you,' she said, feeling close to tears. 'You've saved my life.'

'Ah, sure it was nothing,' Mick said, with fake modesty.

'It was a pure miracle,' Edwina said. 'You convinced a lot of people I'm doing them a favour.'

'He does that all the time,' Tara said, laughing. 'He could charm the birds from the trees.' She put her hand to her husband's cheek. 'That was amazing, sweetheart. Now nearly everyone loves Edwina's project.'

'And why wouldn't they?' Mick asked. 'I know I was a bit iffy myself about it at first but, now I've had time to reflect, I think it's a grand scheme. And what's the big deal, anyway? Some glamourous people for whom money is no issue will be spending their holidays here and throwing their cash around. So what? It'll be great for business and for the village. I'm all for that kind of tourism, I have to say.'

Edwina laughed and dug into her pizza, feeling a surge of relief. Then she noticed someone at the bar. It was Shane, looking unusually stressed. As if feeling her eyes on him, he looked at her and smiled. Then he walked across the floor to their table.

'Hi, gang,' he said. 'Looks like you're having a lot of fun.'

'Oh yes,' Mick said, getting up and shaking Shane's hand. 'We've just outed Edwina as the owner of Starlight Cottages.

She's building an eight-storey hotel with a huge parking lot and a pool there.'

Shane burst out laughing. 'Gee, that should scare the bejesus out of everyone. But I bet you're just having me on.' His gaze drifted to Edwina. 'Except for the bit that she is the mystery owner of the place. That doesn't surprise me one bit. Always thought she looked like a woman of property.'

'Me too,' Tara quipped. 'But why don't you join us? Pull up a chair and share some pizza. We ordered three different ones, but I doubt we'll be able to finish them.'

'Thanks, but I have to get back home with the ones I ordered. My son Daniel has just arrived and I left him watching some rubbish on Netflix and texting his friends on his phone at the same time. Kids these days can't concentrate on one thing. They have to rot their brains on several things simultaneously. Anyway, he's here for the whole summer, so you'll be watching me slowly going around the bend.'

'Tell him to get a job,' Mick said, sitting down again. 'Plenty of places around here looking for staff. I think Sorcha said to me only today she needs help in her shop.'

Shane looked thoughtful. 'Great idea if I can get him to do it. That'd keep him out of my hair and put manners on him. Anyway, my order is ready, so I'd better go back and feed him.'

'You sound like you're talking about a dog,' Edwina remarked.

'Do I?' Shane shrugged. 'Must brush up on my parenting skills. Maybe you could give me a few pointers, Edwina? You seem such an expert.' His eyes were cold as he looked at her.

'I don't claim to know much about bringing up children,' Edwina retorted. 'It was just the way you talked about your son that—'

'I'd advise you to quit while you're ahead,' Shane snapped.

'The teenage period must be the worst part of having children,' Tara cut in, trying to calm the situation. 'I'm not looking forward to ours being that age.'

'Neither am I,' Mick said. 'Twin girls that are going to be as beautiful as their mother. What a nightmare for a nervous father.'

'They're only six now, so we have a little time before that happens,' Tara soothed, smiling at him.

'They are easier when they're small,' Shane agreed. 'But I must go. I'll catch up with you another time, guys.'

When Shane had left, Tara looked curiously at Edwina. 'What was that all about? The two of you looked as if you hate each other.'

Edwina shrugged and picked up her wine glass. 'No idea. He was probably just tired and stressed. His job is very demanding and then looking after a teenager on top of that must be difficult. That's all it was.'

Mick lifted an eyebrow. 'Yeah? I could swear I felt some vibes between you two...'

Edwina felt herself blush scarlet. 'I don't know what you mean. I don't think he likes me at all. And the feeling is mutual,' she added, hoping they'd believe it. 'Can we drop this now?'

'Of course,' Tara said, shooting a warning look at Mick. 'By the way, how are Max and Allegra these days?'

'Busy,' Edwina said. 'Like me. I was hoping to see more of them but I haven't had the time now that the work on the cottages has started.' She suddenly remembered that Max didn't know her role in the building works. She hadn't told him because she knew he wouldn't approve, and also because he might be upset that she hadn't hired him to draw up the plans. But Andrew was part of the building firm and they wouldn't have wanted to hire in an architect from outside. 'But you have reminded me that I should give them a call. I want him to hear about what I'm doing from me, rather than from anyone else.'

'Better make it soon, then,' Mick suggested. 'The grapevine works fast around here.'

'Yes, I think you're right.' Edwina nibbled on a piece of pizza crust while she considered how she would approach Max. 'I'll call him later tonight,' she said, wondering how she would break the news to her brother. She'd just have to tell him everything without any frills.

'He won't be that shocked,' Mick, as if reading Edwina's mind. 'I'd say he'll think it's great.'

'I hope so,' Edwina said.

'Of course he will,' Tara said.

They finished their pizzas and paid the bill. Mick and Tara drove off, leaving Edwina to wander slowly to her flat, deep in thought. When she was inside the door, she decided to take the bull by the horns and call Max.

'Hi,' she said when he answered. 'I hope I'm not disturbing you?'

'No, I've just managed to get the boys to go to sleep,' he replied. 'They were impossible tonight for some reason. But now, finally, they're asleep in our bed. And we're relaxing on the terrace. It's a beautiful evening. How are you settling in to Sandy Cove?'

'Really well,' she said, feeling her stomach contract with nerves. 'I've just had dinner with Tara and Mick. We're becoming good friends.'

'Great,' Max said. 'They're a nice couple.'

'Yes, lovely.' Edwina took a deep breath. 'I have something to tell you, Max.'

'About what?' he asked.

'About why I'm really here,' Edwina said, sinking down on the sofa in the little sitting room. 'It's not really a holiday or something to do with the Wellness Centre. It's about a new project I'm involved with.'

'Go on,' Max said. 'I'll put on the speaker so Allegra can hear it too.'

'Okay,' Edwina said. 'Hi, Allegra.'

'Hi!' Allegra called from further away.

'So tell us,' Max urged.

Edwina cleared her throat, which was suddenly dry. 'It's about the coastguard cottages and what is being done to them.'

'Yes, there's a lot of noise coming from there, I've heard,' Allegra remarked.

'I know.' Edwina paused, trying to think of how to tell them.

'I wonder what the person who bought them is up to?' Max mused. 'But I suppose we'll find out in time.'

'I can tell you that right now,' Edwina said, having finally plucked up enough courage to come clean. 'Because I'm that person.'

'The person who— What?' Allegra asked.

'Who bought the cottages and is doing them up to rent or sell,' Edwina said very quickly. 'I'm the owner and I've hired a construction firm to refurbish the whole lot. They're going to be exclusive hideaways. Five-star accommodation, if you see what I mean.'

There was a long silence during which Edwina thought Max had hung up.

'I don't understand,' Max finally said. 'Why are you doing this? Where did you get the money? What about your job? Does Mum know?'

'Long story,' Edwina said. 'But yes, Mum knows. She has actually helped me with some money to fund this.'

'She didn't say anything about it when we had dinner,' Max said, sounding sour. 'Was it supposed to be a secret?'

'No,' Edwina replied. 'She didn't know about it then. I met her when you had left and then she agreed to help me.'

'We need to talk about this,' Max said. 'It seems a bit mad to me.'

'It's not mad at all,' Edwina argued. 'It's a great idea, if you think about it.'

'Yes, but...' Max started. 'What do you know about building and restoration? You know that I really like that old coastguard station. It's such a unique row of houses. And now you tell me you're about to have them renovated. Why didn't you ask me first before you jumped into something like that?'

'Because I knew you'd be against it,' Edwina said hotly.

'You're damn right I am,' Max said. 'Can we at least discuss it? I might be able to stop you making a stupid mistake. We have to talk about this, Edwina.'

'Come to dinner,' Allegra shouted from somewhere far away. 'Tomorrow night? Then you can have a good talk. We'll try to keep the kids out of your hair. Stay the night, maybe? I'll clear out the rose bedroom and you can sleep there.'

'Er...' Edwina thought for a moment. Stay the night at Strawberry Hill? She wasn't sure she wanted to. But the rose bedroom was lovely with its rosebud wallpaper, Victorian furniture and the view across the garden all the way to the river. 'Okay,' she said. 'That would be nice.'

'Good,' Max said. 'I think we need to talk. Not only about your mad scheme, but other things, too.'

'Come at eight,' Allegra called. 'We should have the lads at least in their pyjamas by then. Can't promise they'll be asleep, though.'

'It's the long bright evenings,' Max explained. 'It gives them extra energy or something. Anyway, see you tomorrow. We'll talk then. Bye for now.'

'Bye, Max,' Edwina said and hung up, deep in thought.

It looked as if Max was ready to at least talk to her but, on the other hand, he might also be annoyed that she hadn't consulted with him before embarking on this project. And then this family evening made her feel apprehensive. She knew she was expected to get to know the boys better and she truly wanted to. But they were so small and she had no idea how to behave around children that age. Had they been older it would be easier; then she could ask them about school and hobbies and favourite movies and maybe read them a bit of Harry Potter. But toddlers were another matter. Oh well, she'd just have to play it by ear and go with the flow. It would be nice to have a break from everything for a while.

Edwina decided to take the whole of tomorrow off and arrive early at Strawberry Hill. She started to put a few items together for her stay and pulled out the Chanel tote bag she had used at the beach, as it was the perfect size for whatever she needed to bring for an overnight stay. She turned it upside down over her bed to empty it and gave a start as a piece of paper fluttered to the floor. The message she had found in the bottle. Being busy with the building project, she had nearly forgotten about it. She bent to pick it up, reading the few lines again, including the phone number.

The image of that sad young man drifted into her mind. Poor Pearse, whoever he was. What had happened to him? She looked at the phone number. *Why not give it a try?* she thought and picked up her phone from the bedside table. The number was probably discontinued, but then at least she would know.

She dialled the number, not expecting it to connect but, to her surprise, it rang through. There was no answer for what seemed like a long time and Edwina was about to hang up when there was a click and a woman's voice answered.

'Hello?'

'Eh, hello,' Edwina said. 'Is there anyone called Pearse there?'

'Pearse?' The woman gasped. Edwina could hear her breathing heavily. 'No, there's nobody by that name here,' the voice snapped.

There was a brief pause and then a click as she hung up.

12

Bewildered, Edwina sat on the bed with the phone in her hand. How weird. She was certain that woman was lying. She had seemed shocked when Edwina had said Pearse's name, and then she had hung up just like that. It meant to Edwina that Pearse had indeed lived – or just stayed temporarily – at that address twenty-odd years ago. This changed everything.

Edwina hadn't expected to get a reply at all and would have given up on the idea of ever finding the author of the message in the bottle. But now her blood was up and she suddenly wanted to look for the mysterious man, and find out what had happened to him. She had to go to Dingle town and do some kind of research. It might be possible to find the address connected to that phone number and then go to the house... *And then what?* she asked herself. She might just get a door slammed in her face. Well, it was worth a try all the same.

She pulled herself together and resumed packing the bag and then went to make herself some camomile tea before going to bed. Tomorrow would be full of tension and she needed a good night's sleep.

· · ·

The following morning, Edwina went to her yoga class before she left for Strawberry Hill. It would calm her and help her meet any stress with a relaxed, open mind. She would not let Max or anyone else get to her, and she would be cool and collected and, yes, serene, she decided as she sat with the rest of the class in the lotus position on the deck of the Wellness Centre.

It was a sunny day with a soft, salt-laden breeze from the sea and, as Edwina closed her eyes, she felt a calm come over her. She breathed in and then out slowly, letting out all the stress and bad feelings that had cluttered her mind for a long time. This was her third yoga session and she had found it surprisingly healing. As they got up to standing and she went through all the poses led by Billy, she forgot everything except her own body, her own soul. And at the end of the class as she lay in the corpse pose, the soothing music in her ears, letting go of every last shred of tension in her body, she felt as light as a feather that could float into the blue sky.

They all slowly sat up, said 'namaste' and then got to their feet, smiling at each other, talking softly about what they would do for the rest of the day. They were nice enough women, Edwina thought, but not really her type. With their dated outfits and plain looks, they lacked the polish she could identify with. She knew she stood out like a bird of paradise in her designer yoga outfits and gleaming hair held back with a scrunchie. She made a brief comment about the class like always. The other students in turn were nice to her, smiling politely, but never included her in their chats or after-yoga coffee. Not that she would have time for any of that, but it would have been nice to be asked. She felt sometimes as if she had landed on a different planet and she was an alien regarded with suspicion.

Edwina inwardly laughed at herself, shook off the bad feelings, thanked Billy and left, ready to face her stay at Strawberry

Hill and whatever conflicts it would bring. She was ready to fight her corner, and Max wouldn't be able to shake her confidence. Not this time.

She remembered her resolve several hours later as she faced Max in his study at Strawberry Hill. It was a small room that he had furnished with a desk, on which stood a large computer screen beside an architects' drafting board holding an unfinished sketch. There was also a bookcase crammed with books on design and architecture beside the tall window that overlooked the courtyard. This was Max's space, where he worked on designs for both large housing developments and individual houses.

Edwina glanced at the books, wondering if she could borrow something on interior design that might come in useful for her project. But this was not the moment to ask for favours. She had always been slightly awed by her talented brother, whose amazing good looks, blond shaggy hair, bright blue eyes and dazzling smile had got him a lot of favours in his youth. But now she was ready to do battle, and wouldn't be taken in by his charm.

Edwina breathed in the smell of ink mingled with the musty scent of old books as Max stood beside his desk, looking at her.

'So,' he said. 'Tell me all about this mad building project. Five-star accommodation, you said? A complete overhaul, which involves rebuilding the whole interior?'

'I don't remember telling you that...' Edwina began.

'You didn't. I spoke to Andrew, the architect at Seabreeze Construction and Design. It took me a while to find out who were doing the project, but then I took a walk down at the cottages and saw their sign.'

'You snooped on my project?' Edwina asked. 'And then you called Andrew? Why?'

'I needed to know what you had got yourself into.' Max sat down on the office chair and gestured at the stool beside the drafting board. 'Sit down. I can't think when you're hovering around.'

Edwina sat down. 'I'm not hovering. I'm just appalled that you had to go and snoop around. Couldn't you have just asked me?'

'Just like you asked me before you started this?' Max asked.

'I couldn't hire *you*. The firm already had an architect. It's included in the package.'

'That's not what I meant.' Max folded his arms across his chest. 'I wouldn't have wanted to do it anyway. But you should have asked me to do a survey and to recommend a firm.'

'What's wrong with the one I hired?' Edwina glared at him, trying her best to remain calm and serene.

'I don't know yet. Probably nothing, but I've never heard of them.'

'Their office is fabulous and they have some amazing equipment. They're quite new but the designers have been working with other very well-known firms.'

Max lifted an eyebrow. 'Such as?'

'Eh... I can't think of any right now. But it's easy to look it up.'

Max sighed and shook his head. 'Just as I suspected. You didn't do any research and you picked them because their logo was cute or something.'

Edwina bristled. 'You make me sound like a total ninny. That firm was recommended to me by Jonathan, who, as you know, is a very experienced estate agent.'

'And this makes him an expert on architecture and design?'

Edwina felt a surge of anger rise in her chest. 'Now you're being superior just for the sake of it.' She dug her nails into her palms and made a superhuman effort to stay calm. 'Look, Max. I know you can't forget that old grudge you have carried ever since the row about the house. I know I was wrong and I've told you that I regret how I acted. But you can't let go of your anger, can you? You want to throw cold water on everything I do. You can't stand the idea that I might just succeed in this area. And now that Mum is involved, it rankles with you even more.'

'I'm just trying to stop you making a huge, stupid and very costly mistake,' Max said, staring back at her with cold eyes.

'No, you're not. You're just being spiteful. You know very well that the project is underway, so it's too late to stop it.' Edwina walked to the door. 'This discussion is now closed. There is nothing you can do to stop me, so just accept it, okay?' She opened the door. 'And now I'm going to go and play with the boys and try to be a really nice loveable auntie.'

'Another huge challenge for you, I suspect,' Max muttered.

'Possibly,' Edwina retorted. 'But they are small children and not as critical as you. It's time they got to know me anyway. Then we're going to have a family dinner and you are going to be *nice!*'

With that, she walked out of the study, slamming the door behind her.

To Edwina's surprise, once she got into it, she really did turn into a nice loveable auntie. Allegra had asked her to mind the boys while they were playing with Lego in the library later that evening, 'just to make sure they don't swallow those small pieces,' she said.

Getting on with small children wasn't as hard as Edwina had imagined. The trick, she realised very quickly, was to talk to them as if they were tiny adults and, planning to do just that, she went into the library where she found the two boys. Paddy was building something with Lego and trying to stop Chris interfering at the same time. The room was the same as it has always been: the walls lined with bookcases crammed with books of all kinds, the worn red carpet covering the parquet floor, the two velvet sofas flanking the large fireplace and the mahogany desk with family photographs in silver frames. A room full of memories but, for Edwina, not all of them nice.

'Hi, boys,' Edwina said as she entered. 'What are you building?'

Paddy looked up. 'I'm trying to build a fort but Chris keeps wrecking it.' He pushed his brother's hand away from the wall he had just built.

'I want to play Lego too!' Chris complained.

Edwina crouched on the floor and, without thinking, scooped Chris into her arms. 'We'll just watch and then you and I can build something else, okay?'

Chris nodded. 'Okay.' He put his silky blond head on her chest while they both watched Paddy finish building the fort. Edwina breathed in the smell of baby shampoo and hugged the warm little body closer as she discovered how sweet it was to hold a child like this.

Paddy put the last piece into the top of the wall. 'Ta-da!' he said. 'It's finished.'

'Excellent,' Edwina said. 'You'll be an architect one day, just like your daddy.'

Paddy looked at her for a moment. Then he shook his head. 'No, I want to be a fireman. I want to drive a big red truck and save people from fires. Chris can be an architect.'

'No,' Chris said, sticking his thumb into his mouth. 'I don't want to.'

'Maybe when you're big,' Paddy suggested. 'Hey, you can help me make the men now.' He picked up a few pieces from a box and handed them to Edwina. 'You put the legs and the arms onto the body and then stick the head on top.'

'Seems easy enough,' Edwina said and gave the pieces to

Chris. 'Can you try?'

'Yeah, I can.' Chris wriggled from Edwina's lap and started to put the pieces together quite successfully.

Some time later, they were interrupted by Allegra walking into the room. 'Hey, gang, what are you up to?' she asked. 'Are you bothering your auntie?'

'No, I'm teaching her how to build with Lego,' Paddy said. 'Cos she hasn't a clue.'

'That's very true,' Edwina said. 'But I've learned a lot about Lego in the past hour.'

'And I made a man,' Chris said, showing his mother the figure he had just put together.

'What a clever boy.' Allegra lifted Chris into her arms. 'It's nearly time for dinner. Max has lit the barbeque on the terrace. And we have two guests who have just arrived.'

Edwina got up from the floor and brushed off her jeans. 'But then I have to change.'

'No need,' Allegra said. 'They're not dressed up at all.' She gestured at her denim shorts and wrinkly linen shirt. 'It's just a friend of Max's. They went to Trinity College together.'

'Who is it?' Paddy asked, looking up at Allegra.

'Go and see for yourself,' Allegra said.

'Can I do anything to help?' Edwina asked when Paddy had run out of the room.

'Yes, please,' Allegra replied, balancing Chris on her hip. 'Could you bring out the drinks and crisps from the kitchen? It's all on a tray on the table. I'll be out in a moment with the meat and the salad. I'll just pop this little man into bed. He's half asleep already.'

A few minutes later, Edwina walked out on the terrace with the drinks tray but stopped dead and nearly dropped her load when she came face to face with the guest who had just arrived. Her heart did a funny flip as she stared at him.

What on earth was *he* doing here?

13

———

'Oh,' Edwina said, trying to regain her composure. 'It's you.'

It was so unexpected to see him here that she was lost for words. He had occupied her thoughts constantly since the last time they met and now she was startled to be confronted by him.

'Yes, it's me.' Shane took the tray from her. 'I'd better take this or we'll have a nasty accident. I don't think we want any more broken glass, do we?'

'No,' Edwina said. 'But what... I mean, why...?'

'I see you've met,' Allegra said as she came onto the terrace carrying a platter of meat and sausages. 'I invited Shane because I wanted to meet his son, Daniel, and to give Shane a break from cooking dinner. Seemed like a nice thing to do on a Saturday night.' She walked to the far end of the terrace, where Max was tending the barbeque that looked ready for cooking.

Edwina's gaze drifted to the tall young man standing beside Shane. 'So this is Daniel.' She smiled at him and shook his hand. 'Hi there. I'm Edwina.'

'Hi, Edwina,' Daniel replied shyly. He had the same dark

eyes and hair as his father, but his face had a softer, rounder shape.

'So how are you settling into Sandy Cove?' Edwina asked.

'It's okay,' Daniel said. 'I just arrived so I haven't really seen much of it yet.'

Paddy trotted to their side and stared up at Daniel. 'Are you a teenager?' he asked.

'Yes,' Daniel replied with a laugh.

'I'm going to be a teenager too when I grow up,' Paddy announced.

'Of course you are,' Daniel said, smiling at the little boy.

'Will you come and see me climb to the top of the climbing frame?' Paddy asked. 'It's over there on the back lawn behind the roses.'

'Sure,' Daniel said and took Paddy's hand. 'Show me where it is.'

'This way,' Paddy said, pulling at Daniel.

Edwina watched the tall lanky youth and the little boy walk away hand in hand. 'Sweet,' she said to Shane. 'Is that the difficult teenager you described? The one who will drive you nuts all summer?'

'Yes,' Shane said. 'But don't let his cute face and good manners fool you. Street angel, house devil: that's Daniel in a nutshell.'

'Maybe he takes after his father?' Edwina said.

'With me it's the other way around,' Shane retorted. 'Street devil, house angel, that's me.' He winked. 'I'm pretty obnoxious in public, but when I'm at home, I'm a saint. I'd love to prove it to you sometime.'

'That would be interesting,' Edwina said, feeling her heart yet again skipping a beat. She found it hard to stay calm when he was standing this close to her.

'It would.' Shane moved even closer. 'How about putting that to the test?' he murmured in her ear.

'In what way?' She glanced at Max and Allegra standing by the barbeque, tending to the meat.

'By going on a date, of course,' Shane replied.

'A date?' Edwina stared at him. 'The last time we met you seemed to feel very differently about me.'

He shrugged. 'Yeah, well, I didn't appreciate you criticising my parenting skills. But I was wrong, and you were right. Handling my son as if he was a burden wasn't the way to go. So I thought about it and tried to change my tone with him.'

'Is it working?'

'Sometimes. But teenagers are tricky.' He looked at her for a while. 'So how about that date? I have tomorrow off. Daniel is going to spend the day on the beach helping out at the surf school. We could go for a drive, maybe?'

'Oh,' Edwina said, startled. Shane had, until now, not seemed that interested in her, apart from teasing her. She had thought her growing attraction was one-sided. But here he was, asking her out. She tried her best not to show how thrilled she was. 'Well, I...'

Shane frowned. 'Please don't play hard to get by saying you'll be washing your hair or talking to your mother or baby-sitting your nephews.'

Edwina faced him and smiled broadly. 'I'm not doing anything of the kind. Thank you for asking me. I'd love to go on a date with you.'

'Oh great,' he said, looking relieved. 'You looked so shocked I thought you were going to say no.'

'I was a little surprised, yes,' Edwina admitted.

'I don't know what came over me. I had no intention of asking you out. But then, when I saw you standing there with that tray, all flustered and not dressed up to the nines as usual, I suddenly felt an urge to get to know you better.'

'Because I look a mess?'

'No, because you look *normal* and not like a fashion model who'd break if touched.'

'Oh.' Edwina looked away from his probing gaze.

She knew what he meant. She had been doing herself up every time she left the house, but that was an old habit left over from her life in Dublin. She would never leave the house without mascara, even if she was just putting out the rubbish. It was her armour and she didn't feel safe without it. But today, she had been intent on playing with small children and hadn't thought she'd meet anyone apart from Max and Allegra. With that in mind, she had forgotten about applying make-up or dressing to kill.

'Well, I didn't expect to meet anyone except family today,' she tried to explain.

'So you came as yourself instead of Edwina, the guru of fabulousness?' Shane said with a glint of mischief in his eyes. 'I believe you know how to look amazing in all weathers, according to what I read on the web.'

'You've looked at my blog?' she asked.

'Just a quick peek. Must say there's a lot of very good advice there. Especially the one about "how to look fresh even after too many drinks the night before". That's up against "the most natural fake eyelashes that nobody will spot".' He peered at her eyes, moving so close she could feel the heat of his body. 'Are you wearing them now?'

She moved back. 'Wouldn't you like to know? That was just a recommendation that I was paid to do,' she added, feeling a need to explain. 'I'm actually going to take down that blog. It's not at all relevant to what I'm doing today.'

'No, that was in a former life, I suspect,' Shane said.

Edwina couldn't help bursting out laughing. 'Oh yeah, that's for sure,' she said. 'And now you can stop trying to annoy me. I'm not going to take the bait. And you know what? That blog and all that fashion and beauty stuff on Instagram was a lot of fun, but I've grown away from all of that.'

'Grown away?' he asked, lifting an eyebrow. 'You mean grown up, don't you?'

Edwina shrugged. 'Whatever. I loved it then, but now I'm doing something a lot more rewarding.'

He looked at her for a moment and then, as someone attracted his attention in the garden, took her arm. 'Allegra is calling us to sit down at that table under the big oak. And I think Daniel is a little bored with watching Paddy hang by his toenails on the climbing frame so maybe you could cheer him up?'

'Me?' Edwina asked.

'Yeah, you. He seems to like you.'

They walked together across the terrace, down the steps onto the lawn and joined Max and Allegra at the table under the oak while Daniel wandered towards them, Paddy running behind him.

They all sat down, and Edwina found herself between Daniel and Shane. Max was opposite with Allegra and Paddy on her lap. Shane shot her a smile, which made her blush, as sitting so close to him unnerved her. The chemistry between them seemed stronger now after he'd asked her out, and she was looking forward to their date more than she cared to admit.

Then, while the meat cooked, Max and Shane started to chat about rugby and the past season. Uninterested in that kind of sport, Edwina turned to Daniel and asked him where he went to school.

'The same school Dad went to,' he replied. 'Glenstal Abbey. I'm going into sixth year and will be doing my leaving cert next year.'

'Oh, boarding school,' Edwina said. 'That's where you go when parents don't know what to do with you. Especially if they're splitting up.'

'You too?' Daniel asked, looking at Edwina with more interest.

'Oh yeah,' she replied with a little sigh. 'It was called a good education, but I know why they sent me there. But hey, it's not all bad, is it? I mean you get away from all the aggro and make friends for life.'

'Mmm, yes, that's true...'

'Especially if you're a bad girl like me, caught smoking in the loo. Only tobacco, though,' she added.

Daniel laughed. 'Yeah, me too. I just wanted to see what it was like, so a friend and I bought a packet of Marlboro and took a few puffs and a teacher spotted us. We were as sick as parrots by then. And I've also been caught drinking brandy behind the cricket pavilion. That got me a week's suspension. Dad was furious because he had to come and pick me up and then have me for that week.'

Edwina laughed. 'I bet he was livid.'

Daniel shot her a wry smile. 'Sure was. Mad as hell.'

'What do you want to do after school?' she continued. 'Medicine, like your dad?'

Daniel shrugged. 'Not sure. I'm just going to do the best I can and see where that takes me. I have a lot of assignments during the holidays and the English one is especially hard. I have to write a story and I don't know where to start. I'd like it to be about some mystery but I can't come up with anything.'

'Oh,' Edwina said, looking thoughtfully at the handsome young man. Then an idea came to her. 'How about this?' she started. 'The hero in your story finds a message in a bottle when he goes swimming. The message was written more than twenty years ago by a young man in a nearby village who threw the bottle into the sea, thinking it would end up on the other side of the Atlantic. But it seemed to have been bobbing up and down the coast on the currents instead. The message seems to be a cry for help and it moves the hero so much he wants to find out who wrote it and...' Edwina stopped, trying to think how to continue.

Daniel's eyes flashed with excitement. 'That sounds like a great mystery. But how could he find out who wrote the message? And what kind of message should it be?' He shook his head. 'Nah, that couldn't happen.'

'It could because it did,' Edwina said. She lowered her voice. 'I found a bottle on the beach when I went swimming. The message was just as I described, a cry for help in some way. And there was a name and a phone number.'

'What was the name?' Daniel asked.

'Pearse.'

'That's all?' Daniel looked disappointed. 'Just the first name? And the phone number? Did you try that?'

Edwina nodded, forgetting her hunger. 'Yes, and a woman answered. I said I was looking for someone called Pearse, but she said there was nobody there by that name and hung up. She sounded quite upset.'

'Hmm. Was it a landline?'

'Yes.'

'Then we could try to find out the address.' Daniel looked at Edwina with interest. 'This is really cool, you know. I'd love to help you find that person who wrote the message.'

'Really?' Edwina felt a surge of excitement. 'I'm sure you'd be a great help. You probably have better skills than me when it comes to research on the internet. You could start by finding the address for that number. I think it's in Dingle town, actually, because that's where this guy said he was in the message.'

'Where is the message?'

'I think I have it right here.' Edwina took her bag from the back of the chair and started to rummage around in it until she found the crumpled piece of paper. She handed it to Daniel.

'I'd say you're right,' Daniel said when he'd read the message. 'Must be in Dingle town. I think it could fit in my story. Not exactly the way it happened to you, but the idea is great. Could be a huge emotional journey. And the hero's own story could run parallel to his quest to find the man who wrote to message.'

'Absolutely,' Edwina said, impressed with his way of thinking. She was suddenly sure he had a great talent for writing. 'I'd love for you to help me find the address of that number. Give me a call when you've found it.'

Daniel fished his phone from his pocket. 'Okay, read out your number and I'll text you. Then we'll be connected.'

Edwina rattled out her number and Daniel typed it into his phone and put it away. 'Great. Can't wait to get started.'

'Brilliant.' Edwina smiled at Daniel. He was such a nice boy and she hoped Shane might get on better with him in time.

Then everything was ready and they passed around meat, salad and roast potatoes. Max poured the drinks: wine for Edwina, Max and Allegra, water for Shane, who was driving, a bottle of beer for Daniel, while Paddy noisily downed a full plastic mug of Ribena.

The meat was delicious, Edwina found, crisp on the outside, with just enough barbeque flavour, and tender on the inside. The potato salad and the lettuce with herb dressing were equally good and the bread rolls fresh from the bakery in the village.

'Lovely dinner,' she said to Allegra.

'Thank you. Max does a mean steak.' Allegra took a sausage and put it into a roll and handed it to Paddy. 'Here, have this and then it's time for bed.'

'Ice cream first,' Paddy said as he took a bite of the sausage.

'Yes, sir,' Allegra said and saluted. 'Eat your sausage and then I'll give you a bit of ice cream in the kitchen before we go up to bed.'

'Okay.' Paddy quickly demolished his sausage. Then Allegra gathered him into her arms but before she left, she told him to give his auntie Edwina a hug goodnight, which he duly did, giving her a noisy smack on the cheek.

'Nighty night, Auntie Edwina,' he said and then waved like royalty. 'Bye, everyone!'

'Such a ham,' Max said as Allegra left with Paddy in her arms. He smiled at Edwina, which made her feel that the hatchet had been buried. For now anyway.

Shane, having ended his discussion with Max, suddenly turned to Edwina. 'You two seem thick as thieves. What are you talking about?'

'Nothing much,' Daniel said with an innocent air. 'Just school and stuff.'

'Really?' Shane looked from Edwina to Daniel. 'You don't normally like to talk about your schoolwork.'

'Well, I asked,' Edwina said. 'But it wasn't only about school. We had a nice chat about all kinds of things.'

'Yeah, that's right,' Daniel said. 'Nothing you'd be interested in.'

Shane met Daniel's eyes for a moment while Edwina felt a distinct chill between father and son. Then Shane shrugged. 'Well, it's nice that you've found someone to share your *stuff* with.'

They were interrupted by Allegra coming back to the table carrying a bowl of strawberries. 'I finally got Paddy to go to sleep. Now I'm going to enjoy talking to grown-ups. And I brought dessert. There's ice cream in the freezer. Daniel, could you go and get that, please?'

'Sure.' Daniel got up, looking relieved to have an excuse to leave the table.

When he came back with the ice cream, the conversation had become more relaxed and friendly, and the evening continued in a convivial way with chat and jokes and laughter. The only tension left was between Edwina and Shane, but it was more like tiny sparks of attraction and anticipation. She found herself looking forward to their date the next day, even if she had a feeling it would be different from any kind of date she had ever been on.

When Shane and Daniel had said their goodbyes, Edwina left Max and Allegra at the table talking softly over a last glass of wine, and made her way slowly up the stairs. She peeked into the boys' room and found them fast asleep, hugging their teddies. She smiled, feeling a dart of unexpected tenderness. They were such sweet boys, even if they were hard work. She closed the door and went down the corridor to the rose room, where her bed had been made and the curtains across the tall window billowed gently in the warm night breeze.

She sat on the bed for a moment, going through the evening that had passed, and found herself thinking about Daniel and Shane and their strained relationship. She knew exactly where that was coming from as she had been there herself – and still was to some extent, even if she was growing closer to her mother these days. It would probably be a long time before Shane and Daniel found any kind of peace and understanding. She felt sorry for them both and wondered briefly if she could do anything to help them. But maybe it was better to stay out of it, she thought as she got undressed and put on her nightie, finally slipping in between the cool sheets and laying her head on the soft pillow.

Funny, she thought, just before she drifted off, *how I suddenly feel a kind of peace here, in this house where I was so unhappy years ago. Could it be the effect of the small boys, or the two people who not only love each other, but also this old house?*

Edwina was woken up very early the following morning by the two boys and Maureen O'Hara, their little dog, bouncing on her bed, telling her they wanted breakfast.

Max and Allegra were still asleep, they said, so Auntie

Edwina had to get up and feed them. This proved to be only half true, as Max emerged from his bedroom when they made their way down the stairs. After breakfast, Edwina left the boys to his care and went to get ready for her date with Shane. He would pick her up at ten o'clock, he had said, so she had plenty of time to prepare. She remembered his comment about her looking 'normal'. The natural look took a lot of work, but when she had finished, she looked as if she had been on holiday: her cheeks glowing, her green eyes sparkling and her newly washed and blow-dried hair sleek and shiny. She decided to wear the same jeans and a freshly ironed blue-and-white striped shirt, which she had managed to iron quite well, even though she wasn't used to it.

Max, carrying a tray with tea and toast to serve Allegra in bed, let out a whistle when he saw her. 'You look all bright-eyed and bushy-tailed,' he said. 'Where are you going?'

'I don't know,' Edwina replied. 'Shane is taking me for a drive.'

'What?' Max stopped at the bottom of the stairs, shooting her an amused look. 'He's taking you for a drive?'

'Yes, so?'

'You'd better fasten your seatbelt, then,' he said, his mouth twitching as he started up the stairs.

'What do you mean?' Edwina called after him.

'You'll see,' Max shouted back.

Edwina shook her head and shrugged. Max was just pulling her leg. She walked outside, looking down the drive. She could hear the sound of an engine and figured Shane was on his way in his old Toyota. But when he swept up the avenue and came to a dead stop in front of her, gravel flying, she couldn't believe her eyes.

What on earth was he thinking?

14

Edwina stared at Shane, dressed in jeans and a leather bomber jacket, sitting on a huge motorbike, grinning at her. 'Top of the mornin' to you,' he said, raising the visor of the helmet and taking off his sunglasses. 'Lovely weather for a road trip.'

Edwina tried to pull herself together. 'On *that*?'

'Well, yes.'

'You mean you're expecting me to get up on that thing?'

'I was hoping you would.' He took a helmet that had been hanging on the handlebar and held it out. 'Put this on and we're off.'

Edwina touched her hair that had taken over half an hour to style. 'The helmet?'

'Yes.' He sighed. 'Okay, so it'll wreck that lovely hairdo but it'll stop you getting a cracked skull should we come off.'

'I'm not sure I want to go,' she protested.

'You said yes when I asked you yesterday.'

'You didn't tell me about the motorbike!'

'I wanted it to be a surprise.'

'Well, you succeeded with flying colours,' Edwina remarked dryly. 'I was more than surprised.'

'Horrified, I can tell,' Shane said. 'Oh come on, Edwina,' he urged. 'Take a walk on the wild side. Live a little. Mess up your hair for once.'

Edwina met his eyes and saw the challenge there. He was testing her. She looked at the bike for a moment and then took a deep breath. 'Okay then, I'll go with you. But if I end up dead in a ditch it'll be all your fault.'

'What a way to go, though,' he replied.

Edwina couldn't help laughing, both at his good humour and the way he had fooled her and she was suddenly carried away by his sense of adventure and fun. 'You're a holy terror.' She pulled on her denim jacket, put on the helmet and climbed onto the pillion behind Shane. 'Okay. I'm here. Happy now?'

'Ecstatic,' he said and kick-started the bike. 'Put your arms around me and hold tight,' he shouted as they slowly went down the drive.

She did as she was told and, before she knew what was happening, they were through the gates and on the open road. Shane revved the engine and they swept away around the hairpin bends, Edwina with her arms around Shane's waist, pressing her body to his, closing her eyes, both frightened and excited. Then she opened them and began to enjoy the speed, the wind against her face and the contact with Shane's firm body. It was exhilarating, almost like flying. She had never felt such a thrill.

'Okay?' Shane shouted, twisting his head to glance at her.

'It's amazing!' she shouted back, pressing her cheek against his back.

'I knew you'd love it.'

On they went, around the edge of the peninsula, along the coast road with vertiginous views of the deep blue ocean and then through little villages and across hump-back bridges until, nearly an hour later, they came to a stop in front of a grey country house with a tower at one end and a lush garden at the side of it.

'Where are we?' Edwina asked, a little dizzy after all the twists and turns. She let go of Shane and looked around.

'Derrynane House,' Shane said and took off his helmet. 'Home of the liberator.'

'Daniel O'Connell?' Edwina asked as she got off the bike. 'I knew his home was around here. Wasn't he the man who brought Catholic emancipation to Ireland?'

'The very one. He's my hero. I named my son after him.'

'He was quite something, wasn't he?' Edwina said. 'I always admired his courage, even though I wasn't raised as a Catholic. But my father gave me a book about Daniel O'Connell and told me it was important to know what he did.'

'It still is. And this,' Shane said, pointing at the house, 'was his childhood home and also where he died. Do you want to see it?'

'Of course,' Edwina said and took off her helmet, pushing her fingers through her damp hair. 'Even if I look a mess.'

Shane looked at her and smiled. 'You look happy. And very cute.' He leaned forward and kissed her cheek. 'Thank you for being so brave.' He got off the bike. 'We can have lunch at the café in the garden. And then we'll visit the house.'

They walked together up the path lined with trees and shrubs until they came to a café where they bought sandwiches, water, coffee and a slice of cake, which they ate at a table in the garden, overlooking the flowerbeds. There was a glimpse of the sea between the trees and the air was full of birdsong.

'What a heavenly place,' Edwina said with a happy sigh as she bit into her ham and cheese sandwich. 'And this food is really good after that hairy trip.'

'Were you scared?' Shane asked.

'Why do you think I was holding onto you for dear life?'

'Oh,' he said with a slow smile. 'I thought that was because you suddenly realised you fancy me.'

She felt her face flush. Then, feeling suddenly reckless, she decided to reveal all and looked at him squarely. 'Okay, well, that was part of the reason. So now you know.'

She took a slug of water while she waited for his reaction. She knew it might put him off but she had felt such a need to say it as he sat there looking so handsome, his hair ruffled and his face still flushed after the trip on the motorbike.

His eyes softened. 'And I fancy you like crazy. So there we are. We fancy each other.' He took her hand and kissed it, looking into her eyes. 'What do we do about that, then?'

'I don't know,' Edwina replied, smiling back at him, her heart soaring. 'I wasn't planning anything like this. I came here to do a job and then develop it into a business. Flirting and dating wasn't at all on the agenda. But there you were, and it just happened.'

'Nor was it on mine, believe me.' Shane let go of her hand and took a slug of water from his bottle. 'I was looking at two months full of conflict with my son and a heavy workload in the surgery as the summer brings a lot of visitors who seem to get into trouble every moment of the day. Cuts, scrapes, broken bones and tummy aches – and all kinds of other stuff.'

'Like silly women cutting their legs up on the beach,' Edwina filled in.

'Yes, they are the worst.' Shane smiled tenderly and touched her cheek. 'You were in such a state when you came in. But all is well now with your leg, I take it?'

'Perfect. I don't even have a scar. All thanks to you.' She finished her sandwich and brushed the crumbs off her shirt.

'Do you want to see the house?' Shane asked. 'There is a guided tour in a few minutes.'

Edwina jumped up from her chair. 'Yes, I'd love to.'

Shane got up and took her hand. 'Me too. I've actually never been inside it and I'm happy to see it with you.'

'A new thing to experience together,' Edwina remarked, loving the feel of his warm hand and firm grip.

He made her feel safe, she realised, despite the mad trip on his motorbike. Safe and cared for and, maybe eventually, loved. That was a new feeling to her: to be with a man she didn't have to dress up for or impress. How amazing it should happen like this, out of the blue with someone she had been teasing and arguing with ever since they met. But there had been an undercurrent of strong attraction between them right from the start – well, perhaps not when their cars nearly collided, but later, in the pub and during the past month since she arrived... She felt as if she was floating on clouds as they entered the cool interior of the old house.

It was a beautiful home, sparsely furnished with mostly Regency-style furniture and lovely delicate etchings on the walls. There was a peaceful, serene atmosphere throughout, as if the love and affection Daniel and his wife had felt for each other had permeated the whole house, like a benevolent spirit that still floated around in all the rooms.

Edwina couldn't concentrate on what the guide was saying about Daniel O'Connell and his political career, or how he had fought for his country all through his life and achieved many things for Ireland. Her thoughts were constantly drifting to Shane and how she felt about him as she wandered through the sunlit rooms, her hand in his. She kept stealing looks in his direction, studying his features, the little lines and grooves that hinted at struggles with stress and sadness, perhaps the lasting effect of a bitter divorce. She didn't know much about him and desperately wanted to find out about his thoughts and dreams and desires. Who was this attractive, intelligent, fun, caring man really?

As if feeling her eyes on him, Shane turned his head and

smiled as the guide finished her lecture. 'That was interesting, don't you think?'

'Yes,' Edina replied. 'Very interesting.'

They thanked the guide and walked out into the sunshine, Shane laughing and pulling a strand of Edwina's hair. 'You didn't listen to a word she said, did you?'

'Of course I did,' Edwina retorted.

'Nah, you didn't. Neither did I. Couldn't stop thinking about us and how I just want to kiss you.' He stopped on the deserted path, looked around and then pulled her behind a tree.

He put his arms around her and lowered his head, his lips nearly touching hers. He looked deep into her eyes and she felt as if time stood still for a moment before their lips met in a light, careful kiss that soon became more intense. Edwina put her arms around his neck, closed her eyes and gave herself up to the sensation of his body pressed to hers, his soft lips kissing her so tenderly and his hands on her back, warm through the thin fabric of her shirt. It was a moment of absolute bliss as they forgot time and place and everything around them except the contact of their bodies and that incredible buzz the very first kiss always brings.

Then they pulled apart and looked at each other, smiling. 'Oh, Shane,' Edwina whispered, touching his face. 'I've never been kissed like that.'

He pulled away and looked at her quizzically. 'What? Never been kissed?'

'Not like *that*. You made me feel so...' She stopped, lost for words.

'You too,' he said, still holding her tight. 'You make me feel like a million bucks, like I'm on some kind of other planet.' He laughed. 'That's mad. And we hardly know each other. We have to talk. I want to know the story of your life and what makes you happy and sad and angry and all those things that make up who you are.'

'Yes, me too. I'm dying to hear your story,' Edwina said as she pulled out of his embrace. 'Maybe we could go and sit on the beach? I've heard it's lovely here.'

'Sandy, but nice,' he said, as he pulled her away from the tree and down the path.

'We can sit on the grass,' Edwina suggested.

'Good idea.'

They followed the sign to Derrynane beach and were soon looking across a vast expanse of soft white sand bordered by dunes and grass. They climbed up an incline from where they would have a good view and be alone.

Shane sat down. 'There. Nice view, not a soul around and soft grass to sit on.'

Edwina sank down beside him, wrapping her arms around her knees. 'Gorgeous place.'

'Stunning,' Shane said, leaning on his elbow. But he wasn't looking at the view. 'You go first,' he said.

Edwina nodded. 'Okay. What do you want to know?'

'Everything. Where were you born?'

'In Dublin. My parents lived in an old country house nearby then but they moved into town shortly after I was born. So I'm really a city girl, except for the years at boarding school when I was a teenager.'

'And Strawberry Hill? Where does that fit in?'

'My father's aunt owned it and we used to go there for some of the holidays like Christmas and Easter. I never really liked the house. I thought it was dark and old and spooky, but my dad loved it. Mum hated it. She's from a super-wealthy family in England and was used to all the mod-cons. Dad thought it was somehow noble to put up with this old house where nothing had changed since the 1890s. Then, when my parents divorced, I was sent to this posh boarding school for girls outside Dublin.' Edwina paused and turned to look at Shane. 'That's where I was taught all the wrong values.'

'Like what?'

'Like the belief that if you have lots of money, you'll also have a lot of friends.'

'Of the wrong kind, though,' Shane remarked.

'I suppose.' Edwina stared out to sea again as she went on to tell Shane about her father's death when she was a teenager and how her mother had remarried soon afterwards. How she had been sent to Strawberry Hill on her holidays so she wouldn't be in the way as her mother embarked on a jet-setting lifestyle. Then she told him how she had fallen into a career in fashion after studying design and landed a job at the department store in Dublin, where she had been quite successful until recently when she had quit, knowing she wanted to move on to something else.

'Good for you,' Shane said. 'And you and Max?' he asked. 'What's the story there? You don't seem very close.'

'It's all my fault, really,' Edwina confessed. She turned and looked at Shane. 'You'd better hear it all. It's not very pretty. My part in it, anyway.'

'I'm sure it's not that bad,' he soothed.

'You tell me,' Edwina said. 'I was plotting and scheming to get my own way without considering other people. But I was a different person back then. Lost and lonely without an anchor in my life. I thought if we all got rid of the house when our great-aunt died, we'd also get rid of all the sad memories. But Max and Gwen, our cousin, love the place and didn't want to sell. To make a long and painful story short, I sided with a woman who turned out to be a fraud and tried to gang up on them to force them to sell. But I lost in the end, and I also lost my brother in the process. He'll never forgive me for that,' she ended, with a feeling of hopelessness.

Shane sat up and put his arms around her. 'I'm sure he will. Max isn't the kind to hold grudges. I've known him since college and we're still very good friends. I'd say he's just as sad as you are about it all. The problem between you two is a lack of trust. You don't trust him to forgive you, and he doesn't believe you're truly sorry.'

'Maybe. I should really try to talk to him again.' Edwina rested her head on Shane's shoulder. 'So,' she said after a while. 'What about you? Where were you born and what kind of family do you have?'

'I was born in Cahersiveen,' Shane said and continued to tell Edwina about a happy childhood with two brothers and a sister. The eldest son, he had excelled at school and always wanted to be a doctor. He had studied medicine at Trinity College and then worked at various hospitals until he qualified as a surgeon and got a job at Galway University Hospital. His wife, who he had known as a teenager, was then also working in Galway. They reconnected, fell in love and married, and Daniel was born soon afterwards.

'That must have been a wonderful time.'

'Yes. I thought that was it,' Shane said, 'the best moment of my life, which would now be perfect. We'd have another baby, maybe, and then we'd work hard to give these kids a great life. We would be the happiest family and be together until death did us part, and all that. But it didn't last very long.'

'What happened?' Edwina asked, moved by Shane's suddenly sad eyes.

'My wife left me when Daniel was four. She fell in love with someone else. Said I had been too absent and not paid her the attention she needed.' He shrugged. 'In a way she was right. I was working in A&E back then. We were short-staffed and I had to work overtime, sometimes by choice, I have to admit. I felt sorry for the overworked junior doctors so I'd take on extra shifts, especially during the worst times in emergency medicine. All those patients on trolleys waiting for days to be seen to, sometimes. It's tough to watch that. So I tried to help them and neglected my family at the same time. It's a huge dilemma for many doctors.'

'Especially those who care too much,' Edwina remarked, touching his face. 'And if your wife didn't understand that, then I bet there was a huge problem.'

Shane nodded, taking her hand. 'Yes. And we argued constantly. I was tired and stressed and probably said some things I shouldn't have. Maybe it was understandable that she turned to someone else.'

'And now?' Edwina asked.

'Oh, we get on all right. We share custody of Daniel, and we both felt boarding school was the best option. I picked the one I went to, as I was happy there. I'm sure he is too if he'd only admit it. But he's very resentful of me. I think my ex-wife blamed me for our divorce, so he's prejudiced. Well, I'm sure you know what I'm talking about.'

'Of course,' Edwina said. 'Been there too, big-time. I blamed both my parents in turn. But it's really nobody's fault.'

'Yes and no. Of course it's both our fault, really. But what can you do?'

'I know. It's just very sad, for everyone.' She sat back and looked at him. 'I think we should leave all that and talk about other things. Us, for example. And how we feel and what we're going to do.'

Shane smiled. 'Yes, we should. Let's look forwards and not backwards. And right now, I'm in a good place. I love general practice in a surgery like the one I'm in. I love that every day brings something different and a new challenge, like when I have to figure out what is wrong with the person in front of me. It can take a lot of detective work before I find a solution.'

'I'm sure you're very good at it.'

'I do my best.'

They started to talk about themselves, their hopes and dreams, likes and dislikes, sharing jokes and teasing each other at times and laughing at silly things they said. Edwina had never felt so relaxed with anyone and she looked in wonder at Shane when they grew silent.

'This is such fun. I've never talked like this with anyone. Not on a date, anyway. You make me feel so good.'

'So do you.' He kissed her cheek. 'This isn't just a summer fling, is it?'

'It doesn't feel that way,' Edwina said. 'I know summer flings, and this is not it. I had one a year ago that I thought was the real deal, but...' She sighed. 'Wrong man with the wrong ideas. It was really my own fault he dumped me.'

'Stop saying everything is your fault,' Shane protested. 'It takes two to tango, as the saying goes.'

'Yes, but I suppose at my age, women get a little desperate. So maybe I was too clingy and needy.'

'And what age would that be?' Shane asked. 'Thirty-two?'

'Yeah right,' Edwina said with a snort. 'I'll be forty next month and don't pretend you didn't guess that.'

'Of course I didn't,' Shane protested. 'Your age never entered my mind. Why are women so obsessed with that? All I saw was a beautiful, troubled woman who I enjoyed sparring with. You really know how to hand it back. I love that.'

Edwina laughed. 'Yeah, me too. It was fun.'

'And always will be. I'm sure we won't stop teasing each other, will we?'

'Hell no,' Edwina said. 'Except right now I don't feel like arguing with you.' She lay back in the grass and looked up at the blue sky, where clouds drifted across the sun from time to time, casting shadows on the landscape below. 'I feel strangely light and free. As if nothing can ever make me sad any more.'

He lay down beside her and took her hand. 'Me too. But it's just a moment of happiness. Life will catch up with us very soon.'

'I know.' Edwina closed her eyes, letting the warmth of the sun and the sound of the waves calm her.

Shane tickled her nose with a blade of grass. 'Don't go to sleep in the sun, sweetheart. You'll burn to a crisp.'

Edwina blinked and sat up. 'Yes, Doctor. And you're right. I should top up the sunscreen.'

Shane's phone pinged. He looked at the message and sighed. 'What did I tell you? Life is catching up. That's Daniel asking what's for dinner. It's nearly six o'clock. We've been here for hours. I'd better get back and feed him. He eats like a horse, that boy. But then teenage boys always do.'

Edwina laughed. 'I know. Max would put away loads of food when he was that age, while I was constantly on a diet. But that was my school – everyone was stick-thin and wore designer clothes. I thought that was what you had to do to be popular.'

'Do you have many friends?'

'Now? No,' Edwina replied. 'I have one very close friend, Jonathan. He was the one who got me into the property business.'

'Really? Should I be jealous?'

'No,' Edwina protested. 'We're close friends but there has never been anything more than that. He has had a number of girlfriends that I've liked a lot. I hope he finds someone permanent, though. I love him dearly but he's like a brother to me.'

'Just like Billy,' Shane said. 'She's the best friend I ever had. She knows all about me. But that's also a lovely, platonic friendship with no strings, pain or drama.'

'She told me you were friends,' Edwina said. 'And she also said something about you having had a difficult time recently. Was that the divorce?'

Shane's eyes darkened. 'Yes. I told you some of it. Let's not go back there.'

'Of course not,' Edwina said, taken aback by his sudden reaction. 'I'm sorry I mentioned it.'

'Okay.'

They got up and walked away from the beach and, even though Shane took her hand, Edwina felt that somehow the spell was broken and the happiness she had felt slowly drifted away. But when they reached the motorbike, she couldn't resist a little joke.

'It was a test, wasn't it?' she asked as they put on their helmets. 'The bike and the helmets and the mad ride. You thought I'd chicken out.'

His eyes brightened and he smiled. 'Yeah. I wanted to see if you'd risk your hairdo. You looked all polished and perfect and I wanted to see what was behind that shiny shell.'

'And if I had said no?'

He kissed her on the mouth before he got on the bike. 'Then we wouldn't be where we are right now. Like this, starting something great.'

'No, we wouldn't,' Edwina agreed and got on the pillion, putting her arms around him.

Shane kick-started the bike and, as it roared into life, turned and smiled at her, as if he wanted to say that everything was all right.

But as they started down the road, Edwina couldn't forget the way he had looked at her when she asked about the divorce just now... Had he not got over it yet?

15

The following weeks were hectic for Edwina, with both her happy love life and her new career. There was, however, a worry in the back of her mind that Shane wasn't over his divorce. But, busy with the work on the cottages that needed her constant supervision and approval, she decided not to think too much about it. The main building work was finished in early August and now the interiors were being put in, with plumbers and electricians coming and going, and needing to be prompted to appear. Shane was busy too and he also had to consider his son and try to spend as much time with him as he could, at Edwina's insistence.

'If you neglect him this time, you'll never have much of a relationship,' she had said, remembering how her mother had forgotten about her children and only thought about herself while Edwina and Max were sent to spend their holidays at Strawberry Hill.

Daniel had continued his quest to find the author of the message in the bottle. He told Edwina it should be a secret between them as he was sure Shane would laugh at the whole thing. She was sure he would, too. But Edwina and Daniel had both been moved by the feeling of despair in that message and they made a pact to do all they could to find out more.

Daniel had tracked down the address of the phone number but, as far as he could gather, a woman lived there alone and nobody seemed to have heard of anyone called Pearse. Daniel said he wanted to go there, maybe talk to the neighbours who had lived there a long time to see if anyone could cast a light on what had happened to Pearse, who now felt like a real person and not some anonymous figure from the past.

It was obvious to Edwina that Daniel felt a certain affinity with her in some way as, like him, she had also been through her parents' divorce. She had liked him instantly and they often met on the main beach for lunch, having bought sandwiches at the café called The Two Marys' nearby. She had never been with young people like this and she was enjoying her moments with Daniel immensely. They were planning to take a drive to Dingle soon to continue their search for the mysterious Pearse.

And then there was her relationship with Shane, which had grown to something important and lovely ever since that day at Derrynane. They tried their best to see each other away from the village, sometimes meeting in nearby Waterville, where they sometimes had dinner at a quaint restaurant near the golf course, and other times having a meal in Ballinskelligs, on the other side of the bay, where they could sit in the garden of the hotel and gaze out to sea and the view of the Skelligs while they enjoyed a plate of scampi. But they couldn't be together as often as they wanted, mostly because of Shane having to spend every day at the surgery and often having to go on house calls in far-flung places. When she was alone, Edwina thought about Shane's divorce. She had a feeling that he might not have moved on as much as he should have done by now. Would this impact their relationship later on?

But when they did manage a few hours together, it was heavenly. Edwina had never experienced being so immersed in

love and tenderness. And the underlying passion that was
simmering under the surface sometimes emerged when they
embraced during those secret, stolen moments. But, oh, it was so
lovely to meet Shane after a long absence, and she saw his eyes
light up as she walked towards him.

They had also managed a weekend together at Strawberry
Hill when Max and Allegra and the boys had gone to a wedding
in Cork and Gwen was away at a horse event. Edwina had
offered to mind the house and feed the dogs, happy that she and
Shane could at last spend a whole weekend together. That had
been like a honeymoon to them, sleeping in the rose room,
making love for hours, and then wandering through the vast
rooms downstairs, gazing at the portraits of the Courtney ances-
tors, laughing at their wigs and clothes.

'Now I know where your snooty expression comes from,'
Shane said the next morning as he looked at a bewigged lady
from the eighteenth century gazing down at them with a
haughty expression in one of the portraits. 'Strong uppity genes
there.'

'Nah, my snootiness comes from years spent as head girl at
my snooty boarding school,' Edwina retorted. 'Years and years
of training perfecting those stuck-up skills.'

Shane laughed and threw his arms around her. 'That's my
girl. Never stuck for an answer. I actually love that quality in
you. You're the queen of the put-downs.'

'Ah, shucks,' Edwina said, kissing him. 'Didn't know I was
that good.'

'Even better now that I've messed you up a bit,' he said.

Edwina ruffled her hair and smiled. 'Yeah, I love it too. I feel
so free when I'm with you.'

'And just imagine the time you save not styling your hair
and not putting on shedloads of make-up,' Shane filled in.

It was true; she didn't spend as much time trying to look
perfect, even if she never compromised on her skincare routine,

which did take a little time in the bathroom morning and evening. She would never give up on that, even if she had switched to some of the more natural products from the Wellness Centre that Billy recommended. To her surprise, she found that she looked astonishingly healthy and youthful even without make-up. Her skin glowed and the smattering of freckles across her nose were cute rather than something to hide behind a concealer and there was a happy look in her eyes. Being with Shane had changed her, she realised.

And as the weeks passed, she was also beginning to warm to village life, which felt cosy and safe, with everyone watching out for each other. Even the people who had initially been hostile to the renovations she was doing now seemed to have accepted her plans. She felt a growing contentment as she walked down the street on a beautiful summer's day, smiling and saying hello to everyone who greeted her. The bright lights of Dublin seemed further and further away...

Despite doing their best to keep their relationship secret, rumours were soon flying all over the village. Worried about what Daniel would think, Edwina had told him she was seeing Shane and that they were getting 'very close'. Daniel had looked at her for a moment and then smiled and said it was 'cool' and that he was okay with it.

'Sure, I've known what's going on for a while,' he remarked. 'You two are so bad at keeping a secret.'

'And you don't mind?' Edwina asked as they sat on the beach with their sandwiches.

'Nah, it's fine by me,' Daniel replied, wolfing down his sandwich with impressive speed. 'He's in a better mood these days, and he's even bought me some great video games. To keep me quiet while he's out on the town with *you*,' he added, with a cheeky smile.

'And it's working?' Edwina asked.

'In a way. But when he's out so am I, but don't tell him. I've made friends here at the surf school and we meet up in the evenings sometimes. Beer and pizza on the beach,' he added when Edwina frowned. 'Nothing more dangerous than that.'

'That's good,' Edwina said, wondering if she should tell Shane about this. But what was the harm of a few beers with friends in a small village like this? She was pleased that Shane seemed to be getting on better with his son and decided to leave well enough alone. Everything was fine right now and she didn't want to rock the boat in any way.

'I'm going to Dingle for a few days,' Daniel said, cutting into Edwina's thoughts.

'Oh?' she said. 'Where are you going to stay?'

'With my grandparents.'

'But I thought Shane was from Cahersiveen; don't his parents live somewhere in County Clare now?'

'Yes, they do. These are my other grandparents,' Daniel explained. 'My mother's parents. I'd like to see if we can find that guy, or at least what happened to him. He'd be old now, though. The same age as my dad, I think.'

'That's true, he would,' Edwina said. 'Not that he's particularly old, but then I'm not sixteen either. So he might have a family, or at least a partner.'

'He might not live in Dingle any more,' Daniel remarked. 'But we should at least see if we can find any trace of him.'

'Yes, we should,' Edwina agreed. 'But you're working full time here at the surf school now, so I thought...'

'I took a week off,' Daniel said. 'So maybe you could join me in Dingle for a day next week, if that's possible?'

'Yes, I think I can,' Edwina replied. 'The electricians should have finished by then and the hot tubs are being installed on Wednesday. And then we're hoping the furniture will arrive at the end of the week. So yes, I have a little free time before the next phase of the project starts.'

Daniel jumped up. 'Great. Well, I'd better go and help out with the kids. We can sort the details later. See ya, Edwina.'

He ran off in a shower of sand from his feet and Edwina picked up the remnants of their picnic, looking forward to their outing to Dingle on Monday, but even more to her date with Shane on Saturday night. As it was Friday, he was very busy at the surgery and had a lot of papers and forms to fill out as well, and then he was filling in for the doctor in Ballinskelligs that evening. Ah well, that was what life with a doctor was like, so she had to get used to it. It was lucky she had her own project to keep her busy, and her own friends – like Tara and Mick, who were happy for her to join them for dinner at their farmhouse nearby. Tara had called Edwina that morning, revealing she had heard rumours about Edwina and Shane and now she wanted to know everything.

'I'm so happy.' She laughed. 'I think you and Shane are perfect for each other. Of course, every single female in the village is madly jealous as we're all in love with him, just so you know.'

'I'm not surprised,' Edwina replied. 'I know what an amazing doctor he is.'

'Oh yes,' Tara agreed. 'He's that, too. Great bedside manner. But joking aside, I have to say that the way he treats every patient with such empathy and respect is very rare. You have a true gem, there.'

'I know,' Edwina said. 'I only wish we could be together more. But that's what dating a doctor is like, I suppose.'

'Try being married to a politician,' Tara said. 'But hey, would we want our men any different, even if we have to share them with a lot of other people? The trick is to have your own life and your own career.'

'That's true,' Edwina said, thinking Tara had a lot on her

plate, what with two children and a busy schedule with her photography, and the running of the self-catering cottages.

'If you're on your own tonight, how about dinner at our place?' Tara asked. 'The kids are dying to meet you.'

Edwina had gratefully accepted the invitation, happy not to be on her own on a Friday night.

Looking forward to the evening, she wandered towards the village and up the main street to her little apartment that now felt like home. She had sneered at the dated décor when she arrived but now, after two months, she saw past that and found herself loving the peace and its beautiful views. So the colours clashed, the wallpaper was too busy and the shower wasn't always as hot as she wanted, but those were now tiny details in her otherwise lovely new life. She popped into the grocery shop to get milk, bread and a pot of lovely local honey on her way home.

Pauline smiled at Edwina as she checked the items through the till. 'How's things?' she asked.

'Great,' Edwina replied with a happy smile. 'The work on the cottages is going to plan. No problems there at all.'

'Well, that's great, but I meant...' Pauline leaned over the counter. 'I hear you and the doctor are getting friendly,' she whispered. 'Aren't you the lucky duck?'

Edwina smiled. 'Yes. I feel very lucky right now. As if I've won some amazing lottery and now I don't know what I did to deserve it.'

'Ah sure, he's a lucky duck too, though,' Pauline said as she put Edwina's purchases into a paper bag. 'I wouldn't have said that when you first arrived, but now...' She paused and looked at Edwina appraisingly. 'It's as if you've come out of some kind of shiny bubble and now you're just like one of us. Prettier than most of us, but you don't look like you can't be touched any more. Sorry, but all that glam made you look like a mannequin in a shop window.'

'Oh, God.' Edwina stared at Pauline. 'That's terrible. But yeah, it was a little like that. I couldn't leave the house without spending hours making myself look perfect. How ridiculous.'

'It was meeting him that changed you, wasn't it?' Pauline said, handing Edwina the bag.

Edwina thought for a moment. 'Partly, maybe. But also all of you in this village being so nice to me. And all the fun and laughs I had when I went out for dinner, with everyone chatting away to me in the pubs, even though they didn't know me. And people saying "hello, how are you," as if they really want to know how I am.'

'I think that's...' Pauline stopped as her gaze drifted to the window and a car that was coming down the street attracted her attention. 'Wow,' she whispered. 'Will you take a look at that?'

Edwina turned to follow Pauline's gaze and what she saw made her gasp. 'Oh, no,' she muttered. 'It can't be...'

16

Edwina watched, horrified, as the sleek, dark-blue Ferrari glided down the street and pulled up outside the shop. The door opened and a tall man emerged, his wavy brown hair gleaming in the sunlight. He peeled off his driving gloves and looked up at the building. Then the passenger door opened and Edwina's eyes widened in shock at the woman setting her Chanel sling-backs on the pavement, getting out and smoothing her white linen skirt. Her blonde hair was tied back with a silk scarf and the turquoise T-shirt had the Versace logo.

'Oh, not both of them together,' she groaned to herself, looking wildly around the shop for an escape.

'Now that's what I call glam,' Pauline remarked. 'I wonder who they are?'

'Wonder no more,' Edwina said. 'That's my ex-boyfriend and my mother. What on earth are they doing here? And why are they here together?'

Pauline's eyes nearly popped out of their sockets. 'Your ex? You mean you dated that fabulous-looking guy? And your mother? But she looks so young! Can't be more than fifty or so. Can she?'

'Oh yes, she can,' Edwina said between her teeth as the little bells on the door chimed and the pair stepped into the shop. She crouched behind a stack of cans of tomato soup, hoping they wouldn't see her.

'What a quaint little shop,' Pamela said. 'Like something out of a Frank O'Connor novel. This must be the one Edwina mentioned. Hello?' she called, snapping her fingers at Pauline. 'Could you tell me where I can find this, eh, flat, my daughter Edwina is renting?'

Red in the face, Edwina stood up before her mother could say something even more embarrassing. 'Hi, Mum. And, eh, Matt. What are you doing here?'

'Edwina!' Matt gushed, rushing forward to kiss Edwina on both cheeks in that fake French way he always did with women. One of his mannerisms she had always found annoying. 'How lovely to see you.'

Edwina took a step back and only just managed to stop herself wiping her cheeks. 'Very weird to see you too,' she managed. 'And Mum?'

'Hello, darling,' her mother said, coming forward. 'We just thought we'd come and take a look at the cottages. I am your business partner, after all.'

'Yes, but why now?' Edwina asked. 'And why with Matt?'

'Because he wanted to take a look, too,' Pamela said. She glanced at Pauline, who was obviously listening to everything with huge interest. 'Could we go somewhere more private?' she asked under her breath.

'We could go up to the flat,' Edwina said. 'I'll make you a cup of tea.' She turned to Pauline. 'Sorry, Pauline, forgot to introduce you. This is my mother, Pamela, and my... friend, Matthew Donnelly.'

Pauline waggled her fingers at them in a little wave. 'Howerya, Mrs Courtney and Matthew. Love your car.'

'Er, thanks,' Matt said.

'How do we get to your flat?' Pamela asked, opening the door with Matt behind her.

'It's the door to the left of the shop,' Edwina said, following them out. 'And then up the stairs to the top landing.'

'Do you have the keys?' Pamela asked.

'It's not locked.' Edwina pushed past them onto the street and then went to her door. 'Follow me.'

'Not locked?' Pamela said as she climbed the stairs behind Edwina. 'Why on earth not?'

'Because nobody locks their doors around here,' Edwina replied, opening her front door. 'It's a very safe, friendly place, you know.' She walked through the hall and into the living room, opening the window. 'It's a bit stuffy in here today because of the warm weather. Please sit down, and I'll make you a cup of tea.'

Pamela looked around and shuddered. 'This is not what I expected. I thought you said the flat was very nice.'

'But it is. I know it might not be a boutique hotel but it's cosy, and really feels like home,' Edwina said before she went into the kitchen to put on the kettle, taking three mugs from the cupboard, all decorated with sheep and shamrocks, a job lot from the tourist shop Sorcha had bought at their sale. Not the Royal Doulton china cups her mother was used to, she reflected with an inward giggle. *Welcome to the real world, Mum*, she thought as she put the mugs on a tray with a small jug of milk and a packet of ginger snaps.

'So,' Edwina said as she carried the tray into the living room. 'What brings you both here?'

'As I said,' Pamela replied, perched on the edge of a chair, 'I came to see the cottages. I thought I'd stay with you for a few days as there don't seem to be any hotels nearby. Didn't you say there was a spare room?'

'Yes, but it's very small and full of the clothes I brought but never wore.' Edwina laughed and shook her head. 'What was I thinking? Stilettoes and party clothes and all kinds of accessories. I learned very quickly that nobody dresses up here like we do in Dublin.'

'I can see that,' Pamela said, eyeing Edwina's denim shorts, wrinkly T-shirt and wind-ruffled hair. You don't seem to have been inside a hairdresser's since you came, either. Your hair is a mess.'

Edwina pushed her fingers through her tangled hair. 'I know, but I haven't had the time. I thought I'd let the highlights grow out anyway.'

'Why?' Pamela asked, looking horrified.

'Just to look more normal,' Edwina said. 'I kind of like the idea.'

'Well, I don't,' Pamela snapped. 'You should go to a salon and sort it out.'

'But you do look very healthy,' Matthew said, stepping closer to Edwina and taking her hand. 'Before we go on, I just want to say that I'm very sorry about the problems between us.'

'Problems?' Edwina asked, snatching her hand away. 'What the hell do you mean? You broke up with me and you know it. And now you come waltzing back into my life as if nothing ever happened. You might have forgotten what you did to me, but I haven't. So please don't try to start anything again. I don't think I can ever forgive you.'

Matthew frowned. 'Well, maybe I didn't behave so well then. But I've been thinking about you a lot lately, and I've realised I was a little hasty.' He smiled that winning smile she had once found so enchanting but which now seemed false, like switching on and off a light at will. The smile didn't reach his pale blue eyes, either. 'So maybe we can forgive and forget, and move on?' he said, taking her hand.

'Move on to what exactly?' she asked slowly, while she looked at him and wondered how on earth she could have been so swept away.

She had been too impressed with his wealth and style and the glamourous world he lived in, where money was no problem. Champagne and caviar by the poolside in the South of France, parties on yachts and flying off to exotic places on private jets had been so seductive. And the attention of a man who had it all, including amazing good looks, and a body to match, had been hard to resist. They had been the perfect couple, but had never really known each other. The image of Barbie and Ken popped into Edwina's head and she tried hard not to laugh.

'Before you go,' she said, 'could you please tell me what you're doing here?'

'Well,' Matthew said, glancing at Pamela, 'I heard about this project you're doing and I'm really interested in buying it when it's ready. But I have to see it first, of course,' he added.

'You mean you'd want to buy the whole row of four cottages?' Edwina asked, staring at him.

'If I think it's a good investment, yes,' Matthew replied. 'I've been looking for something like this for a while. Kerry is getting to be quite fashionable. A little village like this could be developed into an exclusive resort, I think. Something for nature lovers all over the world. The location is quite amazing, I have to say.'

'Yes,' Pamela agreed, putting her mug on the coffee table. 'Didn't I tell you it was wonderful? The village is so quaint – even with the rather ordinary shops. But they can all be made to look fabulous with a little work and encouragement.' She got up from the sofa and smoothed her skirt. 'So, Edwina. Could we go and take a look at the cottages? Matthew has a dinner date in Killarney and I'd like to shower and change before you and I go out for a bite.'

'Of course,' Edwina said. 'Let's go then. We can walk there; it's only a few minutes down the street. But, Mum, I had plans for this evening.'

And for tomorrow and Sunday, she thought with an inward little sob as she thought about her date with Shane the next day.

'Plans?' Pamela said, looking confused. 'What kind of plans?' she asked, as if it was impossible to have any kind of social life in a village like Sandy Cove.

'Dinner with friends,' Edwina said. 'And I'm not going to change my plans just because you took it into your head to come here on a surprise visit. In fact,' she added, 'I think it would be best for everyone if you both left right now.'

'But I thought I'd stay with you here for a day or two,' Pamela protested. 'I am your business partner, after all, and I haven't seen the properties since you started the project.'

Edwina let out a resigned sigh. 'Yeah, well, if you insist. I can't refuse you access to the site. But Matt is certainly not welcome. I hope you're not planning to hang around.'

'Well, I'll be in Killarney for a few days,' Matthew replied. 'But Pamela has to go back on Monday, I think.'

'That's right,' Pamela said. 'I'll catch a flight to Dublin from Farranfore on Monday morning, if you could drive me there, Edwina.'

'Of course,' Edwina said, thinking she'd drive her mother all the way to Belfast just to get her away from here. She couldn't imagine what she would think of Shane and what she would say if they met.

'We could perhaps have a little catch-up dinner during the weekend?' Matthew suggested, aiming that dazzling smile again at Edwina.

'Sorry, but I'm busy,' Edwina said.

'All weekend?' Matthew asked, looking surprised.

'Yes, that's right.' Edwina paused for a moment. 'I have a date, actually.'

'A date?' Pamela asked, looking shocked. 'You mean you have a boyfriend?'

'Yes, that's right,' Edwina said, with grim satisfaction at Pamela's expression.

'Who is he?' Pamela asked. 'Does he live around here? What does he do? Is it that nice architect at the construction firm?'

'No, it's someone else. I'll tell you later.'

'So you're dating again?' Matt asked, looking as if he didn't believe it.

'Yes,' Edwina said, looking levelly at him. 'A man who, unlike you, has a bit of class and style. Can we go now?'

Seemingly unperturbed by Edwina's scathing tone, Matthew rushed to the door and held it open. 'After you, ladies. I'm really excited to see the cottages. You lead the way, Edwina.'

Edwina walked swiftly down the street while her mother followed behind, her high heels clattering on the pavement.

Matthew stepped forward and took Pamela's arm. 'I'd better keep you steady on this very uneven pavement. And I see that the lane ahead is just covered in gravel. We don't want you to break one of those lovely ankles, do we?'

'We certainly don't,' Pamela said, looking flattered. 'So kind of you, Matt. True gentlemen like you are very rare these days.'

'All my mother's doing,' Matt said. 'She taught me manners, you see.'

'She'd be so proud of you,' Pamela said.

Seething at her mother's betrayal, Edwina glanced back at them over her shoulder, walking arm in arm, so complicit. What was going on here? Was Pamela hoping Edwina and Matt would get back together and have that society wedding she had been hoping for? *That's the explanation*, she thought, *and she has probably picked out her mother-of-the-bride outfit with matching hat and shoes. How could she even imagine that would happen after all I've been through?* She looked again at the two of them, her mind whirling. Were they plotting something else together? No, that couldn't be. Pamela wasn't the secretive kind.

She always laid her cards on the table and never hid her feelings, good or bad. Plotting was far from her nature, but it was that wedding fantasy that had driven her to this. That would suit her to a tee and make her look good. Her daughter marrying one of the most eligible men in Ireland, with a big, glamorous wedding featured in every magazine would be very good for her image. And then there was Matt's interest in buying the cottage on top of all that.

'Edwina!' Pamela called, panting. 'Please slow down. You're running ahead like a racehorse.'

Edwina slowed as they rounded the bend and the row of houses came into view. 'Sorry, Mum. But we're actually nearly there. The cottages are right in front of you.'

'Oh.' Pamela stopped and let go of Matt's arm. She looked at the row of four pretty cottages, now all newly painted white, the doors and the trims around the windows picked out in pastel colours – light blue, pink, pale green and lilac, the little front gardens with roses and geraniums in tubs and the new slate roofs shining in the sunlight.

'They look really nice,' Pamela said. 'So fresh and bright. Can we go inside?'

'Yes,' Edwina said. 'The workmen have finished for the day, so there's nobody here. All the doors are open.' She stepped aside while she pulled her phone from her pocket. 'I just have to give my friends a call to say there's been a change of plan.'

While Pamela and Matt went inside the first cottage with the light blue door, Edwina quickly dialled Tara's number.

'Hi,' she said when Tara answered. 'Sorry about telling you so late, but I'm afraid I can't make it to dinner tonight.'

'Why not?' Tara asked. 'You're not sick, are you?'

'No, it's my mother. She has just arrived out of the blue, with my ex-boyfriend, if you don't mind, and she is staying the night so I'm afraid I have to entertain her.'

'And the ex-boyfriend?' Tara asked.

'He has some kind of dinner date in Killarney, thank God,' Edwina replied. 'But my mum will be here for a few days, so that's my weekend ruined. I would have loved to have dinner with you and Mick and the kids, but—'

'Why don't you both come?' Tara interrupted. 'We're just doing a barbeque with the kids in the garden and we have plenty of food. I'd love to meet her.'

'I'm sure you'll change your mind when you do,' Edwina muttered. 'But why not? If you feel strong enough to meet an older jet-setting woman who hasn't a clue how to make a bed or wash her clothes, I'll bring her along. She'll be delighted to meet a high-profile politician. But be prepared for a lot of non-PC chatter. She can't help it; she hasn't ever lived in the real world. She nearly fainted when she had to drink tea out of a mug with sheep on it.'

Tara burst out laughing. 'Oh my God, she sounds like a lot of fun. Can't wait to meet her. See you tonight. Don't dress up.'

'That would be impossible for my mother, but you asked for it. Bye and thanks.' Edwina hung up, shaking her head. Why had she agreed to bring her mother tonight? She put away her phone and entered the cottage, finding Pamela and Matt in the now smaller living room, about to go outside through the sunroom.

Before joining them, Edwina stopped and looked around. Most of the work had been done: the floors laid with polished oak planks, the wall between living room and the new bedroom erected and the old mantelpiece replaced by a piece of wood that looked like driftwood, the hearth set with flat pebbles. The walls were whitewashed and she knew the pictures she had ordered from an art gallery in Dublin would arrive shortly. Then the furniture would be shipped from America and the house would be finished, except for the kitchens, the decks and the hot tubs that would be installed in a few weeks.

But, even now, she could see how wonderful it would look.

Andrew's design, with the new downstairs master bedroom, the en suite shower and the slightly smaller kitchen that would have Shaker-style cupboards was a stroke of genius. Upstairs, the two bedrooms shared a bathroom that had been refurbished with a rolltop bathtub and a skylight inserted into the new roof, making it possible to lie back in the bath and see the stars. Fabulous idea. Edwina smiled happily as she went outside to join Matt and Pamela, who stood on the nearly finished deck looking at the spectacular view.

Pamela turned as Edwina approached them. 'It's incredible,' her mother said and then turned back to the view. 'It's hard to take in such beauty. I can't stop looking at it.'

'I know. Especially today with this light and no clouds.' Edwina gazed across the bay all the way out to the horizon where the sea and the sky met in shades of blue. She never got tired of looking at this view as the ever-shifting light changed throughout the day. The breeze was soft today, making her hair flutter and caressing her face, bringing with it a tang of seaweed and a slight whiff of grilled fish from the fish restaurant nearby.

Matt nodded, obviously momentarily speechless, looking as if he had just had an epiphany. 'It has that wow factor everyone is searching for,' he said after a while. 'And judging by what I've seen of the house, it's going to be the most covetable little gem on the whole of the west coast.'

'You've done a wonderful job,' Pamela said.

'I'm very happy with it,' Edwina said. 'And now all that's missing is the hot tub on each deck, and the fencing between them, then the furniture and some artwork. Then I can put it on the market. I thought I'd throw an open house party to celebrate and maybe get a few people interested. I'm leaning more and more towards letting these cottages, so it would be great to get the word out there. I might even try to get it on national TV, as it's so unique.'

'But you don't have to do that,' Matt protested. 'I would be very interested to buy the whole lot. It would be a fantastic investment.'

'Yes, but I want to put it on the market first,' Edwina argued. 'I'm even going to ask several estate agents to assess the market value. But then, if you offer the right price...' She stopped for a moment. 'Although I'm not really sure if I want to sell all the cottages, or any of them, actually. Letting them could be a better idea for me. It would create a great income and I could even decide to keep one of them for myself.'

'It's not for you decide all by yourself, though,' Pamela cut in. 'I'm your business partner, remember?'

'Yes, but I also remember the agreement we signed at the solicitor's,' Edwina reminded her. 'I just have to pay you back the money you invested once I've sold the cottages. And if I sell two and keep two, I can do that.'

'Agreement!' Pamela said with a snort. 'I'm your mother, so we don't need any agreement, do we?'

'Yes, we do,' Edwina said. 'That's why I insisted on one. You should never do business with family without an agreement in place. You said so yourself many years ago.' She looked at Matt for support but he didn't appear to be listening.

'That beach down there,' he said, pointing to the left. 'The one below the slopes covered in wild roses. Is that a private beach?'

'Not really,' Edwina replied. 'But the best way to get to it is down those steps, just outside the gate. It's locked for security reasons, but there's a key to open it. Each of the cottages will have one.'

'Is there another access?' Matt wanted to know.

Edwina nodded. 'Yes, from the main beach on the other side. Some like to take the path and then make their way down the slope, but it's a bit steep so not a lot of people do that. The main beach is so nice, there is no need to look for a better place to swim or surf. That little beach is called Wild Rose Bay, for obvious reasons,' she added.

'It's lovely,' Matt said, looking thoughtful. 'It feels like a really private beach from here. But it's not possible to block the access from the other side, is it?'

'Not unless you buy the land,' Edwina replied. 'But that would be awful. Then it would make the beach inaccessible to any of the locals who want to go there. Some people like to fish there as it's so quiet.'

'A private beach like that would be a huge asset,' Pamela said. 'We should see if we can block that path and make sure it's exclusive to the owners of the cottages. It could make it possible to raise the purchase price.'

'I don't like that idea,' Edwina protested. 'Isn't it enough that these houses will be the most fabulous get-aways in this part of Ireland?'

Matt frowned. 'There is no limit to what the potential owners will want. If you hope to sell at top price, you have to offer them everything they could want and more.' He stopped and looked around once more before he checked his watch. 'I have to go if I'm to be in time for that dinner in Killarney. I'll be in touch, Edwina.'

'Okay,' she said without much enthusiasm. She knew she wasn't being very polite but she didn't want to encourage him.

But he still kissed her and Pamela on both cheeks before he left, which made Edwina seethe. She knew exactly what was going on. Once Matt had seen how wonderful the setting was, and what a fantastic job the builders had done, he wanted in. He was wading in on her project, trying to talk her into selling the whole row to him and had also managed to convince Pamela that it would be a good plan. And Pamela was reliving that society wedding fantasy.

Now Edwina had to try her best to get her mother to see that selling to Matt before the cottages went on the market was a very bad idea, and that Matt was a total fraud and the worst possible husband for Edwina, or any woman on this earth. That would take a lot of talking and explaining and she wasn't sure she had the energy. She sighed and pulled herself together, deciding to try to enjoy the evening ahead. But even that seemed like a mountain to climb, with her mother tagging along. Getting her to dress down would be the first obstacle.

As it happened, Pamela made no objections to changing into more casual clothes when she heard they were going to the home of a former government minister and member of the Irish parliament. She fished a pair of white linen trousers and a bright blue shirt from the Ralph Lauren spring collection from the large suitcase she had brought. Suddenly rising to the challenge of sleeping in a room with a bed covered in a bright pink candlewick bedspread, and a bright green carpet, she declared it to be 'fun' and the tiny shower 'a bit of a squeeze'. She emerged glowing, saying that the lack of very hot water was 'just like in boarding school' and that she was looking forward to the evening as she had never actually been to a barbeque before.

'I've been to an asado in Argentina,' she said, 'but that's not the same thing, is it? I mean they're not going to roast anything on a spit, are they?'

'Not a whole animal, no,' Edwina replied. 'Just steaks and sausages over hot charcoal. But maybe white trousers aren't the best choice... There will be children and dogs and we'll be in the garden.'

'No problem,' Pamela declared. 'If I get dirty, I'll just put them in a bag for my maid to take care of when I get back to Dublin. I'm not going to compromise on style because of children and dogs. I'll just stay away from them, that's all.'

'Okay,' Edwina said and went to change into jeans and a sweater. Her phone pinged while she was getting dressed and she didn't check the text message until they were about to leave. It was from Daniel. Edwina stared at the text.

> *I think I found out something! Must check but it has to be an important clue. I'll get back to you when I'm sure.*

How amazing. Daniel seemed to be working hard to find the elusive Pearse. She couldn't wait to hear more and was suddenly excited about joining Daniel in Dingle town on Monday. It would be so nice to meet the writer of the message, this man who had been so desperate that night at the beginning of this century.

What had he been through since then? And what had Daniel found, and where?

17

The evening at Mick and Tara's farmhouse turned out to be huge fun. Edwina and Pamela arrived just as Mick had lit the barbeque on the back lawn that sloped down to the river. They had erected a canopy over the table so that they could sit there until late and avoid the chill of the evening dew. But the sun shone brightly as they arrived, and the swallows swooped around, emitting high-pitched shrieks as they chased after insects.

Tara and Mick's six-year-old twin daughters, Noelle and Michelle, dressed in identical yellow dungarees, rushed towards the guests as they got out of Edwina's car. They were so alike that, if it wasn't for the different hairdos, it would be impossible to tell them apart.

'Hello!' the girl with short hair shouted. 'Are you Edwina? And is this your mammy?'

'Yes and yes,' Edwina said and laughed. 'And who are you?'

'I'm Michelle,' the girl said. 'And the one with long hair is Noelle.'

'Hi, Michelle and Noelle,' Edwina said and shook their hands. 'This is my mother, Mrs Courtney-Smythe Huntington.'

Noelle stared at Pamela. 'That's a very long name. Can we call you something else? Are you a granny?'

'Yes, but you can call me Pamela,' she said graciously. She held out her hand to Michelle. 'How do you do?'

'Do what?' Michelle asked.

'It's a way of saying hello,' said Tara, as she came forward to greet them, dressed in jeans and a blue and pink striped shirt. 'Polite people say "how do you do?" when they meet. It's a little old-fashioned, of course.'

'Why do they say that?' Noelle asked. 'I mean why do they want to know how you do... well, whatever it is?'

'Shush,' Tara said and shooed the girls away. 'Go and help Daddy carry out the food from the kitchen. Sorry,' she said to Pamela. 'They are at the age when everything is a question.'

'They're lovely,' Pamela said. 'Twin girls, how wonderful.' She held out her hand to Tara. 'I'm Pamela.'

'Lovely to meet you,' Tara said and shook Pamela's hand. 'Welcome.'

'Thank you,' Pamela said, glancing at the ivy-covered façade of the big house. 'What a wonderful place you have here. And those girls are gorgeous. It must have been a big surprise to have twins.'

'Not at all,' Tara said. 'Twins run in the family. I'm one myself. My sister is the local GP here, except now she's in Australia for a year and I miss her terribly. But come and meet Mick and I'll get you a drink.'

'I believe you work for Condé Nast publications?' Pamela said as they made their way around the house to the back lawn.

Tara glanced at Edwina. 'Well, I did a long time ago. Now I'm freelance and mostly work for Kerry Tourism and other local publications. Who told you about Condé Nast?'

'I googled you,' Pamela said. 'Edwina wouldn't tell me much, so I felt I had to find out about you.'

Tara smiled. 'I see. Well, I'm flattered. You're welcome in

any case. Lovely to meet Edwina and Max's mother at last. You have two gorgeous grandchildren.'

'I do,' Pamela said. 'Even if I'm quite young to be a grandmother...'

'Of course you are,' Tara agreed, with an amused glance at Edwina. 'But come and sit down and I'll get you a drink. We have a nice bottle of rosé chilling in the fridge.'

'Sounds perfect,' Pamela purred.

They walked across the lawn and sat down at the table while Mick came forward and greeted them with his lovely smile and charming manners. Pamela was soon spellbound and seemed to relax as she sat down and chatted with him, telling him she had seen him on the stage a few years ago before he went into politics, to which he replied that acting was very much part of being a politician as well.

Edwina watched her mother and slowly realised there was nothing to fear. Pamela was on her best behaviour and obviously enjoying herself. And why wouldn't she, in this lovely place with such happy people? Edwina only wished Shane could be here and meet her mother when she was in this kind of mood. Maybe they would get on, after all... Shane was every bit as attractive as Mick, and just as charming when he was in the mood.

The evening continued in this pleasant way, the sun slowly dipping behind the trees and the smell of barbequed meat making their mouths water until they were served a plate of sizzling steaks and delicious sausages accompanied by baked potatoes, various salads and sauces.

'I don't usually eat this much,' Pamela said as she dug in. 'But how can I resist it? The smell alone made me nearly drool.'

Edwina tucked into her meal, chatting with Tara and the girls, while Pamela was deep in conversation with Mick. 'My mother is really enjoying herself,' she said. 'I've never seen her so animated. I think it has to be Mick's charisma.'

'And he's enjoying the attention,' Tara said with a laugh. 'She's hanging on his every word.'

'Pity Shane isn't here,' Edwina said wistfully. 'I'd love him to meet her when she's in this mood.'

'I asked if he wanted to come,' Tara said. 'Daniel has gone to Dingle for a few days, so he's on his own. He said he had a lot of paperwork to get through but he'd come over if he manages to finish it all.'

'Who's this Shane you're talking about?' Pamela asked as there was a lull in her conversation with Mick.

'Shane Flaherty,' Tara replied. 'He's the local GP. And...' She glanced at Edwina.

'He's the man I'm dating,' Edwina filled in.

'You're dating the local doctor?' Pamela asked. 'And he's a GP... Not a consultant, then?'

'No, but he's the best doctor in the world,' Tara said. 'He's saved many lives around here since he came. We love him. Don't we, girls?'

'Yes we do!' Michelle shouted.

'Speak of the devil,' Mick said, looking down the lawn. 'Here he is now.'

Edwina turned on her chair and felt a dart of pure joy as she saw Shane walking towards them. She shot up and started to run to meet him.

'Shane!' she called. 'What a surprise. I didn't expect to see you until tomorrow.'

He stopped and looked at her. 'I need to talk to you,' he said, his eyes cold. He glanced at the group around the table. 'Sorry, folks. I need to have a word with Edwina for a moment.'

'What is it?' Edwina asked, alarmed by his angry expression. 'What have I done?'

'It's not what you have done, but what you are going to do,' he replied, pulling her away to the shrubs. 'I heard some things about your plans for the headland. And if that's true, it's over between us.'

18

'What are you talking about?' Edwina asked, staring back at Shane when they were behind some shrubs to which he had pulled her. 'What am I about to do?'

'Buying up land and blocking the access to the little beach. Wild Rose Bay,' he continued. 'Is that what you're planning?'

Edwina took a step back. 'Where did you hear that?'

'Your boyfriend was in the grocery shop earlier this evening talking to Pauline.'

'What boyfriend?' Edwina asked. 'I only have one, and I thought that was you.'

'I mean that guy from Dublin with the perfect hair and the Porsche.'

'It's a Ferrari,' Edwina corrected.

'Yeah, okay. Much better, I suppose,' Shane said ironically.

'No, but...' Edwina stammered. 'Well, he's my ex, as you know.'

'Yeah, right. Whatever.' Shane pushed his fingers through his already unruly hair.

'What did he say?'

'He was going on about how he's going to buy all of Starlight Cottages when they're finished, and you and he are going to be partners, and let the houses to VIPs, and then the land on the other side of the little beach will be bought up and blocked so the beach is completely private. He was also talking about how the shops and restaurants needed to upgrade so these fancy people would be happy. Then he took off in his *Ferrari* like a bat out of hell and Pauline was standing there looking as if she had been hit by a tornado. So, of course, when I happened to call in only minutes later, she told me the whole thing.' Shane drew breath and looked at Edwina. 'I was going to call you, but then I thought I'd say what I think to you in person.'

'And what do you think?' Edwina asked, hurt and anger boiling up in her chest. 'You believed all that drivel? That man was once my boyfriend, yes. But that was a year ago. I was a different person back then. This summer has been a huge watershed for me. I've learned so much, both about myself and life in general. I've met some amazing people and felt so happy. And meeting you and us falling in love was...' She stopped, unable to continue as tears welled up in her eyes and her throat contracted. 'What is this really about?' she asked, confused.

'All I want to know is if what I heard is true,' Shane said. 'Is it?'

Suddenly angry, Edwina glared at him. 'Do you really have to ask?' she replied, her voice hoarse with indignation.

'Yes,' Shane said. 'I do. Because if you're the kind of person who walks all over people, especially nice people like those who live in Sandy Cove, then I don't want to know you.'

Edwina folded her arms and glared at him. 'Well, if you believe even for a *second* that I could even consider doing what that stupid man said, then I don't want to know you either.'

They stared at each other in silence for a moment and then, without another word, Edwina turned and walked swiftly back down the lawn to the table, fighting back the tears that threatened to well up. How could he think such things about her? Didn't he know her well enough by now to trust her motives? She couldn't believe this was happening, that he had looked at her with such utter contempt and then not even tried to say sorry. She suddenly just wanted to be alone and cry.

'Mum, get your things,' she said to a surprised-looking Pamela. 'We're leaving. Sorry, Tara, but we have to go.'

Tara got up. 'What's going on?'

'Ask *him*,' Edwina said, pointing at Shane, who was still standing where she had left him. 'I'm really sorry, Tara, but I'm not feeling very well right now. Thank you so much for a lovely dinner. Come on, Mum.'

'But, but...' Pamela protested. 'I'm really enjoying myself. This is very rude to our hosts, Edwina,' she chided.

'I know and I'm truly sorry,' Edwina said to Mick. 'But I'm too upset.'

Mick went to her side and put his arm around her. 'I can see that. And Shane is standing over there looking upset, too. Is there anything we can do?'

'No.' Edwina picked up her bag from her chair. 'I think it's best if we go. Shane can... can...' She was about to say that he could go to hell for all she cared, but she realised she didn't have to say it out loud. 'Bye, Mick,' she said. 'Sorry about this. Tell the girls I'll drop by another time to see them. They're gorgeous.'

'I'm sure they'll love to see you again,' Mick replied, giving Edwina a squeeze. 'It was so nice to meet your mother. She's great craic.'

'Craic? My mother?' Edwina asked, astonished. But as she looked at Pamela hugging Tara goodbye, she realised that tonight, her mother had been especially charming and appearing to have really enjoyed herself.

It had to be the Sandy Cove effect – or simply that tonight Pamela had felt no need to prove herself or to show off. Well, that was one good thing about this evening. But Shane's sudden arrival and his accusatory questions had ruined the happy feeling completely. She glanced at the spot where he had been standing but he had left and she could hear his motorbike tearing up the lane as they rounded the side of the house to get to the car.

'What happened?' Pamela asked. 'Was that your new boyfriend you were having words with just now?'

'Words?' Edwina asked. 'It was a lot more than that. But we're not together any more. He was so angry and it made me feel awful.'

'Why?' Pamela asked, putting her hand on Edwina's shoulder. 'What happened?'

'Please, Mum, I don't want to talk about it.' Edwina shook off her mother's hand and got in behind the wheel.

'I see,' Pamela said, as she opened the passenger door and settled on the seat. 'But when you're ready, or even just want to have a good cry, I'm here.'

'Thanks.' Edwina started the engine and drove slowly up the lane, blinking away tears.

They drove in silence back to Sandy Cove and parked outside the closed grocery shop. Edwina got out of the car and ran upstairs to the flat, through the door and straight into her room, where she threw herself on the bed and finally gave herself up to her grief. She was vaguely aware of the door gently closing but then she forgot all else except the cold look in Shane's eyes and his harsh words and her whole body shook with violent sobs, her tears coursing down her cheeks. She felt as if her life was over and she would never be happy again. Shane had been the love of her life, she had thought, the man she would love and who would love her back. But now she knew it had just been a dream and she had been disappointed and rejected yet again.

When she had no more tears, she rolled onto her back and

stared at the ceiling, wondering if she would ever be able to feel happy again. She closed her burning, swollen eyes but opened them when Pamela appeared at the door, peering in.

'I made some hot chocolate,' she said. 'Well, I tried. Don't know if it tastes okay. I'm not very good at cooking, as you know.'

Edwina sat up, hugging her pillow, smiling wanly. 'You're the *worst* cook. But thank you for trying.'

Pamela opened the door wider and came in, carrying a tray with a steaming mug. 'Here, taste it. I might have overdone the sugar, but it's supposed to be good for shock.'

Edwina took the mug and had a careful sip. 'It's a bit too sweet but very chocolatey. Probably a thousand calories a sip.'

'Good.' Pamela sat down on the bed. 'Drink up, then. It'll make you feel better.'

'Nothing can,' Edwina said, sighing deeply. She handed the mug back to Pamela. 'Sorry, Mum, but I'm too choked up.'

'It's horrible, anyway,' Pamela said and put the mug on the bedside table. Then she stroked Edwina's hair. 'Maybe you should wash your face and get into bed properly? It's quite late.'

'I know. But I'll never sleep.'

'Yes, but you'll be more comfortable in your nightie than in those wrinkly jeans and shirt,' Pamela argued. She pulled Edwina up off the bed. 'Come on. I'll help you.'

With her mother's help, Edwina managed to wash her face and change into a cotton nightie. Then Pamela piled up the pillows in Edwina's bed and she lay back, letting her mother tuck her in, feeling like a small, sad little girl.

'Thanks, Mum,' she whispered. 'Stay for a bit, please.'

'Of course,' Pamela said and settled beside Edwina, taking her hand. 'I hate seeing you like this. I could hit that horrible man for doing this to you. What on earth did he say?'

'Oh nothing much. It's all Matt's fault, really,' Edwina said and went on to tell Pamela what Shane had said earlier that evening.

'Oh.' Pamela looked taken aback. 'Well, whatever Matt said to that girl, Shane shouldn't have believed it.'

'What was Matt doing here, anyway?' Edwina asked. 'I mean, you knew what he'd done to me and you still brought him here. Why?'

Pamela looked a little sheepish. 'Well... I thought, you see, that maybe you and he could...'

'That we could kiss and make up and then have that big, fat society wedding you've been dreaming about ever since I was a teenager?'

Pamela sighed. 'I suppose that was at the back of my mind, yes. And that perhaps, if he bought the cottages, you'd be partners and then...'

'And then nothing.' Edwina pulled away from Pamela. 'It was never going to happen, Mum. All you did was cause a lot of problems, and then Matt did the rest with all that rubbish he told Pauline in the shop that Shane overheard.'

'I'm sorry,' Pamela said, sounding contrite. 'It's all my fault. Stupid thing to do, really.'

'Yes it was, Mum. *Really* stupid.' Edwina sighed, feeling tears well up again. 'How could Shane even begin to think such a thing about me? I would never have tried to buy that land and blocked the access to the beach. That would be a very sneaky thing to do.' Edwina looked at Pamela for a moment. 'You thought that might be a good idea too, though, I think.'

Pamela squirmed. 'I might have. But then when I thought about it, I realised it would be very bad PR. And tonight, when I was talking to Mick O'Dwyer, he made me realise a lot of things about this village and the people who live here. *They're as unique as the landscape,* he said. *And as beautiful and friendly as the gentle breezes that blow here on a summer's day.* Such a lovely thing to say, I thought.' Pamela smiled. 'I felt so strange talking to him. He was a famous actor once, and could have gone on to Hollywood. But instead, he came here and worked hard in local politics and now he's a member of the Irish parliament and does his best to serve the people who voted for him.' Pamela drew breath and looked at Edwina with a strange glint in her eyes. 'I feel quite peculiar tonight. As if I've been made to see the world, and the people in it, in a different way.'

Edwina smiled. 'What did they put in the drinks?'

Pamela laughed. 'Maybe it was truth serum?' She leaned her head against Edwina's. 'I'm so very sorry for all the trouble I caused. I didn't realise what was going on with you and how much Matt had hurt you. Can you ever forgive me, do you think?'

'I already have. I don't think you really knew what you were doing.'

Pamela sighed. 'No, I didn't. You've changed a great deal, you know. I've never felt this close to you before.'

'No,' Edwina mumbled, soothed by Pamela's surprisingly gentle voice. 'We were never close. You were always somewhere else. Never at the school plays or parents' meetings.'

'I know.' Pamela took Edwina's hand. 'I was an awful mother.'

'Yes, you were in a way,' Edwina had to agree. 'But then, I was a horrible teenager.'

'Oh yes,' Pamela said with feeling. 'You were. Constantly saying you hated me and that I had ruined your life when I tried a little discipline.'

'I didn't *hate* you.' Edwina patted her mother's hand. 'I was just going through that phase when you think you're old enough to do everything.'

'Yes,' Pamela said. 'Like when you wanted to go to a nightclub at the age of fifteen in one of my party dresses. That's when we were on holiday in Marbella that summer, remember?'

Edwina suddenly giggled at the memory. 'I ruined that

dress when I climbed out the window of the hotel. My God, you were livid.'

'Yes, and when I remember that dress, I still get angry. It was a Chanel number from the latest collection.' Pamela laughed and shook her head. 'That was more than twenty years ago. How time flies. And here we are, me so much older, and you nearly forty.'

'Don't remind me,' Edwina muttered.

'Can you forgive me, do you think?'

'For saying I'm nearly forty?'

'No, for being such a hopeless mother,' Pamela said.

'Oh, that's all forgotten. I like you being here now when I'm so sad.'

'That's good. I'm glad if I can help.' Pamela touched Edwina's cheek. 'Tell me about him.'

Edwina was quiet for a while, thinking about Shane. Then she started to tell Pamela about how they met and the fun times they had arguing and teasing each other and then how they fell in love and how he had made her feel.

'Like I was the most wonderful woman on earth,' she said. 'We seemed so in tune, so perfect for each other. I thought I had finally found the love of my life.' She stared into the distance, out the open window to the view of the ocean, that was now a dark blue, and the nearly black sky with a pink band at the horizon where the sun had just set. As the soft breeze gently moved the curtains, her thoughts drifted and she saw Shane's lovely brown eyes in her imagination. 'I will never feel like that again with anyone else. I'll be alone for the rest of my life now.'

Pamela touched Edwina's cheek. '*Shh.* Don't give up. Maybe you'll get back together and then everything will be all right. He needs to cool down a little, I think. He was jealous, thinking you were getting back with Matt, I'd say.'

'Maybe that was part of it,' Edwina said, slightly cheered by that idea. 'But how can I convince him it's not true?'

'Leave him alone for a bit. Get back to your project and ignore him.'

'Ignore who?' Edwina asked, feeling suddenly exhausted. 'Matt?'

'No, the other one, the handsome doctor. Let's forget all about Matt.' She got up from the bed and took the mug of cocoa.

'Good idea.' Edwina turned her head and glanced at Pamela. 'Don't go. Stay here and talk to me. Tell me about Dad. I mean, what he was like as a husband and what went wrong between you.'

Pamela fluffed up her pillows and sat back beside Edwina again. 'Oh,' she said. 'He was one of those ambitious, driven people. You know how he started as a minor bookkeeper at the company and then, years later, ended up running it? Then he bought it and a few other businesses that he ran simultaneously. A true self-made man. I didn't really understand his obsession with rising to the top. I came from a wealthy family and had never had to work very hard for a living. I wanted to play, he had to work. I had enough money to keep us in style, but he didn't want any of that. He said I could do what I wanted with my money, buy yachts and racehorses and expensive cars if that's what I wanted to do. But he was the one who should support his family. He wanted to teach you and Max to work for what you had. Well, you know that Max is very like him. But you...' Pamela stopped. 'Well, I'm sure you know that a lot of the rows were about you and how I was bringing you up to like luxury and glamour. So I gave up in the end and let him make all the decisions. It was easier that way.'

'So that's why you ran away from us?' Edwina asked.

'Mostly from him,' Pamela replied. 'He was all about duty and hard work. And he said I had duties as a wife and mother. This was forty years ago, you understand, so things were different then between men and women. And your father was ten years older than me as well.' Pamela paused. 'But when we met, he was so different. Charming, dashing and with all that drive, and plans for the future. And incredibly good-looking, of course. He knew how to sweep a woman off her feet, that's for sure. Our first evening together was very romantic.'

'Yes, Dad used to tell us how you met on a train and how he couldn't take his eyes off you.'

'My parents didn't approve, so we ran away and got married in the South of France. His family were against it, being of old Anglo-Irish stock. Very old-fashioned, as you know. They thought I was vulgar and nouveau riche. I couldn't stand them and that old house they lived in. Cold and draughty with no proper bathroom.'

'Strawberry Hill, you mean?' Edwina asked.

Pamela nodded. 'Yes. I must say that Allegra has done a wonderful job with all the renovations. But back then it was not a nice place to live for a young couple. And Great-Aunt Davina ruled the roost then. So we bought a very pretty house in the country near Dublin and then we moved into town. But by then it was all over. We fought constantly and it became quite ugly – to the point where we knew we could never patch it up and continue living together.'

'So you walked away?'

'Yes. We decided between us that he should have the main custody. We wanted to spare you a huge custody battle in court. I knew your father would look after you and that I would have you on holidays, which didn't always work very well.' Pamela sighed. 'Well, you know how hopeless I was.'

'You didn't pick very nice men after Dad,' Edwina said, remembering her two stepfathers, who had been very much like Matt: handsome, superficially charming but not very caring or nice deep down. Neither of them had been happy to spend time with Pamela's children.

'No. I fell for good looks, which was a mistake. But let's not go there. Not tonight.'

'Or ever,' Edwina said. 'We're getting on really well now. Why bother with that old stuff? It only makes us sad.'

'Yes,' Pamela said. 'Better to look forward.'

'You might meet someone else one day. A nice man who'll look after you.'

Pamela let out a little snort. 'No. It's too late. Men my age want younger women. And those who are older than me are looking for a nurse. I've given up on that idea a long time ago. Now I just want to have a little fun and be with my family.'

'Sounds good.' Exhausted after all that had happened today, Edwina began to feel sleepy. She vaguely heard Pamela say something and then leave the room and gently close the door. She closed her eyes and sank deeper into the bed until she fell asleep.

A ping from her phone woke Edwina up. She groped around until she found it and saw a missed call from Daniel. She sat up, hesitated for a moment and then rang the number.

Daniel answered at once. 'Hi. Did I wake you up?'

'Yes, no, what time is it?'

'Eight o'clock.'

'That's early for you,' Edwina remarked.

'I know but my granddad is taking me out on his boat in a minute. I only wanted to say... to ask if we can still be friends even if you and Dad have broken up?'

'Oh. Who told you?' Edwina asked, the memory of the row making her heart sink.

'He did. Last night. Said I should hear it from him before anyone else told me. I'm really sorry about that. I thought you and he were great together.'

'Did he say why we broke up?' Edwina asked, her voice hoarse.

'It was something about him being stupid and jumping to

conclusions,' Daniel said. 'And that you were not having it. He does have a bit of a temper, you know, so maybe... Could you try to talk to him and...?'

'No,' Edwina said. 'We're not going to make up any time soon. But hey, you and I can be friends, of course. And we still have to solve the mystery of the message.'

'Oh great,' Daniel said, sounding relieved. 'And I do have a lead but it might not prove anything. You're still coming here on Monday?'

'Of course. I'm going to drive my mother to the airport and then I'll head straight to Dingle. Just tell me where you want to meet me.'

'Grand. There's a café on the pier that's just opened. Very cool place. It's called the Ocean café. Easy to find. We could meet there whenever you want.'

'I'd say I could be there at eleven or so. But I'll text you when I leave the airport.'

'Brilliant. I might have found out more by then. I think I'm getting close.'

'Close to what?' Edwina asked, intrigued.

'Can't tell you yet. See you Monday,' Daniel said and hung up.

Edwina put down her phone and sat up in bed. What had Daniel said? Shane had been stupid and jumped to conclusions... Yes, he had. And she had been so hurt and angry that he could believe something like that about her. And then he had left, tearing away on his motorbike, without saying sorry or admitting he had made a mistake. That made her feel that they just weren't meant to be together, that their romance had been what they had denied: just a summer fling. But it didn't feel like that; it felt as if her heart was broken. Would she ever get over this? She shook her head and decided to stop fretting about it and think of other things, like finding out who had sent the message in the bottle. Daniel had said he was getting closer.

Could there be a connection between his mother's family and the mysterious Pearse? She couldn't wait to go to Dingle and find out.

The trip would, if nothing else, help her take her mind off her heartache.

19

As Edwina sat on the edge of the bed, she could smell something strange. Something that made her mouth water. Bacon and eggs? What was going on? She got out of bed, pulled back the curtain and saw that it was yet another lovely day with blue skies and tiny clouds drifting across the sun from time to time. The ocean glittered in the distance and a flock of seabirds settled on the water. She made her way to the kitchen and stared in astonishment at Pamela, in a green silk dressing gown, standing by the stove, poking at something in the frying pan.

She turned around, beaming. 'Good morning. I'm cooking breakfast!' she said, looking proud. 'Never done this in my life, but just look at it! I found a YouTube clip that showed how to do it, and I seem to have succeeded.'

'Amazing.' Edwina looked at the splatters of butter on Pamela's dressing gown, at her face bare of make-up and her hair still tangled from sleep and wondered if aliens had abducted her mother during the night and replaced her with this slightly dishevelled clone. Then she saw the crisp bacon and brown sausages in the pan beside a perfectly fried egg.

'This looks incredible,' she said in amazement. 'You haven't

burnt anything. And where did all this come from? I hope you
didn't go shopping in your dressing gown?'

Pamela laughed. 'No, of course not. I rang down to the shop
and that nice girl delivered this to the door. There's fresh bread
from the bakery, too. Very kind woman who didn't mind deliv-
ering at all when I said you were poorly. Told me to take care of
you after the break-up. They're all sad for Shane, and for you
too, of course.'

'What?' Edwina said, appalled. 'It's all over the village
already?'

'So it appears,' Pamela said. 'Unfortunate, but what can you
do? This is a small place.'

'Very small,' Edwina remarked sourly. 'Too small for me, I
think.'

'Maybe,' Pamela agreed as she loaded two plates with food.
'Just look at this. A hundred thousand calories that will clog up
our arteries. But doesn't it smell divine? Just the trick for a
broken heart.'

'Your heart isn't broken,' Edwina remarked.

'No, but I will eat it in solidarity with you,' Pamela said with
a mischievous smile. 'Let's go and sit on the window seat in your
room and look at the sea and tuck into this truckload of pure
sin.'

Edwina shook her head at her mother's strange behaviour
but they did what Pamela suggested and enjoyed a lovely,
lazy morning eating all the food Pamela had cooked and then
they took turns in the bathroom and got dressed ready for a
day at the beach, which Pamela had wished for. Mick had
recommended that she have lunch at the beach café and
meet the two Marys – saying it was a 'must' for a visit to
Sandy Cove. It would have to be a light lunch, though,
Edwina had remarked, as the huge breakfast would take a
while to digest.

'This is like the Girl Guides,' Pamela said when she

emerged from the bathroom after nearly an hour. 'Like camping and braving the elements.'

'You were never a Girl Guide,' Edwina remarked dryly from the kitchen as she put away the dishes she had just dried. 'And you haven't been near a campsite in your life. I wouldn't say having a shower in that bathroom is remotely like camping but I suppose to you, it would be.'

'Well, it's putting up with primitive conditions,' Pamela retorted from the living room. 'And anyway, it's kind of fun to cope with a challenge like that. I think I'm very brave, actually.'

'Yes, of course you are, Mum,' Edwina soothed. 'And it's nice to have you here. You were great yesterday. Made me feel a lot better.'

'That's wonderful,' Pamela said with a tender smile as Edwina sat down beside her on the sofa.

'I'm glad you came.' Edwina returned her mother's smile. 'I'll try to make it a fun weekend for you. We'll go to the beach now and swim and then have lunch at The Two Marys'.'

'Lovely. But what will we do tonight, then?' Pamela asked.

'We should go out for dinner,' Edwina suggested. 'We'll go to the Harbour pub and sit outside as the weather is set to stay nice. That's something you might find even more of a challenge. There, we'll sit at the long table with everyone and have grilled steaks and drink beer out of the bottles.'

'You mean we'd sit with other people?' Pamela looked doubtful. 'And drink beer straight from the bottle?'

'Yes. Another new experience for you. The Harbour pub is fun on Saturday nights. Shane and I used to...' She stopped. 'Well, that was then. Maybe this isn't such a good idea. He might be there and then what will I do?'

'You will smile and say hello and then ignore him,' Pamela said sternly. 'Best way to treat a man who has behaved like that. Stay cool and don't show you're upset. It's up to him to apologise.'

'Cool?' Edwina repeated. 'If I see him, cool is the last thing I'll be.'

'Yes, you will,' Pamela said sternly, getting up from the sofa. 'I'll be there to support you. Now, let's go to the beach for our swim and then lunch. I've packed my beach bag. I only need an umbrella to protect me from the sun.'

'I think there's one in the broom cupboard,' Edwina said, jumping to her feet. 'Sorcha, my landlady, said I could use any of the beach things if I need them.'

They found the beach umbrella, which was small and easy to carry, and set off on foot to the beach in the bright sunshine, stopping to talk to the people they met, Edwina introducing Pamela to everyone who seemed delighted to meet such an elegant woman, all dressed up in her Riviera finery. She looked a little over the top for Sandy Cove where shorts, T-shirts and flip-flops were the usual attire, but Edwina didn't mind as Pamela was charming to everyone and chatted happily about the weather and how lovely the views were, and how much she loved the quaint shops and the little pubs and restaurants.

They settled down on a blanket on the beach and put up the umbrella so that not a single ray of sun would touch Pamela's complexion. She made sure Edwina put on enough sunblock to cover an entire family and then sat back to look at people enjoying all kinds of water sports. Edwina announced she was going for a swim and Pamela lay back under the umbrella, saying she would have a little snooze.

Happy her mother was enjoying the trip to the beach, Edwina waded into the water and enjoyed a long swim in the crystal-clear water, which helped her momentarily forget her sorrows. Life wasn't so bad, she thought as she made her way back, looking up at the sky where a seagull glided around, emitting a squawk from time to time. The sound of the waves pounding the shore and the occasional cry from the seagulls added to the pleasure of the beach and Edwina emerged from the water feeling refreshed and relaxed, looking forward to a nice lunch at the café above the beach.

The two Marys always served up a lovely meal and she was idly wondering what was on the menu, when she was startled to hear screams coming from the direction of their beach blanket. Something was wrong with Pamela. Edwina started to run towards the red and white umbrella and arrived, breathless, finding Pamela in a panic.

'I've been stung by a wasp,' she panted, her face ashen. 'I'm allergic. I can't find my epi pen! I think I forgot to bring it.' She clutched her throat and stared at Edwina with huge, terrified eyes. 'I can't breathe,' she croaked. 'Help me!'

Without thinking, Edwina quickly got her phone from her bag and dialled the only number she could think of.

He answered straight away. 'Edwina,' he said. 'What—'

'My mother has been stung by a wasp and she's allergic and she can't find her epi pen. Please help me!'

'Where are you?' Shane asked.

'On the main beach. Under a red and white umbrella. Please hurry!'

'I'm on my way,' Shane said and hung up.

Edwina fell onto her knees beside her mother. 'The doctor is coming. Try to stay calm,' she said.

Pamela nodded, her breathing laboured, her face now turning a deep red.

Only moments later, Shane came running with his bag and crouched beside Pamela with an epi pen ready in his hand. 'I'm a doctor and I'm going to push this into your thigh, okay?'

Pamela nodded.

Shane plunged the epi pen into Pamela's thigh. 'Just try not to panic, eh... What's her name?' he asked, turning to Edwina.

'Pamela,' Edwina said.

Shane nodded and turned back to Pamela. 'Okay. Now, Pamela, lie back and it won't take more than a second or two before you begin to feel better.' He put his hand on her arm. 'Breathe slowly, in... and out... That's it. You're doing fine,' he said as Pamela's colour slowly improved and she started to breathe more normally, still wheezing but looking a lot better. He took her wrist and checked her pulse and then nodded, looking satisfied. 'Nearly back to normal. That stuff is great when it's given in time.'

'Oh what a relief.' Edwina sat back on her heels. 'Thank God you were nearby.'

'I was in my car on my way to a house call up the mountain road,' he said. 'Half an hour later, I would have been too far away. It would have been a better idea to call the emergency number.'

'They would never have been here in time,' Edwina said. She brought her hands to her face. 'My mother nearly died.'

'No, I didn't,' Pamela said. 'I'm still alive, thanks to the nice doctor here. Could you put that little cushion under my head, Edwina?'

Edwina sighed and laughed while she found the cushion and put it behind Pamela's head. 'She's fine. Thank you, Shane.' She stood up, shivering in her wet swimsuit, more from the fright than from feeling cold.

Shane got to his feet and looked at her with a strange expression. 'You'd better get out of that wet swimsuit, or I'll have another patient to take care of.' Then he picked up a towel and wrapped it around her in a surprisingly caring way. 'Put on some dry clothes,' he said.

'I will,' Edwina replied, still shivering.

'Good.' He stood there, staring at her for a while. 'I have to go,' he finally said.

Edwina nodded. 'Yes, I know. Thanks again. If you hadn't been here...' She stopped, trying her best not to burst into tears but failing. 'I don't know what I would have done,' she said, tears running down her cheeks.

'Well, I was here, and she'll be fine,' Shane said. 'And she won't ever forget her epi pen again, will she?'

'No, Doctor, I won't,' Pamela piped up from her cushion. She was looking nearly back to normal again, to Edwina's relief. 'Thank you so much for saving my life.'

'You're very welcome,' Shane said, smiling at her. 'Nice to meet you, Pamela.' He moved away, picking up the epi pen that was lying on the ground. 'Please get Edwina to take you to the hospital in Killarney when she's ready. I'll phone them and tell them what happened. Take care,' he said over his shoulder before he moved off.

'Well, that was awkward,' Edwina said, looking at Shane's departing figure as she dabbed at her wet cheeks.

Her feelings were all confused, but she was deeply grateful for what he had done. Pamela could have died right here on the beach had he not arrived so promptly with that epi pen. She knew he would have done the same for anyone, and he had put his feelings aside while he tended to Pamela struggling to breathe. But then he had put the towel around her and looked at her like that...

'Handsome man,' Pamela said. 'But difficult.'

'I know.' Edwina quickly changed into her T-shirt and shorts behind the towel and pulled on a sweater. 'But I'm pretty difficult, too.'

'You were made for each other,' Pamela said, slowly getting up. 'And he's totally and utterly besotted with you. Can we go and have lunch once we've been to the hospital?'

After a brief visit to the hospital in Killarney, they had a late lunch, enjoying a delicious shrimp salad at an outside table at The Two Marys', meeting both owners, who Pamela declared were wonderful and had 'the true Sandy Cove spirit', which she said was unique and would be highly appreciated by the people who bought the cottages.

'I'll be back very soon,' she announced. 'At the end of the summer, probably. It will be a good rest after all the partying in Saint-Tropez. So exhausting at my age.'

'What age would that be?' Edwina teased. 'Forty-two?'

Pamela flicked back her hair. 'Oh, I usually go for fifty-two at the moment. It seems less of a lie, somehow.'

'You look much younger than your real age. But how about not mentioning your age at all?' Edwina suggested. 'I think I'll go for that once I turn you-know-what. I'll be mysterious and let them guess.'

Pamela looked thoughtful. 'Not a bad idea, darling. That's fine when you're that age. But once you hit sixty, you have to have a number.'

Edwina laughed and shook her head. 'I was joking. What does it matter anyway? I know I'll never look as smooth or polished as you. I won't be doing Botox or fillers. I'm too scared of needles to go through all that.'

'Then you'll have to work on your charm and personality,' Pamela said, stabbing at a shrimp with her fork. 'Hard work, but in the end it might be the best policy. I think you're doing a great job with that already. You're a lot more smiley and fun than before. Must be this place,' she said, gazing out over the beach and the glittering ocean. 'It makes you feel so far away from all those things. I nearly skipped my make-up this morning, but then I pulled myself up and applied a little bit, enough for the beach. I would never go out in public without looking my best.' She looked sternly at Edwina. 'You're letting yourself go a little bit. I mean, looking a mess is not going to get you far, even with great charm and a wonderful personality.'

Edwina touched her hair that, despite pulling a brush through it, was still rough from the salt water. 'I know. I'm sure

Shane thought I looked awful, judging by the way he was looking at me.'

'That's not what I saw,' Pamela said with a knowing smile. 'He's mad about you. I think he wants to apologise, but doesn't quite know how. Maybe you should take the first step?'

'I have nothing to apologise for,' Edwina said hotly, Shane's harsh words still fresh in her mind. She felt the hurt again, and the shock and disappointment at how he had jumped to conclusions about her. 'So if he doesn't have to guts to admit he was wrong, that's it as far as I'm concerned. I don't think we're compatible, actually. We were not meant to be together.'

'Meant?' Pamela asked. 'By whom?'

'I don't know. The forces out there.' Edwina waved her hand. 'The universe, maybe.'

'What utter rot!' Pamela exclaimed. 'So you're going to let him stew? For how long?'

Edwina shrugged. 'Who knows? When does hell freeze over?'

'You're too stubborn. Men like that don't grow on trees. If I were you, I'd grab him and hang onto him for dear life before someone else does.'

Edwina pushed her plate away and drank some water. 'I wouldn't have thought he was up to scratch in your world. He's not rich or anything, just the local GP.'

'Oh, but he has other, more important qualities. He reminds me of your father.' Pamela's eyes were suddenly sad. 'I didn't handle him well, you know. I was stubborn like you, always looking for excitement and not prepared to be the wife and mother he wanted.' She sighed and finished her salad. 'Well, that was then, and this is now. And here I am, all alone and getting older by the minute.'

Edwina grabbed Pamela's hand. 'You're not alone and you never will be. You have me and Max and those lovely little boys. And Allegra, of course.'

'I haven't been a very hands-on grandmother,' Pamela said sadly.

'But you *can* be,' Edwina urged. 'I'm getting better at being an aunt, so you can work at being a very nice granny to them. Go and see them. Play with the boys, take Maureen O'Hara for a walk with them.'

'Who?' Pamela asked, confused.

Edwina smiled. 'That's their Jack Russel. Allegra called her Maureen O'Hara as a joke when they got her and it stuck.'

'Sounds like fun,' Pamela said, looking only half convinced. 'But also quite frightening. Small boys are so... frisky. Climbing all over, jumping, running, shouting...'

'You just need to practise a lot. I'm sure you'll be great with a bit of time,' Edwina said. 'Why don't you go and stay with them for a weekend soon?'

'Oh well...' Pamela looked thoughtful. 'I might. But you know how I feel about Strawberry Hill. Too many sad memories.'

'Yes, but now you can make happy memories there with Max and his family. That might erase the bad ones,' Edwina suggested. 'It did for me. Or at least it's beginning to,' she added. Then she had an idea. 'You know what? I have Sunday free now that I'm not going to spend the weekend with...' She swallowed. 'The way I had planned,' she continued. 'Let's go and see Max and Allegra tomorrow.'

'Just like that?' Pamela said. 'I'm not sure we should just barge in.'

'I'll call them and tell them we're coming,' Edwina said and pulled her phone from her handbag. 'I'm sure they'll be happy to see you.'

'I'm not sure about that,' Pamela protested.

But Allegra had already dialled Max's number. 'Hi,' she said when he answered. 'Mum and I thought we'd come for a visit tomorrow. Would that be okay? Just for her to see the boys and have a cup of tea or something.'

'Of course,' he said. 'But I was just going to call you about something else.'

'What?' she asked.

'It's about that construction company that's doing the cottages. Seabreeze Construction, isn't that what they're called?'

'Yes. What about them?'

'Have you heard the news?' Max asked.

'What news?'

'They've gone bust.'

20

'Bust?' Edwina said, nearly dropping her phone.

'Yes,' Max said. 'I heard it from a colleague just now. They're bankrupt. Completely broke. Can you hear what I'm saying?'

'Yes,' Edwina said in a shaky voice. 'But, but... I mean, I spoke to them yesterday. We were talking about the final work. The electricity, the plumbing, the hot tubs...' Her mind whirled while she tried to understand what was happening. Was it true? Had their construction company, which had seemed so solid, really gone bust? 'It can't be,' she said. 'Where did you hear this?'

'From a colleague in the construction business.'

'I still can't believe it.'

'Try calling them today,' Max said. 'I bet there'll be no answer.'

'It's Saturday, so there wouldn't be. They don't work at the weekend.' Edwina felt tears of despair welling up. This couldn't be happening. Her lovely project was now going to be a huge failure.

'I suppose.' Max paused. 'But on Monday you won't find anyone. Except maybe the architect who's working for them? Do you have his number?'

'Yes, but that's probably a business number. Oh God, what am I going to do?' Edwina moaned while Pamela looked worried.

'We can talk about that tomorrow when you come here,' Max said. 'Not that I really have a clue how to get you out of this mess. I did warn you.' He sighed. 'But we won't go there right now.'

'No, I don't want to hear you say "I told you so".' Edwina glanced at Pamela, trying to stay calm. 'We'll be there in the morning.'

'Stay for lunch,' he suggested, sounding a little friendlier.

'Okay. Thanks, we will.'

'Good. See you then. Bye,' Max said and hung up.

'What has happened?' Pamela said. 'Who's gone bust?'

'Seabreeze,' Edwina said, staring back at her mother while she tried to take in what she had just heard.

'Our construction company?' Pamela asked, looking alarmed.

'Yes, Max heard it from a colleague. They're completely bankrupt, he said.' Her voice shook as she tried to pull herself together. What was she going to do? Blinking away tears, she picked up her phone again and searched in her contact list. 'I have Andrew's number here. I don't expect to get a reply but I'll give it a shot.' She dialled and waited and then a voice said the number was not available. 'He's disconnected this number,' she said with a sigh. 'I might have known. He was too nice to be true. And that company was too slick, when I think of it. The shiny company car, Karen's designer gear, the amazing computers... They seemed to have overspent on a lot of things, including that fancy office. Now what are we going to do?' she asked Pamela, beginning to panic. 'The houses are nearly finished but we have to get builders, electricians and plumbers to do the rest of the work. Where on earth are we going to find anyone in the middle of summer?' Edwina looked at her mother, feeling a wave of hopelessness. 'This project has cost a lot of money so far, but at least we were still within the budget. But we have paid for work that hasn't been done. And for furniture that won't be delivered now, I'm sure. We'll have to fork out a lot more so we can finish the houses. Maybe we should just sell the lot the way they are?'

Pamela stared back at her daughter without replying. Then she took a deep breath and sat up. 'We are not going to give up. There isn't that much left to do. Some painting and putting up picture rails and those thresholds. But we might skip those for now and see if we can get workmen in to finish the essentials. But we are not going to sell the houses the way they are.'

Edwina stared at her mother. 'We aren't?'

'No. We are going to finish them, but we'll have to move the goalposts a little so we can still get in below the budget and come out smiling.' She looked at Edwina, her eyes sparkling. 'This is a huge challenge, but we'll win in the end. I have a few ideas...'

'And you're not going to tell me what they are, I bet,' Edwina said.

'Not yet. I need to think first. You know thinking isn't one of my usual occupations, so you'll have to be patient.'

'But you're supposed to go to Dublin on Monday,' Edwina said. 'Is that off now?'

'No, of course not,' Pamela said with a mischievous smile. 'That's very much on and part of my plan. But let's have a coffee and enjoy the rest of the afternoon. Then we'll go down to the cottages and look around and I'll take photos. And tomorrow we'll go and see the boys at Strawberry Hill.' She leaned forward and fixed Edwina with her bright blue eyes. 'Just leave it to me and don't worry. Everything will work out in the end. In a different way than we planned. But it will be so much better, believe me.'

'Do I have a choice?'

'No,' Pamela said in a firm voice. 'Let it go, Edwina. Let me be in charge now. You have other things to think about.'

Startled by Pamela's determined look, Edwina nodded. 'Okay, Mum.'

'Good girl,' Pamela said as if Edwina was eight years old. She wouldn't have been surprised if her mother had patted her on the head.

But deep down she was grateful. She needed a break after all that had happened. And she wanted to go to Dingle and meet Daniel and find out what he had discovered. He had seemed excited about something and she couldn't wait to find out what it was. Her thoughts turned to the message in the bottle. Those few lines had got to her in a strange way. It had seemed to her like a desperate cry for help.

Who was Pearse and what had happened to him? Would her trip to Dingle reveal the mystery?

After lunch, they went back to Starlight Cottages and walked around, Pamela documenting and photographing the unfinished work, including the bathrooms, wires hanging out of bare walls and those nearly finished decks with the space for the hot tubs. The kitchens were still empty as the old cupboards had been removed and the new, Shaker-style ones they had ordered had still not arrived. Probably because the company hadn't been paid, Edwina assumed with a bitter twist to her mouth. She felt like bursting into tears as she looked around the unfinished site, her dream all shattered. Pamela, however, was busy peering into every nook and cranny, not appearing to be the least bit downcast. In fact, she seemed oddly cheery and excited.

But Edwina wished she had never started the project, wishing for a moment she was back to her carefree, lazy life in Dublin, where everything had been so easy. But then she looked out across the deep blue water of the bay and felt the fresh ocean breeze and realised that she could never go back. This place, the people, and the man she knew she would always love, no matter what happened, would never leave her, even if she went to the ends of the earth. The past two months had changed her, and she felt like a different person.

It was changing Pamela too, even after just a few days, but maybe that was for another reason. Her mother was in a new place in her life, when she was beginning to feel her age and to take stock of her life. It was important for Pamela to feel she had achieved something and that she had both security and the love of her family. And now she was all excited about rescuing Edwina and maybe earning her love and appreciation. She just had to let Pamela take the lead, even if it meant they would have to take a financial hit. It was lovely to watch her mother forget all else and be so excited to be in charge. Edwina had to smile as she heard Pamela mutter to herself, taking photos and writing in her little notebook with the silver pen. At least one of them was happy.

Edwina was startled out of her thoughts by the sound of footsteps inside the house. She turned to look, shielding her eyes from the sun and saw the shape of a man coming through the door. For an instant she thought it was Shane, but then she saw clearly. It was Andrew, carrying a small box.

'Andrew?' Edwina said. 'What on earth—'

'I came to say...' Andrew started. Then he stopped and cleared his throat. 'I'm really sorry about what happened with Seabreeze. I had nothing to do with their finances, you understand. I was hired by them on a contract.'

'Oh, but I thought you were part of the management?' Edwina said, confused.

'No, I certainly was not,' Andrew said. 'They hadn't paid me for a few months, but I thought that was just because they had to juggle funds or something, so I said nothing. But then it came to a head when I had to ask for at least a month's pay and I realised that they were completely broke. They had mismanaged their finances so much that they had debts of over a million they couldn't pay back. And now they have gone underground and nobody can reach them. I'd say they'll be sued by a lot of companies they had placed orders with and hadn't paid.'

'So my money went into some kind of bottomless pit, while they pretended that all was going to plan?'

Andrew shrugged. 'I really don't know how they operated, but I have a feeling most of their problems were just about mismanagement. They thought they'd be able to meet all the orders, but they were just very incompetent.'

'I suppose,' Edwina said slowly.

Andrew's gaze drifted to Pamela, who was walking around the terrace of the last house in the row. 'Who is that?'

'My mother,' Edwina replied. 'She thinks she can salvage some of the project in a way that she won't share with me. No idea what she's up to but what the hell, she might have hidden talents I never knew about.'

'Better than giving up,' Andrew said. 'You could do worse than sell the place the way it is.'

'She thinks we can still make a profit.' Edwina smiled. 'She seems to be enjoying it, anyway. In any case, you did a wonderful job with your plans. The houses will be great, thanks to your designs. Especially what you did with the ground floor.'

'I'm glad you're happy with it.' Andrew held out the scuffed cardboard box he was carrying. 'Oh, I nearly forgot. I found this box when we were redoing the kitchen areas. It was wedged into the back of a cupboard in one of the utility rooms.'

Edwina took the box. 'What was in it?'

'I haven't opened it,' Andrew said. 'But it says something about letters on the top. Hard to make out.'

Edwina looked at the top of the box where she saw some words that were hardly visible. 'It says... letters from... P...' Then she realised what the name was and her heart nearly stopped. 'Letters from Pearse,' she whispered.

21

'What's the matter?' Andrew asked. 'You're suddenly very pale. Do you know someone called Pearse?'

'Yes... no, not really,' Edwina said, holding the small box with shaking hands. 'But it could give me the answer to so many questions.'

'Oh. Okay,' Andrew said, moving away. 'Anyway, all I wanted was to give you the box and say sorry and all that. It was very nice to meet you, Edwina.'

'And you,' she said, smiling at him. 'I'm sorry for you too. I hope you'll find someone better to work for.'

'Thanks.' He looked out at the view and sighed. 'This was a wonderful place to work and a great project. It will be fine, I'm sure. Who wouldn't want to live here?'

'I hope you're right.'

'I am. Well, bye, Edwina. I'll be off now.'

She said goodbye to Andrew and then looked at the box she was holding. 'Letters from Pearse,' she said out loud, reading the faint words on the worn box again. 'Oh my God, how strange.'

She sank down on the steps just outside the door to the sunroom and opened the box with shaking fingers. Inside, she found a small stack of letters, about five of them, bound together with a bit of string. There were no envelopes with a name or address, just pieces of paper with messages in handwriting that was hard to decipher. Edwina looked through them to see if there was a name of the recipient somewhere. But all she could make out were words like *'my sweet girl, dear darling, my love'* and other endearments. She wondered how they had ended up here in a cupboard in one of the cottages and not been kept by whoever had received them. Squinting at them in the bright sunlight made her eyes water, so she decided to put them in her bag and read them later. In any case, Pamela was walking towards her along the path behind the back gardens, beaming from ear to ear.

'All done,' she said. 'We can go home now and have a rest and then we'll go and have dinner at that pub you were talking about.' She looked happier and younger than ever.

Edwina looked at her mother's radiant face and couldn't help feeling that Pamela was entering some kind a new phase in her life. She seemed to be casting aside all the glamour and fashion and was discovering that the simple life was a lot more fun than she had ever realised. Maybe the collapse of the building firm was a good thing? Pamela looked as if she was thriving on the challenge of rescuing the project. This way, she could show she was more than an ageing socialite, and prove to everyone that she could tackle what many people would see as a hopeless task and just give up. Edwina decided to leave her mother alone and concentrate on her quest to find out about the mysterious Pearse, and to whom he had written the letters Andrew had found. She couldn't wait to read them. She smiled at her mother and got up from the step as she put the box into her bag.

'Brilliant, Mum,' she said. 'Let's go, then.'

Pamela looked at her daughter curiously. 'Aren't you going to ask what the new plan is?'

'No. I'm going to leave you alone and let you do what you want. I can see you're dying to get started.'

Pamela nodded and put her phone and notebook into her bag. 'That's excellent, darling.' She glanced at Edwina and laughed. 'Except if this is a way of giving me enough rope to hang myself, then you'll be trying to push me out of the whole thing.'

'Of course not,' Edwina protested. 'I'm really happy for you to take the lead and give me a bit of breathing space.'

'Maybe that will give you time to work on getting your handsome doctor back?' Pamela suggested. 'A tricky man like that will take a while to reel in.'

Edwina had to laugh. 'He's not a fish. And I'm not going to reel him in. Or do anything at all.' She felt a dart of sadness at how her relationship with Shane had ended and wondered if he felt the same. But if she was too proud to take the first step, and he was too stubborn to admit he had been wrong, then there was no use trying to patch things up.

'You'll be sorry, if you don't,' Pamela stated, going back into the cottage. 'Come on. I have a lot of work to do.'

Edwina followed, feeling as if those letters were burning a hole in her bag. Once back in the flat, she would be able to read them in the privacy of her room. Would they prove to be connected to *that* Pearse?

Later, back at the flat, Pamela went into the bathroom for 'a little freshening up', which Edwina knew meant she'd be there for a good half hour, if not more. An excellent opportunity to examine the box with the letters and try to figure out what they said.

Sitting on the bed, Edwina pulled the cardboard box from her bag. She took out the bundle of letters and opened the first one. The date at the top said: *14 August 1999*. Well, that would fit with the same Pearse who had put the message in the bottle, Edwina thought. She began reading the text underneath with some difficulty, but she could eventually make out what it said.

My sweet darling.

If you read this, you got this letter that I gave to S. Please reply soon if you did. It seems a little childish to act like this, but it's the only way for me to write to you as we can't meet in person at this time. I could send you an SMS but I'm worried someone will see it on your phone. I hope that one day we will be together again, but right now it is not possible. I just wanted to tell you how much you mean to me and that I know you want us to be together one day, even if we can't right now. I just wanted the dust to settle for a bit and for everyone to have calmed down after all the drama. We both know whose fault it was, even if we were all involved in what happened that night. But let's keep writing to each other. S said she doesn't mind being our 'postman' and has promised not to tell anyone we're in touch.

Hoping to hear from you soon.

Love and kisses,

Pearse

Edwina took a deep breath and stared at the faint words on the page. The letter told her something had happened that had caused a lot of upset to some people. But what was it? And who was this 'S' who had acted as postman? Was the recipient of the letter a young woman who had lived in one of the cottages twenty years ago? The mysteries around Pearse seemed to grow and grow. She wondered what Daniel had found out and if these letters might be an important piece in the puzzle. But was this Pearse the same young man who had put the message in the bottle on New Year's Eve that year? It seemed to Edwina that it had to be. She picked up the next letter and started to read, now more familiar with the slightly cramped style.

14 August 1999

Hello, lovely,

It's been hell here the past week. Everyone shouting at me and asking questions as if I were the kind of person to tell on a friend. What happened was an accident and nobody's fault, except perhaps that the real culprit shouldn't have been driving that night. But it wasn't really his fault either, and thank God nobody was killed. I hear that you're much better and that you will be going home for rehab soon. I also heard from someone who knows Dr Pat that you will make a full recovery, even if it will take time and a lot of hard work. But I know you have what it takes. The only sad thing for me is that you will be across the ocean and we might never meet again, except if you really want to. Let me know.

Bye for now.

Pearse xx

Edwina started to piece together the story in her head. So there had been an accident. Young people in a car late at night, maybe? Someone driving who shouldn't... Could it be that he had been drinking – or worse, on drugs? And perhaps then this young woman had been injured and needed rehab? Pearse was probably blamed for her injuries, if she was his girlfriend, and then maybe her parents stopped them from seeing each other and the only way he could reach her was by these letters. It all became clear to Edwina now and the message in the bottle began to make sense. Pearse had been desperate and lonely and the girl he loved had left for America. Putting that message in the bottle was like making a wish, or lighting a candle in a church, sending a prayer for someone you loved, a symbolic gesture on a dark evening when everything seemed hopeless. She was now sure the Pearse who had written the letters was the young man who had also put the message in the bottle she had found. She suddenly understood his sadness at having lost the girl he loved. She felt the same about Shane and wondered if they would ever be able to mend what was broken. It was the trust between them that was gone and maybe they would never find that feeling again?

The door suddenly opened and Pamela peered in. 'Casual tonight, yes?' she asked.

Edwina looked up from the letter and smiled. 'Yes. If that's possible for you. I'm wearing jeans and a stripy long-sleeved T-shirt.'

Pamela looked disappointed. 'Oh, that kind of casual. I thought it was more like relaxed but chic. I'll have to have another look in my suitcase. I think I brought a navy pair of slacks and maybe there's a white linen shirt and a pink...' She stopped. 'Back in a moment. You'd better get dressed, too. It's nearly seven o'clock and you said the tables will be gone if we're not there by then.'

Edwina nodded and pushed the letters back into the box. 'I'll be ready in a minute.' She put the box away, had a quick shower, changed into the jeans and top and applied the bare minimum of make-up. Pamela, dressed in the pants and shirt she had mentioned, was studying her reflection in the hall mirror, looking doubtful. 'This looks a bit drab, I have to say.'

'You look perfect, as usual,' Edwina remarked. 'But bring a sweater in case you feel cold.'

Pamela ran back into her room and returned seconds later with a pink sweater draped across her shoulders. 'There, let's go. I'm suddenly hungry.'

'Me too,' Edwina said and grabbed her red fleece from the hallstand before they left. Once in the street, she linked arms with her mother and they walked to the harbour, chatting about what had happened that day.

'So what's this grand plan you're cooking up?' Edwina asked.

'You said you wouldn't ask,' Pamela chided. 'I'm not going to tell you yet. Not until I have all my ducks in a row.'

'Ducks?' Edwina laughed. 'There will be ducks in the cottages? That'll be a fun detail for the VIPs.'

'You know what I mean,' Pamela said, sounding cross. 'But I will have to tell you one thing. We're downsizing a little. I have a feeling the next owners or tenants will not be VIPs. Just people who want to live in a unique spot, who will truly appreciate what this village has to offer.'

'Oh?' Edwina glanced at Pamela. 'You have changed your tune, I have to say.'

'Yes,' Pamela said. 'I think I have changed a lot in just a day or two. I feel as if a fresh wind is blowing through me, somehow. I've been so locked into style and appearances and the latest fashions all my life. But now, here with you, I just want to live a little and have fun.'

'I know what you mean,' Edwina said, giving Pamela's arm a squeeze. 'The same thing happened to me, but it took a lot longer.'

'I'm still going to Saint-Tropez for what's left of the summer season, though,' Pamela announced. 'Only now I'll be more down to earth. Not that I'll compromise on my standards when it comes to fashion,' she added.

Edwina laughed. 'Won't they all be surprised by the new you? Even if you'll look the same, you'll be a different person inside. It's beginning to show already. You have a different look in your eyes.'

Pamela stopped walking and stared at Edwina. 'Do I?'

Edwina looked back at Pamela and nodded. 'Oh yes. Your eyes are sparkling and you're a lot more bouncy.'

'Bouncy?' Pamela laughed. 'I like that.' She resumed walking, pulling at Edwina. 'Let's bounce all the way to this pub, then. I think I might break my diet and have fish and chips. Do they have that on the menu?'

'The best fish and chips in the world,' Edwina said.

'Well then, what are we waiting for?' Pamela said.

22

They arrived at the pub and found it already very busy, but the cheery waitress found them a place outside, at a long table on the terrace, where a party of four people were already having pints of beer. Edwina recognised Maggie and Brian, who she had met on her first night at the Harbour pub. Beside them were Billy with a tall, nice-looking older man with white hair and lively hazel eyes, whom she introduced as her father. His name was Philip and he was driving up the Wild Atlantic Way in his campervan and had stopped off in Sandy Cove to see Billy and spend a few days catching up with old friends in the village.

Philip turned out to be a charmer, kissing Pamela and Edwina's hands in turn and telling them it was an honour to meet such lovely sisters, to which Pamela waved her hand and laughed, telling him he was overdoing it. But her cheeks were pink as he pulled out her chair and her eyes sparkled even more. Then he asked her where she was from and when she said she grew up in London where he had also lived in his youth, they were soon deep in conversation about London in the seventies and the music and fashion in the good old days.

'We were just about to order fish and chips for everyone,'

Billy said when the introductions had been made. 'Would you like that too?'

'Oh yes,' Pamela piped up. 'I've heard it's the best in Ireland.'

'So it is,' Philip said and gestured to a waiter, who arrived at once to take their orders, including drinks. That done, he resumed his conversation with Pamela about the hotspots in London in the seventies.

Edwina turned to the others and smiled. 'Great to be young in those days, I gather.'

'Oh, I'm sure it was,' Maggie said. 'But my best days were actually the summers here in this village. My parents owned one of the Starlight Cottages then.'

'And I had a huge crush on her,' Brian cut in, putting his arm around his wife. 'But she didn't see me.'

Maggie pushed him. 'Of course I did. I thought you were sweet.'

'She didn't really notice me until thirty years later,' Brian filled in.

'When I came back here to go down memory lane,' Maggie said. 'Except I went down the wrong lane for a bit.'

'So you lived here when you were young?' Edwina asked, trying to figure out how long ago that might have been. Maybe Maggie knew something about the young woman who had received Pearse's letters.

'We spent our summers here. But my parents sold the cottage more than thirty years ago and then I didn't come back until two years ago,' Maggie said.

'So you wouldn't have known anyone spending the summer there around twenty-three years ago?' Edwina asked.

'No,' Maggie replied, looking at Brian. 'What about you?'

'Twenty-three years ago?' Brian asked. 'No, I was away for a bit then. Studying veterinary science and then I was doing an internship in Cork. Why do you ask?'

'I'm trying to find out about someone who might have been there for the summer in 1999,' Edwina explained. 'An American family, I think.'

'I wouldn't know about that, but Sorcha might,' Brian said. 'She was here then. That's when she had the baby and lived in the flat over the shop.'

'Of course!' Edwina exclaimed. 'Why didn't I think of her?' Then a thought hit her. Could Sorcha be the 'S' mentioned by Pearse? The person who had acted as 'postman'? It suddenly seemed like the only possible answer. A person running a shop would have been the perfect go-between.

Edwina jumped at a touch on her shoulder. She turned to see the waiter standing behind her. 'Someone wants to see you outside the pub by the front entrance,' he mumbled in her ear.

'Oh? Why didn't they come out here and find me?'

He shrugged. 'Don't know. Said he wanted a word in private.'

'Oh okay,' Edwina said, hoping it wasn't Matt coming back for that catch-up he had been talking about. 'I'll go and see what it's all about.'

'I'll hold your dinner until you come back,' the waiter said.

Edwina thanked him and got up, telling the group she'd be back in a minute. Maggie and Brian nodded, but Pamela didn't turn from her chat with Philip. Billy winked at Edwina as if to say their parents were getting flirty. Edwina smiled back before she went through the pub to the main entrance on the other side that led to the lane. It was darker there and she had to look around to find the person who was waiting for her. But then someone came out of the shadows, his tall frame looming in front of her.

Edwina looked up at him, and felt so drawn to him, despite the hurt he had caused her, that she had to take a step back.

'Shane,' she said, trying to catch her breath, fighting to stay cool and distant. 'What are you doing here?'

'Looking for you.'

'How did you know I was here?'

'Well, you weren't at home, so I assumed you'd gone out for dinner with your mother. How is she, by the way?'

'Absolutely fine,' Edwina said. 'Completely recovered. She's out there on the terrace flirting the pants off Billy's father.'

Shane smiled. 'Philip? He's a real charmer when it comes to the ladies. I'd say they're perfectly matched.'

'Yes. Probably. But why did you come here like this?'

'I didn't want to go in and disturb you and have everyone staring at us, so I thought I'd ask you to come out here so I could say... tell you that...' He stopped. 'Well, to apologise for what I said to you yesterday at Tara and Mick's place. It wasn't fair.'

'No it wasn't,' Edwina replied, her anger rising again at the memory. 'Not fair at all.'

'I know.'

'Good.'

They stared at each other for a while, the tension between them nearly crackling in the air.

Shane cleared his throat. 'Okay, well, that's what I came to say. I was wrong and I hope you can accept my apology.'

'I'll think about it,' Edwina said, even though she was dying to simply throw herself into his arms. But something held her back. She didn't want to give in that easily.

'Let me know when you've thought about it, then,' he said, moving away. He sounded both tired and irritated.

Edwina softened. 'It's okay,' she said. 'I accept your apology.'

'And you forgive me?'

'Well... I suppose I do.'

He let out a long sigh. 'Oh, good. But we need to talk. I think we rushed into something a little too fast. Can we cool it for a bit? I still feel... Well, I don't know how I feel.'

Edwina nodded, taken aback by what he had just said. But

maybe he was right. Her feelings were confused, even though she was irresistibly drawn to him. 'You're right. We should take a break.'

He nodded. 'Good. Let's meet up in, say, a week?'

'Okay,' she said, even though a whole week without him seemed like an eternity. But it would give her a chance to take stock of her feelings for him and look at whatever the future held for them. 'A week sounds good. Do you want to meet up then somewhere?'

'Are you free next Sunday?' he asked. 'I have the whole day off. Let's go for a walk somewhere out of the way.'

'How about the little beach below the cottages?'

'Wild Rose Bay?' He nodded. 'Great. I'll meet you down there next Sunday at eleven. And we can have lunch later if you like.'

'Let's do the talking first,' Edwina suggested.

He smiled wryly. 'Yes. The talking might put us off our food. See you then, Edwina,' he said and, without another word, turned to walk away up the lane.

Edwina watched him disappear into the darkness, her mind full of questions that had no answers. But she decided to leave it alone for now and go back to the terrace and the group that seemed to be having a lot of fun. She would do a lot of thinking during the week that followed.

Pamela looked up from her plate of nearly finished fish and chips. 'There you are, darling. The waiter said he was holding your meal until you came back. Very nice of him. It's truly delicious, I have to say. And,' she said with a proud smile, 'I even ate the mushy peas. Never knew they were so good.'

'Must be,' Edwina replied as she sat down. 'You never eat chips or anything breaded. And you have always turned your nose up at mushy peas.'

'Oh, one has to make exceptions from time to time,' Pamela said. 'Live a little, you know?'

'I agree,' Philip said from Pamela's other side. 'Even though your healthy glow shows an impressive amount of self-control.'

'Well, thank you, kind sir,' Pamela said and flicked back her hair. 'Very nice of you to notice.'

'Only a dead person would not,' Philip quipped, to which Pamela let out a giggle.

Edwina stared at her mother, amazed at the change in her behaviour. She would normally have met comments about her appearance with a frosty stare, but tonight she seemed totally charmed by anything Philip said. But then, he was amazingly beguiling with such a sweet expression in his eyes that you'd forgive anything he said.

'Everything all right?' Billy asked on Edwina's other side.

'Fine,' Edwina said as the waiter placed a fresh plate of fish and chips before her. 'And this is just what I need,' she continued, breathing in the smell of the expertly cooked fish with its crisp batter, dipping the golden chips into a little bowl of homemade mayonnaise. The waiter came back with a glass of cold pinot grigio and Edwina took a swig, feeling that right now, everything was, if not perfect, quite a lot better than before. 'Shane came to say he was sorry,' she whispered to Billy. 'And I forgave him.'

'Oh that's wonderful,' Billy said with a warm smile. 'I know he can be difficult at times so I thought it would put you off him for good.'

'Oh, everyone can be difficult,' Edwina said, biting into a piece of fish. 'God, this is delicious!'

'The best,' Billy agreed. She leaned closer. 'I have a feeling my dad and your mum are getting very friendly. I'm so happy for him; he's been so lonely since my mother died.'

'It would be nice if they made friends,' Edwina agreed. 'My mum is a little spoilt, though. Used to luxury and high society. But let's leave them alone and see what happens.'

'Good idea,' Billy said.

Edwina knew this was the best option, even though she hoped Pamela would be nice to Philip, should she decide he wasn't the kind of man she wanted. Right now, she seemed very taken with him, but that could be the wine and the food making her feel especially benevolent to everyone. She glanced at the two of them and felt happy Pamela seemed so content.

Then her thoughts drifted back to Shane and what he had said to her. His apology had come from the heart and then, when he looked at her, he had seemed to want to say something else, something she had been yearning to hear from him ever since that weekend at Strawberry Hill and their night together. But that was another thing that couldn't be forced. It had to be allowed to grow naturally and she needed to be patient. It was enough that he wanted to talk to her about how he felt, even if he had said they had rushed into things. But that was true. They had become intimate soon after they started dating, which might have been a mistake. She pushed all those thoughts away, deciding to leave it alone. She didn't need to worry about it right now.

Edwina looked forward to seeing Shane when the stipulated week had passed, but first she had to go to Dingle to meet Daniel and see what he had found out. The riddle of the message, the letters and the identity of the man who had sent them just had to be solved. She was sure the letters Andrew had found had to be the ones Pearse had mentioned in his message, the ones he had sent to this young woman who had apparently been injured in some kind of accident. What Daniel had said led her to believe there was some kind of connection with someone in his family, which was intriguing. She suddenly remembered what Brian had said earlier that evening. Sorcha. Maybe she was the 'postman' Pearse had mentioned? There was only one way to find out. She would call Sorcha as soon as she got home.

Edwina finished her meal and wine and then looked at her mother. 'It's getting late, Mum. Maybe it's time to go home?'

Pamela turned and looked at Edwina with a smile. 'It's not that late. But you go on home. I'll stay for a bit and make my own way back to the flat.'

'I'll make sure she gets home safely,' Philip promised.

'If you're sure?' Edwina said and gathered up her bag and jacket.

'Oh yes, I'm sure,' Pamela said, smiling at her daughter. 'I'm having fun. Don't want to end the evening just yet. See you later, sweetheart.'

Edwina said goodbye to everyone and left the Harbour pub, walking slowly up the lane, thinking about what she would say to Sorcha, hoping she would have the answers to at least some of her questions, the most important one being: who was the young woman who had stayed in the cottages that summer?

23

'Oh yes, that was me,' Sorcha said on the phone later that evening when Edwina had explained why she was calling. 'I was the postman and delivered the letters from Pearse to Alison. Can't believe you found them after all this time.'

'Alison? Who was she?' Edwina asked. 'And what happened to her?'

'She was Canadian. From Nova Scotia. She and her family spent a summer at one of the Starlight Cottages. Very pretty girl, around nineteen then, I think.'

'And who's Pearse?' Edwina asked, her heart beginning to beat faster.

'Pearse was a boy she met in Dingle. She used to go there to stay with someone her family was related to. I think they were called O'Riordan.'

'And Pearse?'

'He was actually called Padraig. Pearse was his middle name. Called after Padraig Pearse, the revolutionary hero. His full name was Padraig Pearse Keane, but everyone called him Pearse for some reason.'

'And he was Alison's boyfriend?'

'Something like that,' Sorcha said. 'They were in love, anyway. But I have a feeling her parents didn't approve, especially after the accident.'

'What happened?' Edwina asked, gripping her phone tighter.

'They were in a boat one evening with a gang of young people. A motorboat that belonged to someone's uncle. I don't know the details, but it appears they were drinking a lot of beer. On the way home, there was a fire on board. The engine was old and hadn't been properly serviced and I think it exploded. In any case, Alison was thrown overboard and nearly drowned. One of the friends saved her, but she damaged her back. Broke a vertebra or something and was in a wheelchair for a bit. It wasn't really anyone's fault but the guy who was at the wheel of the boat was blamed for it all. Pearse was innocent as he was sitting at the back, but he wasn't the one who saved her.'

'Who was it?'

'I don't know... It was all kind of confused and I think none of the gang wanted to tell on anyone so they refused to talk. Told the Guards they didn't know how it happened. The case was closed and nobody was charged or anything. That's all I know.'

'And what happened to Alison?'

'I think she recovered. Her parents took her back to Canada when she was able to travel. She had treatments there and she was eventually back to her old self, I heard from one of her relatives in Dingle. Her parents wouldn't allow anyone to see her while she was in the cottage after the accident, except me, because I used to deliver groceries there. That's how I was able to bring Pearse's letters.'

'I see.' Edwina paused for a while. 'So who is this Pearse? Is he still around in Dingle?'

'No idea,' Sorcha said. 'I didn't know him that well. That gang were a bit younger than me, and in any case, I had just had a baby and my marriage was beginning to wobble, if you see what I mean.' She sighed. 'Tough days, but now after all that, I feel that I have finally landed in a good place. My Tom is a wonderful man and we're so happy.'

'That's so nice to hear,' Edwina said. Sorcha's voice made her smile. 'Great that you had such a happy ending.'

'Oh yes,' Sorcha replied. 'Was there anything else I could help you with?'

'Not unless you can tell me more about Pearse and that girl.'

'Afraid not. That's all I know.'

'It was a big help, though,' Edwina said. 'It might seem strange, but I was anxious to find out about what happened because of the letters I found.' She was about to tell Sorcha about the message in the bottle but then something stopped her. It seemed as if she was betraying a secret. If Pearse was still around, still living in Dingle, he might be embarrassed if that came out. 'Thanks for telling me all this, Sorcha.'

'You're very welcome. I had nearly forgotten about those letters and their story. It seems such a long time ago.'

'A little over twenty years,' Edwina said. 'I suppose that is a long time ago, even though sometimes it feels like yesterday.'

'Time flies,' Sorcha remarked. 'How are things with you and the big project? I heard the building firm went bust. Have you found someone else to finish it?'

'Well,' Edwina said with a resigned sigh. 'We had paid them quite a lot for work that hasn't been done and we'll never get that back. But my mother has taken over and she says she is going to fix everything and get it all finished at the end of August with very little extra cost. I really hope she's right.'

'She might surprise you,' Sorcha said.

Edwina laughed. 'She seems full of surprises at the moment.'

'Oh,' Sorcha interrupted. 'Something just popped into my head. I had completely forgotten that Shane's ex-wife...'

'Yes?'

'I think she had some kind of connection to Alison. Don't know how or in what way, but maybe you could ask him?'

'I... might,' Edwina said, wondering how Shane would react if she mentioned his ex-wife. But she could ask Daniel on Monday, of course.

Edwina thanked Sorcha for the information and hung up, turning to the little stack of letters, flicking through them to get to the ones she hadn't read. There were two more, much in the same vein as the first two but with little information about what had happened. Then there was a sweet little poem and a final card in an envelope with a heart saying simply: *I will never forget you.*

Edwina put the little bundle of letters into her bag to show Daniel when they met in Dingle. What Sorcha had said went through her mind again and she wondered if what Daniel had found out would fill the gaps in the story. But she was beginning to see the whole picture and felt sad for Pearse, who probably never heard from Alison again.

Such a sad ending to a sweet summer romance between two young people.

24

Sunday at Strawberry Hill turned out to be a happy day once Edwina and Max had had a frank discussion in the library.

They had been wary of each other at first and Max had been nearly hostile when they started talking about the cottages. But when Edwina had explained to him what was happening, and that Pamela was now in charge, Max had mellowed and seemed to accept the outcome of the whole affair. In fact, he declared, he was relieved they were no longer involved with Seabreeze and that, as Pamela had said cryptically, they were now working on their own. Max said he just wanted it all to be finished and that he would help if they needed it.

Edwina stared at him in astonishment. 'You mean that? You'll actually help us?'

'Yes,' Max said from his place at the desk. 'I'm sorry I was so hostile before. I really want to help out now.'

Edwina, standing by the window, still couldn't believe what she'd heard. 'You're not trying to pull my leg or anything?'

A smile played on Max's lips. 'You mean like when I used to fool you when we were kids that I was giving you a sweet and then put a spider down your neck?'

'Yeah. Something like that.' Edwina met Max's eyes, surprised at the warmth she saw there. 'But maybe you've grown up since then.'

'We both have,' Max said, getting up. 'You especially. You seem to have handled the project really well.'

'Until that company I was stupid enough to hire went bust,' Edwina said bitterly.

'That wasn't your fault. And they did look good on their website. I wouldn't have hired them, but I get why you did. Quite understandable.'

'You mean that?'

'Of course. So I think we can close that subject and let Mum make the best of it.'

Edwina stared at him in astonishment. 'You mean we don't have to fight and argue any more?'

'No. I'm tired of that. The boys need their aunt and their grandmother,' he said, glancing out the window at the back lawn where Pamela was throwing a ball to Paddy. 'What on earth has happened to Mum, though? She's quite human these days.'

'She's met someone,' Edwina said, grinning. 'Last night at the Harbour pub. I think it was love at first sight. He's a university professor. She was so impressed with all the things he knew. And the fact that he looked at her as if she was the most beautiful woman on earth. I think he meant it, too.'

'Really?' Max said incredulously. 'A university professor? Not the kind of man she fancied before.'

'No, but she has changed. I think the collapse of the construction firm and then taking over the project has given her a new look on life. She's determined to get it finished and come out ahead.'

'Well, good luck to her,' Max said. 'I hope it comes off the way she wants.'

'I have a feeling it will,' Edwina said. 'She always gets what she wants, as you know.'

'Yes, but this is a lot more than a designer handbag.'

'But much more rewarding,' Edwina remarked. 'So we're okay then? You and me? The hatchet buried and all that?'

'Absolutely,' Max said with feeling, shooting her one of his thousand-watt smiles nobody could resist. 'You can relax. The war is over.' He held out his arms. 'How about a hug, just to seal the deal, so to speak?'

Edwina hugged him tight. 'Oh I'm so happy,' she whispered, wiping away a tear. 'It's so nice to have a brother I'm actually friends with.'

'For now,' he grunted and let her go. 'I'm sure we'll argue from time to time.'

'Yes, but never like before,' Edwina said.

'No. I trust you now.'

'Why?' Edwina asked. 'I mean, what's changed?'

'You,' he said. 'All through this summer, I've watched you become a different person. You're more down to earth and seem to have understood what's important in life.'

Edwina laughed. 'Yeah. Not designer handbags in any case, that's for sure. I've had a lot of fun this summer.'

'And fallen in love?' he said.

'Yes, I suppose.' She looked away to hide her confusion. 'But I'm not sure it will last.'

'Shane is a good person. I hope you two will work it out.'

'I don't know how, but I hope so,' Edwina said.

'Me too.'

They were interrupted by the two little boys rushing in, Maureen O'Hara at their heels, barking loudly.

'Where's your grandmother?' Max asked. 'I thought she was playing with you.'

'She's stuck,' Paddy said. 'Up the tree. The ball landed in

the branches and she climbed up to try to get it. And now she can't get down. You have to come and pull on her legs.'

'Oh God!' Edwina exclaimed, rushing out through the French windows to the back lawn and the oak, where she could see Pamela hanging from a branch.

'Get me down,' Pamela moaned. 'Get a ladder. I can't hold on much longer.'

Max ran to Edwina's side. 'Come on, Mum. Let go of the branch. I'll catch you.'

'Jump, Granny!' Paddy shouted while Maureen O'Hara barked.

'I'll break my neck,' Pamela protested, sobbing.

'No, you won't. Let go and I'll get you,' Max promised.

Then the branch gave way and Pamela slid down into Max's arms. She wobbled slightly as he let her go and caught his arm, pushing her hair back from her face. 'Well, that was a near miss,' she said. 'But hey, I climbed a tree! Never done that before in my life.'

'And she had fish and chips last night,' Edwina said. 'That's another first.'

'And mushy peas,' Pamela added and started to laugh. 'I'm getting really brave these days. I might even go into that place – what's it called... Mac-something?'

'McDonald's!' Paddy shouted, hugging Pamela's legs. 'Let's go there today.'

'It's in Killarney, and no, not today,' Max said and picked Paddy up in his arms. 'Today we're having lunch in the garden and then we'll go for a ride this afternoon on the new pony Auntie Gwen got for you.'

'You're not putting that little boy on a horse!' Pamela protested. 'He's too young.'

'It's a *pony*,' Paddy corrected. 'And it's very small. And I'm a big boy now.' He wriggled out of Max's arms and slid down to the ground. 'Come on, Granny. Let's go and see him.'

'I don't like stables,' Pamela said. 'The smell of horse sticks to your clothes for hours.' But despite her protests, she followed Paddy as he raced down the lawn, Maureen O'Hara at his heels.

'Should we go down there and help?' Edwina asked. 'I mean, Mum isn't great with horses.'

'Gwen is there. She'll look after them. Let's go and get the barbeque organised.'

And then the day continued in a very jolly way, a real family gathering that hadn't happened before. Edwina felt so relaxed she nearly forgot about her trip to Dingle until they were on their way back to Sandy Cove in the evening. Pamela told her Philip had offered to drive her to the airport the next morning in his campervan, which she was very excited about.

'He's a very interesting man,' she declared. 'And not bad looking. Lovely manners too. Do you know what he said to me?'

'No?'

Pamela's eyes sparkled. 'He said I was *intelligent*. Nobody has ever said that to me before.'

Edwina laughed. 'But he's right, Mum. You *are* intelligent.'

'Thank you, darling,' Pamela purred. 'That's very sweet of you. So if he drives me to the airport, you can get going to Dingle earlier. And we'll say goodbye before you leave.'

'When are you coming back?' Edwina asked.

'Not sure. But as soon as I have everything organised. Then when whatever needs to be done is underway, I can go on holiday for a bit.'

'To Saint-Tropez?' Edwina asked.

'I might go somewhere else,' Pamela replied. 'But I haven't decided yet.'

'Sardinia?' Edwina asked. 'Or Marbella?'

'I'll let you know.'

'Send me a postcard when you've arrived,' Edwina said.

'I will,' Pamela promised.

After that, Edwina gave up trying to get any more information out of Pamela and they drove home in companiable silence, as the evening sun sank into the deep blue ocean.

A light rain fell as Edwina made her way to Dingle the following morning. It was a gentle summer shower which made the air smell of grass and flowers. Edwina found a parking place opposite the little café near the harbour where they had agreed to meet and quickly texted Daniel to tell him she had arrived. He agreed and she waited in the car until she could see his tall, gangly frame dressed in an anorak, hurrying down the street. She got out and ran inside the small café, smiling at Daniel as he entered nearly at the same time. They found a free table by the window and sat down, carefully taking off their wet jackets.

'This is a change from the sunshine yesterday,' Edwina said, pushing her hair out of her eyes.

'I know.' Daniel hung his jacket on the back of his chair. 'That's Kerry for you. The weather changes all the time.'

'I like it. You never know what it's going to do next,' Edwina said.

'That's for sure.'

She breathed in the smell of coffee and newly baked buns while she looked around at the tiny room with its round wooden tables, tiled floor and rough, whitewashed walls. 'This is the smallest café I've ever been in. But it's really cute and unusual, I have to say.'

'I like it,' Daniel agreed.

'What do you want?' Edwina asked, studying the blackboard on the wall behind the counter.

'Latte and some kind of bun?' Daniel suggested. 'I just had breakfast so I'm not that hungry.'

'Okay,' Edwina said and went to the counter to order from

the smiling waitress, who promised to bring it all to the table for them.

'So,' Edwina said when they each had a steaming mug of latte and a bun. 'I think we'll start with this.' She took the bundle of letters from her bag. 'Read them and then I'll tell you what I found out.'

'What are they?' Daniel asked, taking the bundle.

'Letters written by Pearse to a girl called Alison who was staying in one of the Starlight Cottages twenty years ago. They were found while we were doing the renovations. Have you heard that name anywhere while you were looking around for clues?'

'Oh yeah, I know who you mean. I can tell you something about her.' Daniel pulled out the first letter.

'Read them first,' Edwina ordered.

'Okay.'

Edwina sipped her coffee while Daniel read the letters. He looked up from them to take a bite of his bun and then kept reading, looking moved at the words on the page. 'Wow,' he mumbled. 'That poor guy.'

'I know,' Edwina said. 'I felt so sorry for him too.'

When he had finished reading, Daniel handed the letters back to Edwina. 'I don't think Alison replied to any of these.'

'No. I have a feeling she didn't.' Edwina hesitated. 'Do you want me to tell you what I know? What happened to Alison that night?'

'I think I already know,' Daniel said. 'A bunch of teenagers went out in a motorboat and then there was a fire and Alison was thrown overboard, right?'

'Yes. Someone saved her, but it wasn't Pearse.'

'No. But I know who it was.'

'Who?' Edwina asked.

'My dad,' Daniel said.

Speechless, Edwina stared at him. 'What? Shane was there? And he saved Alison's life?'

Daniel nodded. 'Yes. I found this out from my grandparents. My mum and dad were both in that boat. Alison is my mother's second cousin.'

'Oh,' Edwina said, her mind whirling. 'But I thought Shane was from Cahersiveen?'

'He is. He went to school there. But that summer, he had a job here in Dingle. He worked in a restaurant and that's where he met Mum. They were just friends then, and didn't start dating until a few years later, when they met up in Dublin where they both went to university.'

'I see. But back to that summer and the boat trip,' Edwina urged. 'Tell me more.'

'I don't know much more.' Daniel frowned. 'Funny, but the whole thing just came up by accident. I was asking my grandparents if they knew someone called Pearse who might have been one of my mum's friends when she was a teenager. And then Granddad told me about the accident. Pearse was only here for a year and then he left in the spring the following year. Nobody knows what happened to him after that. I actually went to the address of that landline. Got it from a friend who knew how to find the location.'

'Did you?' Edwina stared at him with bated breath. 'And what did you find out?'

Daniel shrugged. 'Not much. There was a woman there who said her family used to rent out rooms. Said she remembered Pearse from that time. He stayed there for about a year and then he took off. She had no idea what happened to him but she said he had been a bit strange. Didn't talk to anyone much and kept himself to himself. I think that's why she sounded so shocked when you rang and asked about him.' Daniel stopped. 'You know what I think?'

'What?' Edwina asked.

'You should ask Dad about it. He can tell you exactly what happened. I would ask him myself but I think he might feel awkward talking to me about it. I'm guessing that there's a lot more to this than what we know.'

'You're probably right.'

'I know I am.' Daniel eyed Edwina's uneaten bun hungrily. 'Are you going to eat that?'

She laughed and pushed the plate towards him. 'No. I'm not feeling very hungry, actually. You have it as you're a growing lad.'

'Thanks,' Daniel said and pushed most of the bun into his mouth.

Edwina laughed as she watched him devour the rest of the bun. 'I knew you'd eat it.'

'Pity to waste it,' Daniel said. 'Hey, I'm so glad you came and showed me the letters. That made me feel closer to Pearse, even if we'll never meet him.'

'Doesn't seem very likely,' Edwina remarked. 'But isn't it amazing to have found out all of this?'

'Really cool,' Daniel agreed. 'And it has given me a lot of ideas for my writing assignment. I want to turn this story into a novel a bit later on. I'd love your take on it when I've finished it. If you can bear to read it, that is.'

'Of course I'll read it.' Edwina smiled at him. 'I can't wait to see your take on our story, and what you make of it.'

'I'll dedicate it to you,' Daniel promised. 'But it will take a while. I have to do my leaving cert first and try to get into college.'

'It'll be worth the wait.' Edwina met Daniel's earnest brown eyes and felt a surge of affection for this young man with such a passion for writing. She was sure the story would be wonderful and that, one day, she'd see his name in print.

'Thanks for all your support,' Daniel said. 'It's great to have an adult on my side. Neither of my parents think I should work on my writing. They want me to do what they think is more useful. But I can't bear the thought of doing something I don't enjoy. I mean, if my heart isn't in it, how could I be good at it?'

'I know,' Edwina said. 'You have to stand your ground.'

'I can if you help me. Could you talk to Dad? I know you're... close, so maybe he'll listen to you?'

'I wouldn't bet on it,' Edwina said. 'I don't think he'd appreciate me butting in about your education. In any case, I'm not sure we're that close any more. We had an argument, you see, and now we're kind of drifting apart, or so it seems.'

'You didn't make up?' Daniel asked, looking worried.

'Well, not exactly. Whatever happened wasn't my fault, actually. Your dad got a bit hot under the collar and said some things and then I got mad and then...' Edwina stopped.

'He can fly off the handle sometimes,' Daniel cut in. 'But he doesn't mean it.'

Edwina nodded. 'He has apologised, and I forgave him. But then we haven't resolved some things so...'

'I hope you do,' Daniel said. 'I know Dad is very much...' He stopped and squirmed. 'Kind of in love, yeah?' he finished, his face reddening.

'You think?' Edwina asked, her spirits lifting.

'I'm sure. He talks about you all the time. It's really boring.' Daniel's mouth twitched. Then he pushed away the plate and took his anorak from the back of the chair. 'I have to go. I promised my gran I'd help her with some computer stuff. Thanks for coming, and for the coffee and buns.'

'You're welcome, Daniel.' Edwina stood up. 'I'd better get going too.'

'You're meeting Dad?' Daniel asked with a hopeful look.

'No. We're meeting next week. We thought we should take a little break and think about things for a bit.'

'Oh.' Daniel looked at her. 'I hope you get back together. It's been fun having you around.'

'I've enjoyed our chats,' Edwina said. 'And trying to solve the mystery, even if we didn't have all the pieces of the jigsaw, if you know what I mean.'

'I think Dad has the last piece,' Daniel said as he moved away.

'Maybe he does,' Edwina said to herself when Daniel had left the café.

But would he tell her what she wanted to know? She would find out next Sunday when they met on that little beach below Starlight Cottages, the beach where lovers used to meet.

But would they ever be lovers again?

25

During the following week, Edwina was still struggling to gauge her emotions regarding Shane. She knew she was in love with him, and that perhaps he felt the same about her, but where would that lead? Would their feelings be strong enough to last once the summer was over? She was trying to find answers to her questions while trying to have that week off he had suggested. But how could you have any time off loving someone as much as she did?

Deep in thought, Edwina was wandering around the cottages at the end of the week, when she was startled to see a van appear by the first cottage, followed by another, and then a third, followed by someone in a small car who pulled up behind the vans and tooted the horn several times. Then the door opened and Edwina was startled to see her mother, dressed in navy chinos and a white denim jacket, her sunglasses pushed into her hair, stepping out of the small car and waving both her arms at the drivers in the vans.

'This is it,' she shouted. 'Please start unloading the furniture according to the lists I gave you.'

Edwina stared, open-mouthed, as men started unloading the vans and carrying all sorts of furniture into the cottages.

'Mum?' she finally said. 'What's going on?'

'We're furnishing the cottages,' Pamela replied as a pleasant-looking woman with grey hair got out of the passenger seat of the car. 'This is Anne, my friend and assistant, who has helped me source these pieces.'

'Hi, Anne,' Edwina said. 'Nice to meet you.'

'Hello,' Anne said and shook Edwina's hand. 'Nice to meet you too. If you'll excuse me, I'll go in and take a look and see if all is according to plan in the cottages. The electrician should have started a few days ago.'

'What? An electrician?' Edwina asked when Anne had disappeared into the first cottage. 'When did that happen?'

'He should have been here on Monday, according to the invoice he sent,' Pamela said. 'Did you come here then to look around?'

'No,' Edwina replied. 'I was in Dingle all day Monday.'

'That's good,' Pamela said. 'You needed the rest. But I've been busy, as you can see. A lot has happened since I left on Monday.'

'Yes, I can see that. But it's only Friday. Where did you get the furniture in such a short time?'

'Anne got it all for me. She already had most of this in her warehouse. I sent her the plans and we talked for hours on this FaceTime thing. And then we met for lunch when I was up in Dublin and she had it all organised in record time. She's an interior designer and specialises in beachfront houses. So we decided on a country-cottage-meets-beachcomber feel in the houses while maintaining a period look with a modern twist.'

Edwina stared at her mother. 'Gosh. That sounds... complicated. Where does she get all this stuff?'

'All kinds of places. Antique shops, second-hand shops, architectural salvage yards. She has a warehouse full of all kinds of furniture. So all we had to do was to pick out what would suit. It's been great fun and I think we got a good mix of styles that will come together nicely. The kitchens will be done next week and then it will all be finished.' Pamela drew breath.

'Holy God,' Edwina exclaimed. 'That's a lot of work in such a short amount of time.'

'You're telling me. I'm exhausted!' Pamela said, looking energised rather than tired.

Edwina took a step towards the first cottage where one of the van drivers had just carried in a wicker chair. 'I'll go and take a look.'

'No, you don't,' Pamela said, pulling Edwina's arm. 'No peeking until it's finished at the end of next week. I don't want you poking your nose in and telling me it's all wrong.'

'I wouldn't dare,' Edwina said, laughing. She held up her hands. 'Okay. I'll leave you to it. Let me know when I'm allowed to go inside.'

'I will. Once it's all done we have to discuss what we're going to do. Sell or let, that's the question.'

'I'll think about it,' Edwina said. 'I'll also have a chat with Jonathan and see what he says. He knows the market so he'll be able to advise us. He owes me after what happened with the construction firm he recommended.'

Pamela nodded. 'Good idea. Not that I trust him after that. But he was suitably horrified when I called him.' She patted Edwina on the shoulder. 'Off you go and do something fun. If you'll excuse me, I have to go and supervise now.'

'Where are you staying?' Edwina asked.

'With you,' Pamela said. 'As you don't lock your door, I went in and put my bag in that little spare room.'

'Oh.' Edwina felt a dart of irritation.

'Only for a few days. I'll be gone again on Monday. Anne is staying in a B&B in Ballinskelligs and she will be handling the kitchen installations. After that, I'll pop back and show you the finished houses and we'll have that meeting. And then...'

'Then?' Edwina asked.

'I'm going away for a long break. You can handle the marketing and whatever else we decide to do. How's that?'

'Sounds good.'

'Perfect. Off you go, then,' Pamela said and started to walk away. 'I'll see you tonight. We could perhaps try to cook something?'

'That would be interesting,' Edwina said with a wry smile as she started on her way back to the village.

She could hear Pamela shouting orders, which made her shake her head and wonder what on earth would happen next. But she would stay out of it and concentrate on how she would deal with Shane when they met on Sunday. She tried her best to figure out what she was going to say to him, but came up with nothing. All she wanted to do was tell him she loved him. But what if he didn't love her back and told her it was all over? That would change everything, and might even drive her away from Sandy Cove.

The sun appeared behind dark clouds on Sunday morning. After a restless night, Edwina told her mother she was going for a walk and might have coffee at The Two Marys' later. Pamela replied with an absent-minded 'fine' while she looked at her notes. Feeling relieved, Edwina left her mother to her plans and walked away making her way to the cottages where everything was momentarily quiet.

Shane, dressed in jeans and a red fleece, waited for her at the bottom of the steps that led down from Starlight Cottages. He held out his hand to help her down from the last step, but she ignored it and jumped down onto the sand. The hazy sunshine was warm and Edwina eased off her jacket and smiled at Shane.

'Hi,' she said shyly.

He smiled back. 'Hello. Nice morning after the rain.'

'Lovely,' she replied, as they walked slowly across the beach.

Edwina looked at the steep slopes on the other side of the beach where butterflies fluttered among the wild roses and larks could be heard singing high up in the blue sky. She breathed in the sweet air, feeling a sense of peace come over her, even though she knew their talk might be full of conflict. But she didn't want to argue with him any more, whatever they decided to do.

'Let's sit on that rock over there,' Shane said, pointing ahead. 'Then we can talk.'

'Good idea,' Edwina agreed and followed him to the rock where they sat down side by side on the flat surface, warmed by the sun.

'So,' she said, turning to him. 'What's on your mind?'

Shane looked at her and sighed. 'I was going to say... You know... that...' He stopped and pushed his hand through his hair. 'Oh God, I'm not good at this.'

'At what?' Edwina asked.

'At saying I'm sorry.'

'But you already did when you came to the pub the other day.'

'Yes, but not properly. I should go down on my knees and ask your forgiveness for the way I acted and for what I said to you that night. But...'

'But what?' Edwina inquired. 'If there's a "but", it's not a proper apology.'

'The "but" is about my own stupidity. So that's part of the apology,' Shane said, looking frustrated. 'Do we have to do this? I mean, all the arguing?'

'Who's arguing? Go on. But what?'

'But I was insanely jealous.'

'Jealous? Of *Matt*?' Edwina shook her head. 'How could you possibly think...' Then she stopped. 'Is it your divorce coming back to haunt you? Your wife left you for someone else, you told me. Maybe you're all confused and you're mixing me up with... her?' She looked at him, suddenly understanding what he had been going through. Jealousy had been eating into his heart. She knew how that felt as she had also had her doubts, worried Shane was still in love with his ex-wife.

Shane nodded, slightly shamefaced. 'I suppose that has something to do with it...'

'You still love her?' she asked in a small voice, her stomach contracting. It had been on her mind for a long time and now she felt she needed an answer to her fears.

'No, of course not!' Shane exclaimed. He turned and stared at Edwina. 'I think you hit the nail on the head, though. Not that I'm still in love with Sharon, my ex-wife, but the trauma of the rejection is still there. So I was scared it was happening again. That I would lose you to someone else.'

'Oh.' Touched by the desperate look in his eyes, Edwina put her hand on his shoulder. 'I understand it now. But there was no need for you to worry. None at all, okay?'

His eyes were tender as he looked at her. 'I see that now. But that day... When I saw that guy sail out of Sorcha's shop and slip into his Porsche like a hand into an expensive glove, I went a little crazy.'

'Ferrari,' Edwina cut in.

'Oh okay. Ferrari. Whatever. The fact is, I looked at him and thought I could never compete with all that.'

'Who's asking you to compete?' Edwina said.

'Oh, I know. Stupid thought. But yeah, I was jealous of all he could give you that I never could, so that's what all my anger was about. Not about me thinking you could do what I accused you of. That all came from him.'

'He's a shit,' Edwina said hotly, 'if you'll excuse my expression. And he could never compete with you and what you have already offered me.' She took Shane's hand and looked into his troubled eyes. 'Can we forget him, please? I'm painfully aware that I was once taken in by all the bling. But you showed me what truly matters in life, to be loved and love someone back with all your heart. When I'm with you, I feel like a better version of myself. Forgive you? Of course I do. That was the best apology ever. Just do one thing, though.'

'What?' he asked, his eyes brightening as he looked at her.

'Kiss me,' she said and leaned into him, closing her eyes.

'Only if you promise there will be no helicopter pad on the headland.'

'I promise,' Edwina said, her eyes still closed.

'Okay.' Shane pulled her up from the rock and took her in his arms and kissed her, long and hard. Edwina melted into his arms and felt as if that kiss was what she had been waiting for ever since the row that Friday night, but had thought would never happen. Now she relished the feel of his lips, his body pressing into hers. His arms around her and his special scent of soap and aftershave made her feel dizzy with love and desire. But what was that he had said?

'Helicopter pad?' she asked when they broke apart. 'Where did that come from?'

'I made it up,' he mumbled into her hair. 'Just to annoy you.'

'You can say what you like if you kiss me like that,' she said and pushed back a stray lock from his forehead. 'You need a haircut.'

'I know. I'll never be as polished as Ferrari-man.'

'Oh please,' Edwina said with an exasperated sigh. 'Can we forget about him?'

'I will if you will.'

'He's gone from my memory bank forever,' Edwina

declared. 'Do you want to go somewhere for lunch? You must be hungry.'

'Only for you,' he said and kissed her again. He let go of her and smiled. 'I'm so happy you forgave me.'

'Did you think I wouldn't?'

'I was afraid you might still be angry about what I said.'

Edwina smiled. 'I was, but your apology swept all my anger away.'

'Oh good.' Shane touched her cheek. 'You're amazing and beautiful and smart and funny and truly unique. And you were right about what you just said. I do love you. With all my heart and soul.'

'Oh sweetheart, me too,' Edwina said, overcome with emotion. 'With all my heart and soul and body and... everything,' she ended as tears welled up in her eyes.

'Why are you crying?' Shane asked, hugging her.

'I'm so happy,' she sobbed into his fleece. 'I feel as if I was lost and now someone found me and will take me home, wherever that might be. Where will it be?' she asked, looking up at him.

'Wherever we are together,' he said. 'We'll work it out.'

'Oh yes,' she said, smiling through her tears. She stood on tiptoe and kissed his cheek. 'Can we go and have lunch now? There is something I need you to tell me.'

'What?' he asked.

'It's such a long story. And I'm hungry.'

'Then I'll feed you,' he said. 'We'll get a pizza at the Harbour pub. It's early, so it won't be crowded.'

As they walked back across the beach hand in hand, Edwina hardly noticed the glorious views across the bay, the cry of the seagulls or the wind in her hair. All she could think of was Shane and what he had said to her. He loved her. She had never felt so close to anyone before and the feeling both scared her and made her heart soar. This was it: real, true love. At last.

26

Shane had been right; the pub was nearly empty except for a few people sitting on high stools at the bar. They sat down at a small round table in an alcove with views of the harbour where the sun shone on the little brightly coloured fishing boats riding at anchor as seagulls swirled around, dipping down into the still water from time to time to catch fish.

'So peaceful,' Edwina said, looking out. 'The sea like a mirror, those little boats and the seagulls the only living things out there.'

'An oasis,' Shane agreed, looking around the pub. 'No waiter. I'll go to the bar and order. What do you want?'

'Something plain,' Edwina said. 'And maybe a glass of wine, if you don't think it's too early.'

'I'll get us both a margherita,' Shane said. 'And a glass of chilled rosé.'

'Perfect.'

'They'll be ready in a minute,' he said when he came back carrying two glasses of wine. He put the glasses on the table and sat down, looking at her. 'So what was it you wanted to ask me?'

Edwina ran her finger around the rim of her glass. 'It's about

something that happened a little over twenty years ago,' she said
and launched into the story of the message she had found in the
bottle and then the letters, what Sorcha had said and finally
what Daniel had found out.

Shane stared at her without interrupting until she had
finished. 'Holy God,' he exclaimed when she came to the end.
'I'm shocked. That was an incident I'll never forget. I can't
believe you didn't tell me any of this.'

'I had a feeling you'd think it was ridiculous,' Edwina said,
giving a start as the waiter placed her pizza before her. 'In any
case, I never thought I'd find out who Pearse was until I found
the letters. I couldn't believe the two were connected until I
spoke to Sorcha. And then Daniel was also on the case. He
wants to write a novel based on this story.'

'Does he?' Shane said, looking doubtful. 'Well, why not? As
long as it doesn't affect his studies.'

'I'd say it will help him,' Edwina said. 'But let's not get into
Daniel's plans for the future. They're none of my business.'

'Not really,' Shane agreed. 'But he likes you a lot, so that
might help me handle him.'

'Maybe.' Edwina picked up a wedge of pizza. 'Sorry, but I'm
starving. I'll just have a bite while you tell me your part of the
story. I mean, you were there that night, weren't you?'

Shane looked thoughtful. 'You know I was. And so was
Sharon, my ex-wife. We weren't even dating then, just friends.
We were all in this gang having a lark on a summer evening.
Thought we'd go out to see Fungie, the dolphin who used to live
in Dingle Bay and swim around the boats. But we were a bit
young and stupid and didn't think about security. Nobody had a
life vest on or anything. Then the engine caught fire.'

'Was there some kind of explosion?'

'No, not really. Just a lot of commotion when the fire
started. We all stood up and that made the boat rock and Alison
fell in, hitting the side of the boat as she did. Someone put the

fire out with a fire extinguisher and I, without thinking, jumped into the water to save her.'

'And Pearse?'

'As far as I remember, he just sat there, looking shocked. I think he had drunk a lot of beer to deaden the pain of Alison dumping him. They had had a fight just before the fire started and she told him it was over between them.' Shane paused and took a swig of wine. 'To be honest, Alison wasn't a very nice girl. One of those pretty-pretty girls who are so into themselves they don't care about anyone else. All the guys fancied her like mad, of course.'

'Did you?'

Shane nodded, smiling at the memory. 'Sure did. I think I even kissed her one night under the stars. But she kissed everyone so that didn't mean a thing. Just a little flirting, you know?'

'I think I know what you mean. Hey, eat your pizza. You can tell me the rest in a minute,' Edwina urged, trying to digest what Shane had just told her.

So Alison was a pretty girl who was sure of her looks and her powers of attraction. She knew that kind of girl; maybe she had been one herself when she was a teenager. It had been fun, even if a little heartless.

'Okay.' Shane picked up a wedge of pizza and took a bite.

'What happened to Alison after the accident?' she asked.

Shane swallowed his mouthful. 'She injured her back. Broke a vertebra or something.' He picked up another wedge. 'All I know is that she stayed at the cottage for a few weeks until she was able to travel. Then I heard from Dr Pat, who was the GP here at the time, that she would make a full recovery. She was Sharon's second cousin and were in touch for a bit after Alison went back to Canada. I think she married and moved to Montreal.'

'And Pearse?'

Shane shrugged. 'I didn't know him that well. He was in Dingle for a year working at the Skelligs Hotel and then he left. I had no idea he had written to Alison. Her dad was so angry with everyone after the accident and wouldn't let her see anyone from the gang. I think Sharon went to see her a few times while she was in laid up in bed.'

'But they weren't close?'

'Not really. They lost touch when Alison went back home.' Shane drank more wine and smiled at Edwina. 'Memories, eh? Makes you feel relieved you're no longer young. That accident was hugely traumatic for me. I kept thinking of how much worse it could have been. That's partly the reason I wanted to study medicine.'

'You were a hero to save Alison. I'm sure she was very grateful.'

'If she was, she didn't say anything. But you know, I didn't do it to earn her gratitude. I didn't even like her much after the way she had been behaving all summer. Poor Pearse was devastated. That's what drove him to get drunk on New Year's Eve and put a message in a bottle, of all things. What a strange thing to do.'

'He must have been feeling so desperately sad and lonely,' Edwina mused. 'When you're young you feel those things even more strongly.'

Shane nodded. 'Yes. All those emotions and hormones swilling around inside. I prefer middle age, to be honest.'

Edwina laughed. 'Oh yes, me too. I like being middle-aged with you.'

He took her hand and looked deep into her eyes. 'I want us to grow old together. I want us to be like those old, old couples holding hands and helping each other across the street. All wrinkly and saggy, but still in love.'

'Can we do middle age first?' Edwina asked, laughing. 'I mean, you'll have us in our graves, the way you're talking.'

Shane grinned and squeezed her hand harder. 'Yeah, let's be gloriously middle-aged together.'

Edwina raised her nearly empty glass. 'Here's to us and middle age. And to growing old together. Eventually.'

Shane looked fondly at her. 'You're so cute, sitting there all rosy and smiley.' He half rose and leaned across the table and kissed her on the mouth. 'I can't wait for you to be an old lady with white hair and still those dimples. Oh, look,' he said, squinting at her. 'I can see a wrinkle just there, across your forehead.'

Edwina laughed and pushed him away. 'Stop. I know you're teasing me. But this time, I won't rise to the bait.'

'That's very disappointing. I was hoping we'd have a rip-roaring row.'

'I'm not going to give you that today. I'm far too happy.'

'I know. And that makes me happy too.' Shane sat down and gripped her hand again. 'I have something to tell you. I was saving it for the right moment. And the moment seems to have arrived.'

'The moment for what?' Edwina asked, forgetting about her pizza.

'To tell you that the HSE have approved for the surgery to be split between two GPs. And that Kate is coming back when her year is up in January. So I... well, we need a place to live. That is, if you want to live here with me...'

'If I want...?' Edwina stared at him while her heart beat faster and happy tears welled up in her eyes. 'Are you asking me to move in with you?'

He nodded. 'Yes, that's what it sounds like to me.' He kissed her hand. 'Sweetheart, do you think you could leave the big smoke and designer gear to live here in the back of beyond with a lowly GP?'

Edwina nodded, unable to utter a single word.

'Is that a yes?'

'Of course, you eejit,' she exclaimed. 'I can't think of anything better than living here in this gorgeous village with you in some nice...' She stopped and clapped her hand to her mouth. 'Of course! I know the perfect place for us.'

'I think I can guess,' Shane said, his mouth twitching. 'I'd go for cottage number one. It's the nearest to the beach and the back garden is bigger so we can put in one of those hot tubs that you were thinking of but never got around to putting in.'

'Yes,' Edwina said, feeling her heart nearly bursting with joy. 'Oh, how perfect it will be. I have to talk to Mum, though, to see what kind of financial agreement that would demand. We haven't decided whether to sell or let the houses yet.'

'Will she object to us living there?'

'No, she'll be delighted. She likes you a lot after you saved her life. But if we want to own one of the houses, we have to see what kind of arrangement that would entail.'

'I could lease the house for a year while you decide,' Shane suggested. 'But we'll iron out the details later.' He let go of Edwina's hand and picked up his wine glass. 'A toast. To us and to our future. Whatever that will hold.'

Edwina picked up her glass and clinked it with Shane's. 'To lots and lots of wonderful days like this.'

'And nights,' Shane said with a wide smile as he picked up her hand and kissed it, looking deep into her eyes.

EPILOGUE

The stars sparkled in the dark sky like a million diamonds set in black velvet. The steam from the hot tub swirled around the terrace and Edwina sank deeper into the warm water. She leaned her head back and looked up at full moon rising over the bay casting an eerie glow over the still water. It was early December and she had just spent a long day working on a building project on the far side of Waterville. This was her first job as project leader and it was hard work, but a wonderful challenge.

She had taken this on when Jonathan had recommended her to a construction firm that needed someone to run their various contracts, a firm with good reputation and solid financials. Her brand new career had taken off at last, after she had finished an online course in construction development. It suited her well, as she could do a lot of the planning at home and then simply visit the sites when she needed to, working with architects and builders and coordinating all the work that needed to be done. It meant using her leadership skills that now came in very handy. Shane said that she just loved shouting orders at people, which made her perfect for the job.

Edwina smiled as she thought of the past months and all that had happened since that day last August when they sat outside the Harbour pub making plans. The first thing was the big reveal of the renovations of Starlight Cottages. Pamela had arrived back two weeks after the delivery of the furniture and the installation of the new kitchens and started to put up posters all around the village inviting everyone to the open house. But Edwina was allowed to inspect the cottages before the official viewing.

The long wait was over and she could step inside the cottages and finally see Pamela's designs that had been realised with the help of her friend Anne. The cottages were charming and the eclectic mix of furniture and textiles were perfect for seaside cottages. The living rooms all had a comfortable Chesterfield sofa in front of the fireplace and two easy chairs upholstered in muted colours. Then there were occasional tables in various woods and rugs in warm colours on the wide oak planks. Large framed photos of the ocean, sailing boats and birds in full flight adorned the whitewashed walls, giving the indoors a light and airy feel. The bedrooms had been sparsely furnished, each with a double bed, and various kinds of bedside tables, and the cupboards in the now smaller kitchens had been salvaged from old country cottages and painted a distressed white. The whole effect was charming, cosy and very inviting.

Edwina beamed at Pamela, who was standing in the living room of the last house looking apprehensive as Edwina finished her tour. 'So? What's the verdict?'

Edwina laughed. 'The verdict? It's absolutely fabulous! You're a genius, Mum.'

Pamela brightened. 'I am? Or are you just humouring me?'

'No, of course not. I'm amazed. You've done a wonderful job.'

'That's lovely to hear.' Pamela looked at Edwina with sparkling eyes. 'I'm so happy. But what do we do? Sell or let?'

'I'd say sell,' Edwina said. 'Let Jonathan put them on the market. All except one. The first cottage. I want that one for me and Shane. We're back together, you see. And it's even better than before.'

'Oh how wonderful!' Pamela rushed to Edwina's side and hugged her tightly. 'I'm so happy for you both. I knew you'd come to your senses.'

Edwina laughed. 'Yeah, that's a good way to put it.'

'And you want to live here? In one of the cottages? As a summer home?'

'No, as an all-year-round forever home,' Edwina replied. 'Shane is going to be a GP here permanently.'

'And what are you going to do?' Pamela asked.

'I'm not sure, but I'll think of something,' Edwina said.

'I think you should do what you've been doing all summer,' Pamela suggested. 'Leading projects like this one.'

'Why?' Edwina asked, surprised. 'It all went pear-shaped until you stepped in.'

'Oh, you were doing fine until that company went bust,' Pamela argued. 'And that wasn't your fault. If you make sure the people hiring you are doing well financially, you'll be fine.'

Edwina looked thoughtfully at Pamela. 'It's not a bad idea. I'll have to think about that for a bit. We'll see when the cottages have been sold and I've talked to Jonathan about it.'

Edwina parked that idea at the back of her mind while the inauguration went ahead, with the whole village turning out to look around the cottages, everyone declaring that the renovations were truly wonderful. Then they all gathered on the terrace of the Harbour pub for wine and nibbles which went on until the small hours with Irish music and dancing under the stars. By then, Pamela was the darling of the village and everyone wanted to congratulate her and slap her on the back for doing such a grand job with the coastguard station.

Now that everything was finished to their satisfaction, they could relax and take it easy, leaving the sale of the properties to Jonathan, who spent time putting a brochure together and doing some advertising, both in Ireland and abroad. There were three cottages for sale, the first one having been sold to Shane and Edwina, who were now joint owners. They moved in a month later, after Edwina had sold her apartment in Dublin and they had managed to sort out their belongings and buy some additional pieces of furniture to make their own stamp on their first home. And then, as a surprise for her fortieth birthday, Shane had had a hot tub delivered and installed when Edwina was in Dublin moving out of her apartment.

Pamela had disappeared after the inauguration on that mysterious holiday she had mentioned to Edwina, who had assumed it was somewhere either in France or Spain. But all had been revealed when Pamela sent a postcard with a beautiful view that Edwina didn't recognise.

'Where is this? It's not anywhere on the Riviera,' she said to Shane, waving the postcard in front of him as they sat in the living room of the surgery with a cup of tea one evening.

'What?' He took the postcard and studied it for a moment. Then he burst out laughing. 'The Riviera? No, it's Clew Bay in County Mayo.'

'Are you sure?' Edwina looked at the front of the postcard. 'But what would she be doing there?'

'What do you think?' Shane asked, still laughing. 'She's gone up the Wild Atlantic Way with Philip in his campervan.'

Edwina joined in the laughter when the penny finally dropped. 'Of course! The sly old thing. Well, I hope she's having a good time.'

'I bet they both are,' Shane said. 'And good luck to them.'

Edwina smiled at the memory as she lay there in the hot tub

looking up at the stars. The image of Pamela in a campervan had made her laugh at first. But then she was amazed at the change in her mother, who would previously only have accepted five-star accommodation. Pamela had been on a journey ever since she had arrived in Sandy Cove and the snobby, discontented woman was now positively blooming, which was wonderful to see.

The sound of footsteps on the deck interrupted Edwina's thoughts and she turned her head to see Shane walking towards her in the dim light. He dropped his dressing gown, climbed into the tub and slid into the water beside her, letting out a long, contented sigh.

'Long hard day?' she asked.

'Yeah. But this sure makes up for it.' He leaned his head against the edge of the tub and closed his eyes. 'What a perfect way to end the day: sitting in a hot tub with the woman I love looking up at the stars.'

'And the moon,' she whispered. 'Just look at it.'

'Incredible.' He took her hand under the water. 'Edwina,' he said. 'You know I love you to that amazing moon and back, don't you?'

'Yes,' she whispered, her breath coming out in a plume of steam. 'And I do love you, so very much.'

'That's good because I want to give you a ring. An engagement ring with an emerald to match your eyes. Would you accept such a ring?'

'I'd adore it,' she said.

'I know you would.' He sighed. 'There is only one problem. I can't afford it. I could do something in plastic for the time being, of course.'

'I'd love that even more,' Edwina said.

'You would?'

'Of course. It's not about the value of the ring, it's about why I'd be wearing it.'

'We'd be engaged,' he said in a dreamy voice. 'And then, eventually, we'd be married. That's what I want, anyway. You and me forever.'

'Forever,' Edwina repeated, looking up at the stars that shimmered and glimmered in the vast expanse of the black sky.

A LETTER FROM SUSANNE

Thank you for reading *The Lost Letters of Ireland*, which I so enjoyed writing. If you want to keep up to date with my latest releases, just sign up at the link below. Your email address will never be shared and you can unsubscribe any time.

www.bookouture.com/susanne-oleary

I hope the book swept you along to the beautiful south-west of Ireland that I love. Sandy Cove is a fictional village but there are plenty of such villages all around Ireland, especially in Kerry. I do hope that reading my book cheered you up a little bit and provided a brief escape from the stress and worry of the times we live in, wherever you are in the world.

I would really appreciate it if you could write a review as I love feedback from readers. Your take on my story is always so interesting – and even surprising, sometimes. Your comments might also help other people discover my books. Long or short, a review is always helpful.

I also love hearing from my readers – you can get in touch on my Facebook page, where I post news about my books. Many of my readers also have chats with me there, which is great fun! You can also catch up with me on Twitter, or my website.

See you soon again in Sandy Cove!

Susanne

KEEP IN TOUCH WITH SUSANNE

www.susanne-oleary.co.uk

 facebook.com/authoroleary
twitter.com/susl

ACKNOWLEDGEMENTS

Huge thanks yet again to my wonderful editor, Jess Whitlum-Cooper, for her hard work to make my book shine. Also all at Bookouture – always such a delight to work with.

My husband, Denis, deserves an extra enormous hug and thanks for all he does for me, and my family and friends who are there for me. With all these wonderful people in my life, I feel incredibly lucky.

Last but not by any means least, I want to thank my readers for your kind messages and comments. You are the reason I keep writing and your enthusiasm and support are my best inspiration.

THANK YOU!

Made in the USA
Columbia, SC
20 December 2022

74675815R00152